THE LONDON TRAM MURDERS

VANCE AND SHEPHERD MYSTERIES BOOK 2

JOHN BROUGHTON

CHAPTER 1

BECKENHAM, GREATER LONDON

Oliver Waterman, a creature of habit, walked his cocker spaniel, Luna, the same way every early morning. Their relaxed stroll allowed plenty of time for the amiable bitch to satisfy her olfactory curiosity and to re-establish her territory by sprinkling it with urine. An endearing creature with a sensitive nature, the well-groomed spaniel often succeeded in rescuing her owner from moments of deep despair by putting her head on his knee and staring up at him with soft, half-moon eyes. Since redundancy had left Oliver feeling worthless and embittered, for he considered himself an expert at his job of twenty years, it was easy for him to lose hope of further employment as a precision grinder in this period of economic recession. One of his few reasons for living, after a messy divorce, was the little animal bouncing by his side, occasionally distracted by tufts of grass sprouting from the pavement in this generally well-kept residential area between Penge and Beckenham.

Their morning perambulations took the owner and his dog along a path flanked by tidy allotments, where Oliver paused with a half-formed idea of applying to the council for a plot.

His gaze swept over the admirable rows of tight cabbages and white-topped cauliflowers and he imagined how much soil preparation had gone into producing these pristine green sentinels standing to attention. He enjoyed gardening at the rear of his small semi-detached house, but there was not enough room for a vegetable patch; besides, his ex-wife had severely vetoed anything other than a floral contribution. Now, he had grown fond of his gladioli and dahlias and would be loath to exchange them for onions and carrots.

Luna barked at him to snap him out of his reverie and to continue their walk. Still, he thought, an allotment would give him something worthwhile to pass the time and stop him from brooding about his future.

At the end of the allotments, he and Luna came to an old, abandoned railway bridge where a tight curve of the disused line passed over the road. Now, the overhead bridge had gone, but either side's high brick walls remained, flanked by a pair of neat, black, cast iron bollards. Passing through, Oliver considered, *we might as well be on the moon; there's not a living soul around.* They continued until they came to another forsaken bridge, this time in the form of a tunnel.

Ordinarily, Luna loved sniffing around the delightful odours that her owner found so repugnant because less civilised humans than himself tended to use the secluded underpass as a urinal. Today, though, Luna dug in her heels and whined.

"What's up, girl?" Oliver had a bad feeling. His little dog never behaved like this.

She trembled and whined continuously so he bent to comfort her, but, so unlike his little girl, she wriggled free and, nose pointing to the tunnel, began to bark, stopping only to turn her head to stare at him as if asking why he did not understand. Then, once again, she bristled, hackles erect, gave a series of short yips, and the whining restarted.

A dreadful presentiment gripped Oliver Waterman. Commanding the spaniel to sit, he reached into his tweed jacket pocket, pulled out his mobile phone, switched on the torch facility and headed into the gloomy tunnel, only slightly lit at the entrance by the early-morning light.

His torch beam picked out a huddled form on the ground. There was no doubt, it was a body. The corpse of a young woman, her blonde, braided hair stretched behind her, lay head towards him. He presumed she was dead. Common sense told him not to touch her. He caused a booming echo by calling out, but there was no response from the inert form, so, refusing to approach too closely, he dialled 999 and asked the operator for the police and an ambulance. He gave directions and told the professional-sounding operator that he thought the young woman was dead, but hadn't gone close to avoid contaminating the scene.

At New Scotland Yard, Detective Inspector Vance of the Criminal Investigations Department had just finished lamenting his lack of recent activity with his ex-Sergeant, Brittany Shepherd, now promoted to his rank, ostensibly for her role in saving the Commissioner's nephew's life, but on merit for her superb intu-itions and lively intelligence. She still considered Jacob Vance her boss, although they shared equal grade. Old habits die hard; besides, they were good friends with an almost telepathic rela-tionship as colleagues. Vance looked at the ringing phone on his desk with the expression of a ravenous wolf in the harshest winter. Action at last? He was tired of routine reports and staff assessments.

"Do you want to share this one with me, Brit? It might be something or nothing, but if Francis Tremethyk smells a rat, that's good enough for me."

"Count me in, Jake. I'm bored out of my mind in here. What is it? What's alerted our dear old Cornish medic?"

"A young woman in her thirties. Dr Tremethyk says it looks like a heart attack, but his instincts tell him there was foul play."

"Where is it?"

"Under the tramway at Avenue Road."

Brittany Shepherd frowned. "That's a quiet part of town." she murmured. "Will you drive, or shall I? I won't bother my sergeant. We can deal with this."

Vance grinned. "Just like old times, hey, lass?"

"Except that I can safely give you more lip to keep you in line!" She giggled. "I take it I'm driving?"

Once inside the vehicle, an unmarked BMW, Vance asked casually, "You said it's a quiet part of town. Do you know that area? I can't bring it readily to mind."

"Not really, but I connect Avenue Road with the tramway. Surely you remember the disaster at Croydon, the derailment that cost several lives and injured scores of passengers? That was in 2016 and since then, they've introduced loads of safety measures. I reckon the tram's the best way to transport people without pollution and it's so smooth for the traveller. I don't know why they did away with them in the first place."

"Before you go off on a long ecological ramble, Brit, maybe you could stick to the point."

"Oh, yeah, well…" She turned her sapphire blue eyes on him momentarily. He knew that look. She used that when she was annoyed with him, so he smiled into her pretty oval face and gave her an encouraging nod. Her attention returned to the busy road, and she continued, "… that catastrophe didn't put me off riding the tramway. I use it regularly to go from Merton Park to Gravel Hill."

"Merton Park, I get that, but why would you regularly go to Gravel Hill?"

"My brother lives there. His wife died of cancer two years ago."

"I'm sorry, how come you never mentioned it?"

Brittany's jaw tightened. "There are some things you don't bring to work."

There followed a long silence broken only by traffic noise, until Shepherd swore at a motorcyclist cutting in front of her vehicle. Vance seized the opportunity. "So, what about Avenue Road?"

"There's nothing there, Jake. The station is composed of only a green footbridge and a couple of litter bins, while very few people come and go there. I've read that it's the least-used tram station, with an average of only about one hundred and sixty-nine passengers a day."

"You're a bit of an expert on trams, I see. I suppose most of those will be at peak times, too."

They lapsed into thought, but soon, Shepherd pointed out the station sign: blue writing on a white background and a thick green stripe above, the logo of the London Tramways. "Here's the station. I'll leave the car. We can take the famous footbridge and walk to join the others."

This they did. Jacob Vance made mental notes of the station. It looked like a perfect place for anyone who loved solitude. Brittany's description had been spot-on. His first thought was: *ideal for anyone who planned to commit murder undisturbed.*

They entered the tunnel from the opposite direction to Oliver Waterman and found white-kitted officers around the body of a young woman. Vance's instincts ran wild. For him, this was a murder scene. There were too many combinations for it to be a natural death.

The Chief Medical Examiner, a middle-aged gentleman, Dr Francis Tremethyk, looked up as the two detectives approached.

"My, my, two inspectors! Welcome, me-dears." The marked Cornish accent meant that the doctor was troubled.

Vance spoke first. "What have you got for us, Doc?"

"Female, foreign extraction, eastern European I'd say, early thirties and, at face value, a heart attack. Dead ten or eleven hours. But it's all wrong, boy."

Vance was used to that form of address, common to southwest England, so passed over it to say, "What's going on in that grizzled head?"

Tremethyk grinned. "I've got competition in that area, I can see." He referred to the distinct greying at Vance's temples. "I have to ask myself, a heart attack, here in this tunnel? It's too conveniently deserted and if my time of death is accurate, which it's sure to be, it would have been pitch black down here. Besides, there's no apparent trace evidence, and the poor lass made no effort to call for assistance. Her phone was in her handbag when we got here. It's all too neat."

"Was?"

"Aye, was. The remarkable Markham has her mobile bagged up along with a pocket diary. Ye'll be wanting to see that, me-dear. That puts the lid on it for me. This is murder. All tidy, as I said, but it's murder, and I'll confirm it as soon as possible."

"So, do we have identification?"

"Passport. The photo matches, so she's Gundega Krūmina, a Latvian citizen aged thirty-two."

"Who found the body?"

"A chap walking his dog. Nice enough fellow, sensible, too. He didn't contaminate the scene of the crime. He's over there by the entrance with a cocker spaniel—the hound alerted him to the body."

"Thanks, Doc and—"

"Don't say it, me-dear. I'll get the results to you as soon as humanly possible. Cheerio!"

The doctor's assessment of the dog walker was one Vance could agree with. He mentally eliminated the responsible Oliver Waterman from his inquiries. Shepherd, a dog lover, spent time petting Luna whilst her colleague sauntered over to Dr Markham, the attractive Head of Forensics. Vance greeted the competent specialist in her forties with a cheery grin.

The large brown eyes, which had won the heart of the department's computer expert, Max Wright, fixed on the inspector.

"Oh, hi, Jacob, I'm afraid you'll have to wait for her personal effects. I'll be as quick as thoroughness allows. I'll bring them over from Lambeth myself. You'll be wanting to read the diary we found in her pocket. I'll lay odds on this being murder."

Vance snorted, his face a mask of frustration. "That's what Doc Tremethyk said. Don't withhold the damned diary a minute longer than necessary, Sabrina."

"You know that I'll be in the Yard as soon as possible—to see Max! Has he told you yet?"

"Told me what?"

She laughed happily. "It's up to him to tell you! I'd have thought he'd have done so by now."

"Well, whatever it is, he hasn't," Vance snapped. "It seems everyone's withholding information from me."

CHAPTER 2

METROPOLITAN POLICE HEADQUARTERS, NEW SCOTLAND YARD, LONDON

VANCE SLAMMED THE PHONE RECEIVER ONTO ITS CRADLE WITH enough force to break the heavy-duty plastic. The same violence used to shut his office door rocked the partition wall, threatening lesions to the plasterwork. Anyone familiar with Jacob Vance's moods should have been diving for cover at that moment. As it was, he stomped straight towards Max Wright's computer station. Max was the resident computer expert and the envy of the other informatics operatives, because such was his standing that he always obtained whatever sophisticated equipment he asked for.

DS Wright sensed rather than saw or heard his superior arrive. He looked up with a sincere grin that faded at the aggression on the detective's face.

"Bad day, is it, sir?"

Vance's sour expression contorted into a snarl. "What is it with you lot? Dr Markham tells me you're sitting on the news you should have given me days ago. If you're—"

Max Wright laughed, cutting his inspector short. "Oh, that! It's just that I hadn't found the right moment, you know. It's that we're engaged! We haven't fixed a wedding date yet, but when we do, you'll be the first to know."

"Bloody hell, Max! You old dog! And what a catch! Congratulations, and I'm sorry if I stormed at you. People are withholding crucial information, and you know how that bugs me."

"So, will you consider being my best man, sir?"

"No, I won't. No need to consider. I'd be honoured."

Max Wright leapt to his feet and, to the inspector's surprise, caught him in a rib-crushing hug. "Sabrina will be delighted when I tell her."

"Tell me what?" A faint Manchester accent broke up the man-hug.

"Sabrina!" they exclaimed in unison before Vance grumbled, "About bloody time!"

Max quickly explained the reason for the embrace, so that for the next few minutes police work firmly took second place to congratulations and excited wedding chatter, with lots of banter from Vance to embarrass the loving couple.

At last, the Detective Inspector put on a serious face. "Before I come to you, young lady, what have *you* got for me, Max?"

"Nothing unsavoury about our poor victim. Quite the opposite. Her grandparents, refugees, came over from Latvia in the twenties. Like many of their compatriots, they settled in Glasgow. Her grandfather worked in the Clyde shipyards. Instead, her parents transferred to Swinging London as a young married couple in the Sixties. No criminal records in the family. Indeed, her father held a steady job on the Tube up to early retirement for ill-health in 2019. He died last year, unfortunately. It's sad, isn't it? I mean, when a bloke works for years, gets retirement and then doesn't get a chance to enjoy it. What's worse," he sighed, "is that we have to contact a widow about losing her only daughter." He uttered the last sentence with a hangdog expression and a wince whilst passing an address to Vance.

"OK, I'll see to that. But what can you tell me about the victim?"

"Gundega Krūmina, an only child, the star of the family. Upper second-class degree in Computer Science and Information

Systems from Imperial College London and worked at Harrods. She held a responsible position as an Online Concessions Assistant. Her task was to meet planned sales targets. You have to be bright for that. I could do it, for example, because it involves data processing, trading, analysis and reporting. I'd say our Gundega will be a big loss to her employers."

"You have been busy, Max. Well done! I'll send my sergeant to Harrods for the usual info-gathering about our victim. As for you, Dr Markham," he had simmered down throughout Wright's detailed briefing; Jacob Vance needed to be surrounded by efficiency and not caprice, "please come with me to my office and enlighten me about your findings. All in your own good time, naturally," he added, dripping sarcasm as he marched off.

Max and Sabrina exchanged conspiratorial grins before she placed a chaste kiss on his forehead and hurried after the occasionally irascible inspector.

"This is what you want, Jacob. Look, I've brought it as quickly as my scruples would allow." She slid a plastic envelope containing a small diary towards him across the desk. "It's an almost unused and outdated Lett's Legacy Slim Pocket Diary. We found it in the victim's coat pocket. But I can say with certainty that the killer put it there."

Vance stared at the dark blue diary and grumbled, "I still haven't heard from Doctor Tremethyk, and until I do, I can't assume foul play."

"Not until you open the diary, that is, Jacob," Doctor Markham purred sympathetically.

He snatched up the plastic evidence bag, opened the seal and slid out the small book. Flicking through the pages, the puzzlement on his face grew. "But it's empty!"

"Not quite. Keep going!"

Then he came to it. Feeling absurdly like Conan Doyle's hero, he took a magnifying glass to read the minuscule printing of a square of white paper pasted onto a page.

"It's typed in Microsoft Word, Jacob, Times New Roman's

smallest font—five-point. The gum is a standard paper latex glue, and, as with the whole diary, there's no trace evidence. I believe that our murderer knew exactly what he—or she, more likely—was doing."

Detective Inspector Vance was too absorbed in his reading to follow her with sufficient attention. Several expletives were followed by, "Eh, sorry?"

"Now that you've read it, you can see why I'm sure the woman was murdered."

"There's no doubt at all. Now, would you mind repeating what you said? I was distracted by the implications."

Sabrina Markham nodded and repeated her words.

"It looks that way, Doc. But why do you think the killer is female?"

"You need Miriam Walker on it for a professional opinion, not me. Mine's instinct."

The forensics specialist referred to a psychologist the Met used as a profiler. She had been of great help in several high-profile cases.

"You're right, but share your thoughts with me. I always find them invaluable."

"Max always says that's what makes you a good copper," she beamed fondly at his stressed face, "your ability to listen and analyse. He's right. So, look at the meticulousness in typing so small, without any errors, although she could have done it, say, in twelve-point then reduced it. But it's the concept—it strikes me as unmasculine. Then, she cut the square of paper so care-fully. Study the piece again, Jacob. What can you see? Anything?"

"Do you mean here?" He raised his magnifying glass and pointed to the paper.

"Exactly! Indentation caused by a pair of tweezers. Our murderess placed it accurately into position with the kind of implement I use for plucking my eyebrows."

Vance couldn't keep himself from staring into the pretty

expert's face. The large brown eyes twinkled as he studied her shapely brows.

"It seems our killer is right-handed," he said, slightly embarrassed at his over-appreciation of her comeliness.

"You would think so," she agreed, "otherwise, the indentations would have been on the other side."

"But listen, Sabrina, science apart, what does this document make you think?"

"The same as you, by the look on your face. Tibbet?"

"We're on the same wavelength, Sabrina." He reached for his phone, dialled an internal number and barked, "Shep? Get your carcass up here double-smart!"

Dr Markham protested, "Jacob! That's no way to treat a colleague, let alone a lady."

"Lady? It's Brittany Shepherd I was talking to."

"I know. And if there's anyone more ladylike on the Force, I'd love to meet her."

"If you'd had to work in close contact with Brit, you'd soon change your music."

The object of their exchange knocked and entered, the pretty oval face and turned-up nose under dark hair cut in a 1920s straight bob, confirming Markham's assessment. As was her way, DI Shepherd went directly to the point. "Has the pathology report come through? It's murder, isn't it?"

"No, it bloody hasn't! But yes, it's murder, as our remarkable Doctor Markham can confirm." Mention of the autopsy caused him to use Dr Tremethyk's moniker for the forensic scientist, whose name the CME invariably preceded, out of respect for her professional ability, with *remarkable*. Vance picked up the diary, turned to the pasted passage and read, with the aid of his magnifier:

Arnold Tibbet was innocent.
The Met Police are inept bunglers.
Reopen the case.
Prove his innocence —
Or others will die.

The detective inspector paused for dramatic effect, then read:

Signed, one whose name is writ in blood.

Brittany Shepherd leapt to her feet. "Bloody hell!" she yelled, confirming Vance's earlier statement, questioning her ladylikeness. He gave Markham a smirk and received a wink in return.

"And that is why I want you to work with me on this case, Brit. I know it's been assigned to me, but given the circumstances—"

"Just try to keep me away from it! This note is bloody serious!"

"Only someone close to Tebbit would have ended with that sign-off. Somebody who knew the contents of his diary."

"Exactly, or someone in the know on the Force," Brittany muttered.

"Damn it, Brit. Are you suggesting a bent copper?"

"I'm just keeping an open mind. Don't you think you should hassle Doc Tremethyk for the post-mortem results?"

"The good doctor has his timeframe, Brit. We'll have to wait on it."

The three occupants of Vance's office drank coffee and chatted about Sabrina's forthcoming wedding. "It'll soon be news of the day all around the department," Brittany laughed, after offering her congratulations.

A knock came on the door to interrupt this scene of conviviality.

"Am I disturbing a party, me-dears?"

"No, come in, Doc," Vance beamed at the pathologist. "We were just congratulating Dr Markham on her engagement."

The Chief Medical Examiner did a double-take of the forensics expert's pretty face.

"Well, boy, you could knock me over with a twig."

"I believe the expression is a *feather*, Doc," Vance chuckled. "I must say, I was just as surprised. No offence, Sabrina, but I'd always considered you married to your profession."

"I'll take that as a compliment, Jacob, but there's room in my life for Max."

"The remarkable Max Wright?" the pathologist asked.

Tremethyk looked puzzled when all three laughed.

"The very same, Francis." Sabrina smiled.

"They'll be a *remarkable* couple, won't they?" Vance couldn't resist. "Now, Doc, what have you got for me?"

The Cornishman's benign face suddenly became grave. "Murder, as you already knew. I'm afraid it throws up more problems than it solves. You'll have noticed that the autopsy took me longer than usual. That's because the crafty so-and-so nearly convinced me it was a heart attack. Although I say it myself, I'm to be congratulated on fathoming this one." He stuck out his chest and beamed around the room, scowling only at Shepherd, whose attempt to transform her laughter into a cough hadn't succeeded.

After a pause for his hurt dignity, the good-natured fifty-four-year-old resumed, "Almost certainly, the killer followed the victim silently into that infernal tunnel, where she used a cotton wad, like chloroforming the poor lassie, but not with chloroform, with something more sinister, and therein lies the problem." As if to accentuate his perplexity, he scratched his grizzled locks at the nape of his neck.

Again, he paused, cleared his throat, looked around and, content that he had everyone's undivided attention, continued, "Hydrogen cyanide is a clear colourless or blue liquid; its pre-evaporation time on the wad a mere two or three minutes, so our murderer moved swiftly, sure of himself. The result: seizure, slow heart rate, low blood pressure, loss of consciousness and cardiac arrest. The poor girl would have died almost instantly. Had the body lain there any longer, our killer would have got away with the perfect crime. Finding the cause was challenging. In the end, a blood sample showed a minuscule trace of the substance. You see, it decays— just enough remained to confirm my suspicion which was initially triggered by finding almost invisible cotton fibre in the nasal passage."

Like a professor addressing a tutorial for university students, he expounded, "You see, not anyone can lay hands on liquid hydrogen cyanide. I'd go as far as to say that it's impossible for the general public to get hold of. I'd start my inquiries at Porton Down if I were you, Jacob."

"Good heavens! Are you serious? The government's top-secret biological and chemical warfare research station? I thought our lot had signed up to abandon chemical weapons."

"They did, in 1957," Sabrina Markham intervened, "and since then, they've eradicated stockpiles. In 1996, Britain ratified the Chemical Weapons Convention, but Porton Down is still active, mainly in developing effective *countermeasures* to chemical and biological threats. You'll certainly find hydrogen cyanide in liquid form there."

"I've got an awful feeling about this case," Vance grumbled.

"Here's my full report, Detective Inspector. If you want my opinion, this was a random killing. The young woman was of good character."

"What makes you say that, Doc?" Brittany asked.

"The poor lassie was a virgin. There aren't many of those aged thirty-two around nowadays."

Dr Markham smothered a laugh, remembering the seriousness of the victim's death, but felt compelled to say, "Dr Tremethyk, I'm not sure whether to categorise that remark as old-fashioned or sexist."

"No, no, me-dear gal, you should label it as respectful if anything, but I must be on my way."

When the door closed behind him, Vance summed up everyone's feelings with, "Dr Tremethyk is as old-fashioned as they come, a gentleman, and a damned fine pathologist, but he's given me a right headache with this one."

Dr Markham opened her case and pulled out another plastic evidence envelope. It contained the victim's mobile phone. "I've typed you a list of names that featured in recent calls, Jacob. Nothing unusual strikes me. You'll have to find out who they are. The most frequent is to Anete Krūmina, I presume that's her mother."

"Talking about which, Brit, do you have a female officer available to go round to this address?" He passed her Max's Post-it note. "It's time we informed the poor lady of her loss. Whoever you send should take Dr Markham's list—maybe her mother can clarify whether they are friends, relatives, or colleagues. Notice there are no men on that list. I don't think that she was in a romantic relationship, going by that."

As soon as Sabrina Markham left, Vance and Shepherd chewed over the implications of the latest developments. "I'll have to bring in Big Mal, Brittany."

"Agreed. We'd better do that, given the Tibbet connection. I'm worried."

"With very good reason. Me, too."

Detective Chief Inspector Malcolm Ridgeway joined his officers in Vance's room. Deep-set eyes under marked eyebrows, a firm jaw and well-shaped lips under a slightly crooked nose—an old rugby injury—gave him an uncanny resemblance to the late flamboyant soccer coach, Malcolm Alison: hence, his nickname. All he lacked to be a perfect doppelganger was a straight nose, fedora and fat cigar.

"What's so urgent, Jacob? Good day to you, Brittany."

"It's the Avenue Road incident, sir. As I suspected, it's a homicide, but it's taken a worrying turn." He hurriedly filled in his chief on the diary and the lethal substance used for the killing.

"Good grief! What have we got here, a copycat killer on the loose?"

"That's what it looks like and, after the Quasimodo case, I think we should be alarmed. If you recall, sir, that series of deaths also began with the murder of a thirty-two-year-old blonde. But if Porton Down is involved, we're going to need some high-level clearance."

"Not only that, Jacob, but remember that Tibbet's intended ninth victim was the Commissioner's nephew. I'm going to bring her in on this chop-chop."

No sooner had he gone out of the room than Brittany snorted, "Did he really say *chop-chop?*"

"It's a generational thing, Brit. Your grandchildren will take the mickey out of the way you speak before you realise it."

"Bit of a tricky one, that, Jacob. Having grandchildren contains a whole series of implications."

"Right, sorry I mentioned it." He looked so contrite that Shepherd decided to let the matter drop. There was too much sorrow involved in that argument.

In a phone call from Ridgeway, the DCI confirmed that all three detectives were summoned into the Commissioner's reception room, a plush affair illuminated by blue lighting, as with all the top-floor spaces. Seen from the outside, the blue light at the top of the building reminded the general public that they were under police tutelage. Vance—who rarely came into direct contact with The Black Swan, as he thought of her but would never dare put into words for the motive of political correctness and sheer cowardice, although he occasionally referred to her simply as *The Swan*—gazed at the profile of a Greek goddess. Aalia Phadkar, admired for her career and looks but feared for her iron fist, turned her gaze on him and demanded an update.

He obliged whilst trying and failing not to sound troubled. She picked up on it right away.

"I think we were all disturbed by the Tibbet case, Jacob, but we have to think positively now. There's no reason to suppose that this new killer will possess his skills and cunning." Her large black eyes turned on Ridgeway. "Malcolm, I think that Miriam Walker would be of great help to us with this case. Bring her in immediately. Another thing, you can have as many uniforms as necessary should matters become more complex. I'll see to that myself. And Jacob, good thinking bringing Brittany onto the case. I'll get priority clearance for the two of you and a detective sergeant for Porton Down. I want this matter sewn up as soon as possible. Arnold Tebbit was as guilty as Cain. There's no question of reopening the case. Now, down to work, all of you."

Her jaw set in the stubborn expression Vance had seen before when she refused to apologise for her inaugural speech, which he knew she had got wrong, but secretly admired. After all, in his book, where criminals were concerned, scum was indeed scum. He would never fault The Swan for her plain-talking, however undiplomatic for an inaugural speech.

CHAPTER 3
NEW SCOTLAND YARD, WESTMINSTER, LONDON

MIRIAM WALKER, A FORTY-NINE-YEAR-OLD PSYCHOLOGIST WITH A string of qualifications to her name, greeted Jacob Vance with genuine warmth. Her somewhat frumpy middle-aged appearance, comfortable tweed skirt under a hand-knitted cardigan, flat shoes that looked like they had been rescued from a charity shop and mousy hair pinned back in a bun, combined to mislead anyone who did not know her. Concealed under the aspect prevailed a sharp mind and an empathic personality.

"Well met, Detective Inspector. With so much going on, it seems like a lifetime ago that we last worked together, it must be eighteen months at a guess."

Vance smiled. Long gone were the early days of suspicion towards external interference when the very word *profiler* set his teeth on edge. Miriam was so unassuming and excelled at her work to such a degree that he welcomed her, though not literally, with open arms. "Precise as ever, Doc. It was when you gave us a vital insight into the mind of the evil Tebbit. Frankly, that's why I've asked for your help this time."

"Good heavens! Surely, you haven't reopened that case? I thought it was cut and dried."

"So did we, Miriam." He felt comfortable now using her

given name. "But someone else has a different idea. Come with me to my office and I'll fill you in. Coffee?"

She sipped at her espresso as Vance read out the threatening message pasted in the diary. He fought back the urge to blurt out his thoughts because the psychologist needed to reach unprompted conclusions. He could almost hear the cogs turning in her brain. Miriam Walker was not one to blurt anything, ever. After due consideration, she half-rose in her chair and methodically placed the espresso-style cup and saucer precisely in the centre of a cork coaster.

"Jacob, the most disturbing aspect of this message is that whoever wrote it knew that the original letter sent by Tibbet to the Commissioner signed off with those words. Am I right in thinking that you never circulated Tibbet's letter to the press?"

"Absolutely not."

"That, as I'm sure you will have already concluded, means one of two things: either there's a leak from within, which I doubt, or disturbingly, someone had access to Tibbet or his diary."

"You're right. Both DI Shepherd and I arrived at the same conclusion."

"How is the lovely Brittany?"

"Would you mind if I brought her in on the next part of our conversation? Despite it being my case, we'll work it together, just like old times."

"Vance and Shepherd: just like fish and chips!"

They both laughed and waited whilst Shepherd responded to Vance's call. Within minutes, there came a knock at the door, but it wasn't Brittany. DCI Ridgeway entered. Miriam Walker rose politely to greet him and explained her reaction to the threatening message.

"We're waiting for DI Shepherd," Vance growled. He was always impatient at the beginning of a case when he felt he was making little headway.

The neo-inspector saved him from toppling over into irritability by knocking on the door as he finished the sentence.

Defusing the situation expertly, Miriam said, "Thank you for breaking off whatever you were doing, Brittany. It's a pleasure to see you again." Smiling, she extended her hand to the officer, who equally cordially exchanged greetings.

"Grab yourself a chair, Brit," Vance said, mollified. "I'm about to ask Miriam to hazard—excuse me, it's the wrong word —to *outline* a profile of our killer. But first, some extra information." He told the psychologist Dr Markham's conclusion about the gender of the assassin.

The profiler stared at Vance for what seemed an eternity before curling her lip. "You know, *hazard* wasn't so far wrong at this stage of the inquiries. It's too early for a clear picture. Still, one thing that should put you all on the alert, our murderer has already displayed a close affinity to Tebbit, not only by claiming his innocence and we must ask ourselves why *she*— yes, I agree with Sabrina—would fly in the face of a watertight conviction. It seems that she has an emotional connection of some kind to the serial killer. We should take nothing at face value—that's my motto, by the way—but the copycat nature of the message and the selection of the victim would point to a frighteningly similar psychotic individual, displaying the classic symptoms of dissociative identity disorder. I'm afraid we can't rule out somebody else in the same family."

A collective intake of breath greeted these words. The senior officer present spoke first.

"I seem to remember that there were brothers and sisters in our Tibbet investigation." He glanced from Vance to Shepherd.

Brittany answered him. "Yes, sir, I interviewed each of his three sisters—he was the fifth of five offspring, by the way— Beryl, Brenda and Beatrice. Of those, Beryl is a model citizen. A hard-working mother of two, happily married. Brenda is a bit of a slattern, takes after her mother in that respect, and showed signs of aggression when questioned. I think her husband Nigel is something of a wide boy. Then there was Beatrice; she seemed reasonable and intelligent. She didn't have much time for Arnold. Those were my impressions."

"Mmm, very helpful, Brittany," Miriam said, her tone admiring. "Perhaps you should probe into this Brenda."

"I'll get onto it straight away." Shepherd's jaw clenched. They could see she meant business.

"What about the brothers?" Ridgeway asked. "Refresh my memory."

Vance took up the discussion. "The eldest, Andrew, was in prison serving time for housebreaking at the time of the Tibbet murders. A phone call will establish whether he's still behind bars. I can't recall how much of the sentence he still had to serve. I'll get Max onto that. I interviewed the second brother, Andrew; at the time, he struck me as a regular guy. He had no record and worked as a forecourt attendant at a petrol station in Lansbury. My instincts are usually right, but I'll check him out myself."

Shepherd sat stock still, staring at the wall. Miriam Walker noticed. "Is something bothering you, Brittany?"

"Eh? Yes. But I can't quite pin it down. Something to do with Tibbet's family. I need to read through the case notes again before I race off to question Brenda Tibbet."

"I'll have them sent to this office," Malcolm Ridgeway said, "but don't get bogged down, Shep. I want progress on this one pretty damned quick, given the precedents. Listen, people, I want you to keep me posted on even the smallest development, understood?"

He didn't wait for an answer but made a determined exit from Vance's office, leaving an exchange of meaningful glances behind him.

"Has Ellen reported in yet?"

Vance referred to the latest addition to the team, who DI Shepherd had recruited as a constable from the Vice Squad to be her sergeant. DS Ellen Rhodes had earned herself a commendation and medal for taking on two pimps to save a homeless teenage girl. In the process, she'd also gained herself a broken jaw but still succeeded in cuffing one of the assailants and radioing for help to capture the other, a lumbering brute of Polish origins, to ensure both were arrested and imprisoned. Shepherd admired her pluck and offered the promotion and change of job she desired, which Rhodes seized eagerly.

"Not yet, but speaking with the grieving mother isn't a task you can rush. I expect she'll report in soon. What about Mark?"

She meant Vance's replacement for her as his sergeant, a constable who had shone during the Tibbet case. Jacob had made a point of not letting Shepherd, as he put it at the time, *snitch him from under my nose.*

"I sent him to Gundega's workplace, Brit. Even you'll have heard of Harrods, I expect?"

"Cheeky sod! You're supposed to get mellower with age."

"Pah! Age is just a number. Come on, partner, let's see what Max has turned up."

The pale-skinned computer specialist blushed to the roots of his hair when the attractive Brittany bent to kiss his cheek and congratulated him on his engagement.

"Back to work, you two!" Vance said, but his tone was light.

"Sir, Anthony Tibbet's still inside HMP Wandsworth, so he can't be our killer. They refused his parole for assaulting a prison officer. Tell you what, though, boss. I decided to run a check on the other brother, Andrew, whilst I was at it. He's still working as a forecourt attendant, and although he has no record, police questioned him not long ago about a series of break-ins in the Lansbury area. He had to explain to the local bobbies what he was doing with a new iPhone that they traced from the real owner's tablet. He cooperated fully, and they accepted his explanation of how he'd bought it on the cheap from some shady character already known to us. Tibbet's statement led to the arrest of the burglars. It occurred to me that the fellow might not be as squeaky-clean as he'd like us to think. He must have known that the price he paid for the iPhone was way below its market value."

"Good work, Max. I'll visit our friend Andrew Tibbet to see for myself."

He escorted Shepherd back to his office, which by default had become their operations room for the *Diary Killer* affair. For that reason, Ridgeway had ordered the Tibbet file to be taken there, so it was lying on his desk when they returned.

"Over to you, Brit. Take my chair and take your time, too."

"Thanks, Jacob, I can't shake the feeling that my memory just needs a jog." She set about turning pages, clicking her tongue, shaking her head and grumbling under her breath. Vance watched her for a while, ignored his stress levels and made them both another espresso coffee. After drinking it in two gulps, he tried to decide whether to drive over to Lansbury or wait for DS Allen to report back.

Mark Allen solved that quandary by knocking on his door as he prevaricated.

"Ah, Mark, do you have anything interesting to report?"

"Not a sausage, boss. I spoke to all her colleagues and her direct supervisor. No one had a bad word to say about her. She was always cheerful, professional and reserved about her private life. Some of the girls ragged her for being an ice maiden. One of them is openly gay, but she says that Gundega most certainly wasn't. I don't know whether she came on to her and got repulsed. I didn't press the point. I'm not comfortable with gay people."

"That's something you'll have to work on, Mark."

"Yes, sir." He looked downcast. Vance was his hero and even a gentle reproval from him stung.

The inspector's thoughts had moved on, "So, that's a bit of a dead-end but confirms my theory that it was a random killing—"

Shepherd looked up from her reports. "Unless it's a copycat, Inspector." She didn't want to sound too familiar by using his name in front of the sergeant. "I mean, both blondes, thirty-two years old, and office workers."

"I'm keeping an open mind on that. Arnold Tibbet used colours. His murders were kind of thematic. It's too early to see any pattern here. Certainly, Primrose Street referred to yellow, as did the haiku."

"You may be going grey, but there's nothing wrong with your memory. I'm the one reading the case file!" Shepherd said self-effacingly and laughed. "Besides, Arnold Tibbet signed off his handiwork with a formula, like **9-5=4**. We didn't see that at the crime scene."

"Mmm, perhaps because it was dark in there, and we weren't looking. Sergeant, be a good lad, nip over to Avenue Road, take a decent torch and check for any writing on the tunnel walls."

"I'm on it, sir."

Vance waited for the door to close, heard voices outside, followed by a knock, and called, "Come in!"

The door opened slowly as if the newcomer was hesitant. A head with short red hair appeared around the edge.

"It's alright, Ellen, this is our ops room for this one," Shepherd said.

"Sir, ma'am," DS Ellen Rhodes greeted them deferentially, "reporting back on my house call." She glanced uneasily at Vance as if in awe of his reputation.

Quick to sense her unease, Vance came to her rescue. "Don't mind me, Sergeant, I'm a great admirer of your work. You took one for the Force, didn't you?"

"All in the line of duty, sir." She looked relieved and said, "It was heart-breaking with Mrs Krūmina. The poor woman took an hour before she got a grip. Then the usual stuff, old photos, praise for her daughter, who you'd have thought was a saint. I pressed her on relationships, but she wasn't going out with anybody. She had one friend, a Valerie Brookes from across the road. They're the same age. Before I chased her up, I checked out

Gundega's bedroom. Nothing there, except that she kept a diary."

"Did she, indeed!" Vance muttered. In a louder voice, he asked, "Anything interesting in it?"

"Mostly work gossip and reference to books she was reading. She would copy short passages if she thought something worthwhile. The last entry was from a Portuguese writer, Fernando Pessoa. All of these extracts struck me as intellectual, sir. But there was one thing—"

"Yes?"

"Two days before her death, she wrote that she thought she was being followed home. But then she added, *it's me being silly about the dark. It was only a girl with long blonde hair.* She thought that she should take a sedative because she was too jumpy. I don't know if that's important, ma'am."

"It might be; well done, Ellen. Now, tell us about her friend... Valerie, wasn't it?

"Yes, Valerie Brookes. I had to catch her at work so as not to have to wait till her shift ended. She works on stock replenishment and as a cashier at Whole Foods Market, Fulham Broadway."

"I know it well," Shepherd said ruefully, "I spent long enough on surveillance there on the Tibbet case. It's strong on organic groceries."

"I used my initiative, ma'am and asked Val whether her friend had seemed nervous lately. She insisted she'd been her normal self and had seen her the day before her decease. They'd watched a Netflix film together at Valerie's house. Another thing, she looked amazed when I asked if Gundega had any enemies. She was definite that such a sunny personality couldn't provoke antipathy—my word, not hers. She'll miss her friend deeply. A genuine lass, if you know what I mean?"

"Well done, Ellen. You have the makings of a detective, and you've given us something to work on," Vance said.

"I have?" The slightly chubby features of the sergeant lit up, displaying pleasure and puzzlement simultaneously.

"Put it this way, you've definitely earned yourself the offer of my prized coffee. Want one?" he grinned. She accepted cheerily.

Vance's mobile pinged a notification. "It's an image," he said, "from Mark. Bloody hell! Look at this, Brit!"

The photo, taken on the tunnel's inside wall, showed black-painted graffiti that portrayed a formula, well-known, sinister, and chilling to the detectives: **9-1=8**.

CHAPTER 4

NEW SCOTLAND YARD, AND EALING, OXFORD STREET AND CLAPHAM TOWN, LONDON

AALIA PHADKAR SMILED AT HER REDOUBTABLE DETECTIVE inspectors. "You know when it comes to science, one has to be so careful. We are police officers and can't be expected to have a comprehensive knowledge of anything. Hydrogen cyanide production, for instance, I freely admit, firmly falls into the category of a closed book for yours truly. I called you up here to explain how I've avoided a banana skin." Her exceedingly attractive countenance lit up with an even-toothed smile that transformed it into beautiful.

"To think, I was on the verge of obtaining passes for you to enter Porton Down, which, as you know is a maximum security, top-secret establishment, but fortunately, I had a light-bulb moment and phoned through to them. To get to the point, they passed me to their Chief Scientific Officer, who coolly informed me that anyone can buy hydrogen cyanide on the internet!"

"What a world we live in!" DS Shepherd exclaimed.

"Exactly, Brittany. But as it turns out, it wasn't a wasted call, nor one that only prevented us from looking like bloody fools. The CSO went to the trouble of checking their hydrogen cyanide stock to discover that it tallied completely with the inventory, which it did. So, we can eliminate Porton Down from our inquiries. He also made the point that our killer probably has more than a passing chemical knowledge to be capable of confidently deploying HCN."

Vance intervened. "So, we're looking for a blonde with a degree in chemistry?"

"That might well fit our profile." The Commissioner flashed her white teeth again. "But keep an open mind—oh, and get Max Wright to chase up HCN suppliers on the internet. We might want to check their trading."

"Will do, he's the best at getting results."

"Jacob, Brittany, let's see some progress in this case. If we're dealing with a copycat killer, I hardly need to remind you that another eight lives are at risk."

They both gave her the assurances she sought before taking the stairs down to Vance's office.

"It's only human for the Commissioner to worry about her nephew," Brittany leant close to whisper in Vance's ear. "After all, he was Tibbet's intended ninth victim. Our copycat killer will know that."

———

The person the two detectives were discussing at that moment glared at the coin-operated meter. Her old-fashioned single element electric fire gobbled up electricity units, and her 50p coin had just run out. She blamed herself for her stupidity, or rather, excessive caution. She had a luxury flat in Fulham with a fantastic view over the Thames that she'd inherited on her brother's death. Instead of sitting there in the warmth, revelling in the panorama, she was holed up in this linoleum-floored, pokey hovel, shivering from the rising damp emanating from the walls of a bedsit over a hairdresser's salon. True, she had a fortune and could spend some of it on better-quality accommodation, but her Irish landlady, coiffeuse Ms Kelly, was the type of person who steered well clear of the law and its enforcers. For good or bad, her choice provided her with the anonymity she craved— necessary for what she had in mind.

With a heavy sigh, she fed four more coins into the ravenous meter and decided to buy a cheap but efficient halogen stove from a supermarket as soon as possible. Relatively, halogen heaters hardly consumed any electricity.

But for now, she had to concentrate. She reached for her notepad and began to jot down the pros and cons regarding her next murder. Some elements were quite clear to her. Foremost, she would strike at an off-peak time when passenger flux was at its lowest; secondly, her *modus operandi* would be the same. Her actions would need to be swift and unobserved. The question was how to find a compartment with only one or two passengers.

Firmly in the cons column was victim selection. The awkward business of copying Arnold's victims' profiles limited her. If only she would be satisfied with the unexpected opportunities that chance threw her way. But no! She had decided on this course of action and would stick to it. So, her next killing had to be of an around twenty-five-year-old white male. To avoid detection, she would have to wear a disguise, but she was used to that, so placed the word *disguise* in the pro column. Mostly, it entailed making sure that her giveaway mane of long blonde hair was hidden, but there were other tricks; for example, she could fake being heavily pregnant or pretend to be a boy.

She tossed her pencil down, an air of impatience in the gesture, followed by the drumming of her square-cut, brown-varnished fingernails. Was she scared? Was that why she hesitated before researching the next kill? What reason did she have? The coppers still didn't have a clue except for what she had so recklessly gifted them. She bit her lower lip. Had that been a mistake? Without the diary, though, they would not know that this was a revenge operation, a *vendetta* as the Italian mafia would say.

She carefully locked her notebook in a security case and

pushed it far under the low single bed in the corner of the room so that it wouldn't be seen in the unlikely event of anyone entering the room. The silk sheets on the bed under three heavy blankets were the only touch of luxury she had conceded to herself. Ms Kelly made it quite clear that she didn't provide a laundry service—basically, she didn't provide anything—but the petite blonde wasn't complaining at that price.

She grabbed the keys, locked up and set off to buy whatever struck her as suitable garb to disguise her without catching the eye. Then, her serious research could begin. Unlike the first murder, she would be more exposed to the public gaze this time, so every tiny detail needed to be in place. Thoroughness had been Arnold's watchword, and she intended to outdo him on that score. Her brother had let the coppers catch him. She swore that they wouldn't capture her. After all, she was way smarter than them, wasn't she?

A brisk walk brought her to Ealing Common tube station, where she took the District Line to St. James's Park and, feeling the need for fresh air, she strolled through the park and headed for the Oxford Street shops. She had no worries about paying by debit card because the police weren't on to her yet. Brittany loved shopping, so disguise-hunting pandered to her passion. She began her spree by entering a sportswear shop, where she bought an XS black designer tracksuit with the three iconic stripes down the shoulders and arms and legs. She matched it with the same manufacturer's trainers, again with the famous triangular three-striped logo on the uppers. Pleased that the top had a hood, which would come in useful in the vicinity of prying closed-circuit cameras or in any place she wished to hide her blonde locks, she purchased it willingly. At the cashpoint, she spotted a black Adidas face mask. In this period of Covid 19, this item had become a fashion accessory. How cool was that for incognito work?

Exiting the store, she came to another clothes shop, this time, a boutique. Hats! She adored hats. She entered and browsed through the millinery department. She tried on and dismissed a wool, wide brim, porkpie fedora hat, which made her look pert, but she thought that it caught the eye too much for her purposes, so chose a beige felt trilby with a brown band around the crown. She would be able to pile her hair up under it but would need a scarf to cover the blonde hair at the nape. The foulard would need to match a jacket paired with the hat, and why not buy trousers to complete the outfit? Half the morning had gone by as she strutted in front of mirrors in the fitting room before dodging back into the changing booth to try on a different pair. Finding the right jacket proved more troublesome because she was petite, so the correct cut was vital; otherwise, there could be unsightly bulges at the back of the upper arm near the shoulder. At last, satisfied, she paid and, laden with shopping bags, moved along the busy thoroughfare choked by red double-decker buses. They always seemed to swarm together or not be seen at all! She coughed unhappily at the diesel fumes and thought fondly of her favourite pollution-free trams. Partly to escape from the thick air, and partly because, whilst her Fulham property was well-stocked with size 3½ shoes, she had moved very little of her wardrobe to her bedsit, she veered into a shoe shop. She immediately fell in love with a pair of zipped brown ankle boots and, on a whim, treated herself to an expensive pair of black Elizabetta Franchi décolleté shoes with logoed high heels. This kind of costly impulse purchase had been denied her until her hunchbacked brother's violent death in prison—poor sod! She offered up a silent prayer for his tormented soul as she paid for her extravagant acquisition.

With a smug bounce in her stride, she crossed the road to enter Bond Street tube station. With one change of line, she reached Clapham Town, where she browsed in several shops selling punk gear. She kitted herself out entirely with clothing and boots that made her look like a Goth from head to toe. She drew the line at ear and nose piercing and tattooing—she would have to pass muster without them—but she bought a black wig with a purple crest and, to her jaundiced eye, that compensated for the other missing details. She detested punks. A pity, she thought, that Arnold hadn't included one among his seven victims. She, Bethany, would love to put a punk out of her misery. She particularly loathed female Goths, failing to understand why they would want to look so unfeminine. Having said that, a Goth disguise was tops. It would transform her from an attractive lady into an unremarkable slob: that was the idea. Shopping over for the day, she rode back to her bedsit with her new outfits.

The next few days, she would now dedicate to carefree research on the Tramlink, her favourite, and the only, London tram route.

———

Brittany Shepherd startled her colleague by exclaiming from Vance's chair behind his desk, "I've got it! Damn it, Jacob, that's what was niggling me. Luckily, I reported the conversation. Look here!" He came around the desk, bent over her shoulder and peered at where her short, bitten fingernail—the nails were the only unfeminine part of Brittany—traced a chat with Beatrice Tibbet. "See, Jake, she didn't rule out the possibility of a younger sister, who would have been the baby of the brood. Her slatternly mother didn't care for the little ones—probably too demanding for the lazy sow—and tended to farm them out to aunts. I'll bet you a tenner that there *is* a Bethany Tibbet. Arnold Tibbet tried to pin the blame for his sick crimes on her—his real sister!"

Vance grunted, "The riverside apartment is in joint names. It might not have been a transvestite Arnold Tibbet who signed, acting the part of Bethany, as we presumed, but the woman herself. I suggest we put surveillance on the flat. Let's see if we can observe her movements. Another thing, we should find out where Tibbet's mother sent the kids. If they are still alive, they can update us on the mysterious Bethany."

Shepherd didn't reply, she was staring at the opposite wall. Vance knew the unfocussed look meant that she was deep in thought. He respected her silence and waited. "Casting my mind back to Arnold Tibbet's funeral. Do you remember, there was a small woman dressed in black, standing apart from the others? That's what's been troubling me and dodged my memory. It was you who pointed her out to me: a petite young woman with long blonde hair. When I moved to question her, she'd disappeared among the gravestones. At the time, it occurred to me that she might be the elusive Bethany. At that stage, if you recall, we were both convinced that Bethany, like Lord Robert, was just a voice in Arnold's head. But what if she wasn't? What if she lived in the flat with him? She could have been an accessory to his heinous crimes. Given what we know now, it's not beyond the realms of possibility that she's a psychopath, too, and even committed one or two of those murders with her brother as an accomplice."

"Bloody hell, Brit! Don't go down that track. I'm begging you. We don't want to reopen the whole caboodle! Not that I disagree with your logic, but let's get her for this new crime if she exists. And I'm beginning to think she does. Then we can give her the fifth degree to see whether any of Arnold's eight were her handiwork. Good work, Shep. Let's get the ball rolling on this case by chasing up the HCN suppliers: first stop, Max Wright."

As usual, the computer expert preceded his findings with a display of knowledge. "Boss, you said that our suspect probably has competence with chemicals. That would fit with my findings. You see, HCN isn't exactly user-friendly. Did you know that the French army deployed it in the First World War? Well, not only them, the Italians and Americans tried it in 1918, too. The problem is, the gas is lighter than air and rapidly disperses into the atmosphere, whereas denser agents—such as chlorine and phosgene—tend to remain at ground level. So, it wasn't much use as a weapon. Compared to these agents, it also requires higher concentrations to be fatal."

He consulted his notes, took a sip of mineral water and, setting his plastic beaker down, continued, "Hydrogen cyanide concentration of 100-200 ppm in the air will kill a human being within ten to sixty minutes and concentration of two thousand ppm—approximately two thousand three hundred and eighty milligrams per square metre—will kill a human being in less than one minute. But a French chemist managed to concentrate it into a blue liquid. That's what our killer is using. The liquid evaporates quickly, too. So, she would have to imbue a pad with it and use it immediately to be effective. She could reach the fatal concentration easily enough. Her victim won't have suffered for long."

"Fascinating, Max, all quite clear, but where the devil does she get her supply? Not from the local chemist's shop, I presume?"

"Ha, ha! No way, Inspector. You'd need a manufacturer or a research lab."

"Like Porton Down?"

"Yes, but you said we'd ruled them out."

"We have. What about others?"

"It's complicated, sir. Isn't it always? You see, there are many legal purposes that the chemical serves. It's used in the manufacture of paints, plastics, nylon and other synthetic fibres, also in the preparation of other more sophisticated chemicals."

"So, I take it that there are many manufacturers in the United Kingdom?"

"Not so many, sir. However, I've identified at least fifteen international traders who can supply it via the internet, ranging from Chinese, American, and Indian to European suppliers. When you arrived, I was just checking this company." He turned the monitor for the detectives to see. "It's American, called Norco Incorporated, they trade in it via their Norlab Company. It's all above board and quite legitimate."

"Can we access their dealings with UK citizens?"

"*I* can't, sir. It's a specialised job. We'd need the Informatics Police on this one, strictly with the Commissioner's backing."

"What about in our own country?"

"The news is a bit brighter there. The nearest company is Monarch Chemicals, just forty-five miles from here: in Kent. They're based... let me see," he checked, "in Sittingbourne. I got through to the Managing Director—a real gent and he's expecting a visit from a couple of Met officers. He did specify that it should be under the aegis of the necessary warrants, of course."

"Good work, Max. I'll phone up for the permits. What?"

"Oh, just that there's also a company in Hampshire on an industrial estate in Alton."

"Good, but we'll do this ourselves, systematically. Even if, Brit, we should check out time frames. If the killer is copying exactly, we should know when the next death will be. We might have to accelerate our investigation."

CHAPTER 5

SITTINGBOURNE, KENT, THE UNITED KINGDOM

BRITTANY SHEPHERD DISPLAYED HER DRIVING SKILLS AND intolerance of other less expert drivers as she drove through beautiful, sleepy Kentish villages. Yet, the poor performance of other road users was not her chosen topic of conversation because, on the journey, she was obsessively concerned about the nature of copycat killings.

"I've set Rhodesy"—her fond name for her sergeant, Ellen Rhodes— "to check the precise timeline of Arnold Tibbet's murders. I know it's a long shot, but we might anticipate this killer's next moves and save some lives."

"Good thinking, Brit. Let's hope we get something out of this visit. The last thing we need at the moment is a wild goose chase, lovely as the countryside is in these parts. That pub looks particularly inviting. Forget that I said that! Maybe on the way back," he said wistfully.

"No way, pal. We'll take the motorway back. It's only an hour to Central London. While it's less scenic, it's much faster."

"Fair enough." Vance brooded over a vision of a pint of beer disappearing into nothingness like Lewis Carroll's Cheshire Cat. Only the foam was left as the pint disappeared. The Detective

Inspector was partial to a pint of bitter and if it was unfiltered craft beer, so much the better.

Whatever preconceptions the two detectives had of an industrial estate, they had to abandon when they pulled into the Kent Science Park. The planners had created an environmentally friendly estate containing laboratories and office facilities screened by trees, but including not only those attributes, as they soon found out. Their request for Monarch Chemicals was met by an inscrutable smile from an elegant young woman, who made a phone call, said *u-hum* three times before inviting them to follow her. She led them across a footbridge that arced over a stream to a modern white rectangular building fronted by large, plate-glass windows.

"The Hub," she said laconically, leading them into the bright interior. The two officers took in meeting spaces and a restaurant at a glance. "Monarch's Technical Director is on his way and will meet you here in a couple of minutes. Meanwhile, would you like a coffee, some cake?"

They accepted coffee and Brittany, belying her trim figure, failed to resist a slice of orange cream sponge though Vance, as usual, refused any kind of dessert. Within the promised time, a man appeared, wearing a grey three-piece suit, under it a blue silk tie with unobtrusive white dots, to greet them with outstretched hand and a wide smile. He joined them for coffee.

"Duncan Weybridge," he introduced himself, "Technical Director of Monarch Chemicals." He scrutinised their warrant cards, looked up and gave Brittany a beaming smile. "Congratulations, Detective Inspector, you must be good to have achieved your rank at such a young age."

"The best." Vance leapt in to cover before Shepherd said anything caustic. He knew her only too well. "My colleague is older than she looks, but don't be taken in, she's exceptionally good at what she does."

"I paid him to say that!" Shepherd smirked.

"So, what can I do for you formidable detectives?"

He listened carefully, his gaze occasionally straying to the view over the picturesque Japanese gardens outside. When Vance had finished, he said, "Yes, I remember the request. It came from a Melanie Something-or-other. I can furnish you with her surname if you want. Sorry? Yes, quite certain. No, Melanie, not Bethany. Of course, I only spoke to her on the phone because, you see, I had to direct her to our Sheerness depot. That's where we keep our stock for distribution. So I'm afraid if you need a physical description of the lady, you'll have to slip over there. It's only twenty minutes from here by car. Take the A249, which brings you to Brielle Way, just before the road bridge turn right onto New Road, and you can't miss it."

"What do you remember of that call, sir?" Vance asked.

"First of all, I was impressed. We don't take calls from Porton Down every day."

"Hang on!" Shepherd interrupted. "Did she say she was at Porton Down?"

Weybridge smiled unctuously. "Certainly, that made an impression on me, but so did her knowledge of chemistry, which you'd expect coming from there, of course."

"Did anything strike you as slightly off?" Shepherd insisted.

He looked surprised. "No, not at all. Why do you ask?"

Shepherd decided to come clean. "Because we're investigating a murder. The substance used to kill a healthy young woman was hydrogen cyanide."

"Good Lord! And you suspect this Melanie What's-her-name?"

"Sir, I think at this point, if you could furnish us with her surname, it would be helpful."

The executive whipped out his phone, dialled a number and waited for a second, his eyes never leaving Shepherd's oval face. "Amanda, be a darling and check out a visitor name for me. A Melanie Something, roughly two months ago. He tapped the table rhythmically with three fingers whilst waiting. "Good girl!" he said patronisingly, not noticing Shepherd's wince.

"Bradshaw," he announced, "Melanie Bradshaw. I can also confirm that she paid for an unspecified quantity of hydrogen cyanide at our Sheerness Depot."

Vance stood, proffering his hand, to bring the interview to an end.

"Thank you. You've been most accommodating, Mr Weybridge. But we must be off."

"Might I offer you lunch before you go?"

The detectives exchanged glances and understood each other. Shepherd took it upon herself to reply. "Time is important at this stage, sir. Much appreciated, but we must move on. The excellent cake I ate here will keep me going." She gave him her hand, which he held for a fraction too long, gazing into her sapphire eyes.

"Good luck with your case, Detective Inspector, bring the villain to justice."

"Amen! We'll do our best," she said, releasing her hand.

As she drove out of the park onto the A248, she said through gritted teeth, "It's types like him that create a glass ceiling for the female sex."

"Don't be too harsh on him, Shep; at least he gave us a lead to follow up."

She scowled. "It's not much, just a false name Bethany invented to cover her tracks."

"We can't be sure of that. There might be a real Melanie Bradshaw on the loose for all we know. People read the newspapers, you know. She may be an independent psychopath pretending to have had intimate knowledge of Tibbet!"

"I bow to your greater experience, Detective Inspector."

"Harrumph!"

"Although—"

"What?"

"I don't buy it. Why would a killer who almost got clean away with the perfect murder put us on her tracks with that diary? Doctor Tremethyk, by his admission, almost missed the faint trace of HCN. If he had, and without the diary, he'd have reported a heart attack."

"All of which proves the Met recognises a talent like yours when it has one."

"Are you taking the mickey, Jacob?"

He smiled secretly and said nothing. They were observing the speed limit along Brielle Way when Vance, who had spotted the road bridge ahead, said quietly, "Turn right here."

Shepherd obliged, surprised at the narrow lane, but it led onto New Road. "Right or left?"

He guessed, "Turn right."

They drove for a while, then he pointed. "That's Monarch Chemicals."

"By heck! Next time I enter a car rally, you'll be my navigator!"

"When did you ever participate in a rally, Shep?"

"Just saying."

He snorted, struggling to extract his warrant card from a pocket without unfastening his seat belt. They didn't need their warrants to drive into the large car park. To their left was an impressive fleet of new Mercedes Antos lorries. All a uniform grey, they bore the clever wording on the front, *Delivering the Solution.* Not bad for a chemical delivery vehicle, Vance thought. He also admired the circular logo of diminishing white dots, starting and ending with one large green dot. He considered the symbol striking and effective. The graphics were located on the cab doors.

Shepherd parked, and they proceeded to an office, where an immaculately-groomed secretary greeted them. She soon made a call through to management, then announced, "Ms Johnson, our Quality Manager, will be along in a moment if you'd care to take a seat."

A dapper woman in a power suit and her mid-forties, entered

the office. "Metropolitan Police? I hope there hasn't been an accident. In Europe, maybe? We have several drivers in France," she said, with a faint Irish brogue.

"No, ma'am, nothing of the sort," Vance sensed her apprehension, "don't worry, our inquiry doesn't involve any of your staff, but I believe that someone here can help us in a murder investigation."

If anything, her anxiety grew at these words, but she heard him out without interrupting. When he ended his explanation, she said, "So, you think the killer bought her supply of hydrogen cyanide here? Sweet Jesus, that's terrible!" She hesitated, in thought, then resumed, "I seem to remember my colleague, David Brookes, saying something about a chemist from Porton Down about a couple of months ago. Stephie, be an angel and get David down here, will you?"

The secretary smiled and tapped out a number.

"David is our Area Sales Manager," she clarified, brushing an imaginary speck from her sleeve.

"Hi, Bernadette, what's up?" a man in a beige suit and wide brown tie asked breezily, and gazed curiously at the visitors.

The Quality Manager explained and introduced the Met officers to him. The cheery smile vanished to be replaced by an expression of concern. "That's dreadful," the flaxen-haired manager frowned, "she seemed so competent and above board. All her documents were in order, too. We can't sell hydrogen cyanide to just anyone who turns up here, you know."

"Documents?" the detectives asked in unison and looked at each other in surprise.

"Yes, an order on official headed paper and rubber-stamped. I remember it well since it was from Porton Down. As you know, Porton Down is—"

"We *do* know, sir." Vance interrupted.

"Yes, of course. That's why I had no hesitation in supplying the twenty phials she required."

"I don't suppose you still have that document, sir?"

"No, Detective Inspector, but there will be the other routine paperwork involving the transaction."

"Before you retrieve it for us," Shepherd said, "what can you tell us about the woman's appearance?"

"I'm not much good at descriptions," Brookes confessed, "but I remember that I fancied her at first, begging your pardon, officer. She was slight of build, I'd say about five feet two inches tall, with long blonde hair." The police officers exchanged glances. "She had beautiful blue eyes. That's what attracted me initially, apart from her elegance and evident expertise. She was very particular about the concentration of the liquid. But you know that old saying about the eyes being the mirror of the soul. That's what put me off her. I remember thinking, *you're a cold fish, madam.* You see, Detective Inspector, those eyes held no feelings. It's not hindsight; I felt *I wouldn't like to cross you, young lady.* But with what I know now, let's say, I'm not surprised."

"Young, you say," Shepherd seized on the remark. "How old would you say she was?"

"Not sure, but no more than thirty, maybe less."

"I see. Apart from her eyes, did you notice any particulars? Accent? Distinguishing marks?"

"No tattoos or anything like that. She struck me as too elegant. Pierced ears, though, just normal, she had two round gold earrings about this big." He held up a finger and thumb like a pincer. "But I didn't pick up any accent. A well-spoken, educated type."

"I don't suppose she gave you any idea of where she was going when she left?"

"No, but I noticed she was driving a black Audi TT. I spotted that because I've always longed to own one myself."

"Registration?"

"Why would I notice that? Sorry, I can't help there."

"The paperwork?"

"That, I can do."

"Already done, Mr Brookes." The secretary, Stephanie,

smiling smugly, gave him a sheaf of papers held together with a paperclip.

"Thanks, Steph, as efficient as ever."

He pulled off the clip and shuffled through the pages. "Ah, this might be of interest—her signature." He passed it to Vance, who glanced at it and handed it Shepherd, who whipped out her mobile and photographed the page. "Apart from that, it's just specification of quantity and sales date, all routine stuff."

"Show me, please," Vance said. "Mmm, photograph this, Shep." He turned to the sales manager. "This concentration," he pointed to the letters $500 \ mg/m3$, "is that sufficient to kill in the air?"

"Definitely, and quickly, too, if breathed at close quarters. I'd say it would provoke a coma and almost instant heart failure."

"I think we're done here. Thank you for your cooperation, Mr Brookes, Ms Johnson. Good day to you."

"I hope you catch her. She's got twenty of those phials."

In the car, Vance said, "I'll ring Max. We need to know whether there's a Melanie Bradshaw at Porton Down."

"She faked the document, Jacob," Shepherd said with certainty.

"Probably, but if she was once their employee, it'd make life much easier for us."

Shepherd heard a voice answer. "Max, it's me. I want you to get on to Porton Down. Find out if they've ever employed anyone by the name of Melanie Bradshaw. That's right. If not, chase up the name and see what you can dig up for me. Thanks."

Back at headquarters, and three strong coffees later, a knock came at Vance's door. With an air of triumph, Max Wright sat down uninvited to stare at the inspector with a broad grin on his face."

"Well, out with it, man!"

"Your intuition was correct, boss. Melanie Bradshaw, research chemist, worked at Porton Down until three months ago. She gave notice of quitting six months ago, correctly worked out her contractual twelve weeks, then rode off into the sunset. My contact at Porton says they have no record of where she went, and interestingly, she didn't ask anyone for a reference. But I suppose, with a first-class honours degree in Chemistry with Medicinal Chemistry from Imperial College, she shouldn't find employment hard to obtain."

"There you are, Shep, I told you, Melanie Bradshaw worked at Porton Down. She would have had plenty of time to get her hands on headed notepaper and pilfer an official rubber stamp."

Shepherd looked up from studying Ellen Rhodes's detailed timeline, the tension contorting her otherwise angelic face, "The day after tomorrow, she'll strike again, and this time it will be a white male in his mid-twenties if our scientific brainbox sticks to Arnold's schedule."

"We'll have to move fast then. Max, did you find anything interesting from her matriculation at Imperial?"

"I looked into that, but she, or someone else, beat us to it. I don't know if this Melanie has computer skills, but someone had skilfully removed her personal details from Imperial's records. It looks like our suspect covered her tracks remarkably well. Quite how she breached their system eludes me because it took all my expertise to enter the site. Unless she paid an expert, of course, or bribed someone in their administration, which strikes me as too risky."

"Shame, but we might just trace her another way. I want you to check ownership of Audi TTs in Greater London. Oh, and Wiltshire since Porton Down is in that county. It's not such a common model as, say, an A4, so you might have some joy there, Max."

"I'm onto it, sir." He rose and fairly sped out of the room.

"I wish all our other staff were as efficient as our geek," Jacob muttered.

"Ellen's done a good job. We have a clear overview now of when the killer will strike and the victims' profiles. It looks like we're in for a busy month if she's determined to follow in Arnold's footprints. It's a nightmare, Jacob."

"We won't let her kill nine people, Brit—all we need is a lucky break."

"Listening to Max, though, I get the impression that this psycho is more cunning than Arnold Tibbet—and that's saying something. She's his bloody sister, after all!"

"We don't know that."

"I'd stake next month's pay cheque on it. Melanie Bradshaw is Bethany Tibbet as far as I'm concerned."

"Nothing like keeping an open mind, is there, colleague?"

For a moment, her cheeks turned pink, and she didn't meet his eyes, but then, defiantly, she asked, "Did you put surveillance on the riverside flat?"

"My sergeant's on it. Do you want me to call Mark?"

"Why not?"

"OK." He frowned and tapped a number on his mobile. Shepherd heard the faint ringtone of Mark Allen's phone. "Mark, anything to report?" She listened to the soft drone of the sergeant's voice since Vance hadn't thought of using the hands-free mode. *Jake's something of a technosaur.* She smiled at her newly-conceived expression: a person too old-fashioned to master technology—a technosaur, as in dinosaur. Vance, whose interest in dinosaurs was unknown to her, would have shocked her had she spoken her thought by informing his colleague that the Technosaurus was a genus of Late Triassic silesaurid dinosauriform.

He ended the call and turned to his sniggering partner. "Mark's been busy. He's checked with King Street—the Borough of Hammersmith and Fulham council offices—the apartment is, indeed, registered in the name of Bethany Tibbet, and that's an interesting point because she made the legal change shortly after Arnold's death, signing it into her sole ownership. That means, of course, that Bethany exists and your instinct that the blonde among the gravestones was her was probably correct."

"My instincts never let me down, Jacob. You should know that by now. And I'm telling you that Bethany Tibbet and Melanie Bradshaw are one and the same."

He looked sceptical. "Mmm, I don't know. Without belittling your famous intuitions, I'm keeping an open mind on that one. Mark said that according to the council clerk, all Bethany's local taxes are unimpeachably paid. She pays by standing order. Whilst Mark's been watching the flat there has been no movement. He phoned the UK Power Networks office and found the same thing: she pays by standing order. But hear this; they told Mark that there had been almost zero consumption in the last quarter. What does that say to you?"

"That Bethany isn't in residence."

"Quite! So, I told Mark to put a couple of uniforms on surveillance for forty-eight hours in shifts. They've to look out for a black Audi TT and a petite blonde with long hair. If nothing shows up after that time, we'll call off surveillance."

"She won't show, Jacob. She's too damned cunning for that."

CHAPTER 6
LONDON TRAMLINK, WIMBLEDON TO BECKENHAM JUNCTION

BETHANY CAUTIOUSLY OPENED THE DOOR OF THE BEDSIT'S RICKETY wardrobe. She decided that her landlady had probably acquired it from a rag and bone man, judging by its appearance. The veneer had peeled back in places to make the exterior seem like a person afflicted by some rare skin disease. Paler patches of wood showed through beneath the darker stained lamination. She didn't care, as long as the boxlike structure didn't topple over onto her. Her less than extensive collection of clothing was dangling on wire hangers—had they been sentient beings, they would have suffered the indignity of this imprisonment in the musty interior. All Bethany cared about was the full-length mirror fixed to the inside of the wardrobe door. Like the rest of the bedsit, it was substandard. She peered at the reflection of herself, challenging those blotchy spots behind the glass, where the mirror surface had oxidised, to offer visibility.

A convincing Goth stared back at her, complete with a purple crest. The wig hid her blonde locks to perfection, and the heavy dark makeup around her eyes removed the slightest suspicion that she was an elegant, pale-skinned intellectual. Her black lipstick gave her a sinister aspect. She'd had to force herself to varnish her nails black, too, but all in a good cause. She bounced from one heavy-booted foot to another, chanting the words of *Highway to Hell* to enter into the spirit of the role.

Outdoors, her first realisation that punks are not universally popular, even in tolerant, cosmopolitan London, came when a passing youth badmouthed her. *Lucky for him, I haven't got my phial with me,* she thought. Then immediately cursed herself. She wasn't some maniac who would kill to avenge a meaningless insult. No, she had a master plan, and it involved the London tramways. The spotty youth deserved to feel the full extent of her wrath, though, but not summary execution. She turned to follow him for a while with the idea of lashing one of her Doc Martin boots into his testicles, but, thanks to a momentary distraction, she missed him jumping onto a bus. When she realised what had happened, he was gone. Had she lost her mind? What if the coppers had arrested her for assault on a teenager? She could do without unwanted attention. *Come on, Bethany, get a grip!*

She continued on her way, uncomfortably aware of the stares she attracted. Very few she could categorise as admiring. So what? The point was not to be recognised: a consideration confirmed soon when another female punk approached her. "Hi, you're new around here, aren't you?"

"Piss off! You're not my type. Leave me alone."

The studded Goth recoiled at the aggression, muttering, "Got out the wrong side of the stye, did you, sow?"

Melanie hurried on. She had a stiff march to get to the tram station at Merton Park. Late afternoon had been a deliberate choice, because she needed to study an early evening stretch of tramline to see how busy it was at off-peak times. Her planned journey required her to take two buses, starting with the 65 from Ealing to Cromwell Road bus station. That, she knew, was a fifty-minute ride. She touched her Oyster Card on the yellow reader to pay the fare and took a seat next to a mousy woman with a shopping bag bulging with groceries in her lap. She could swear the woman cringed away when she sat down, but she offered her a timid smile when Bethany stared at her. She nodded back and smiled to break the tension. Another advantage of the punk disguise was that it assured privacy. The mousy woman didn't want to chat with her ilk. They travelled in silence until the woman squeezed past her to get off at Kingston. Nobody sat next to Bethany between there and the terminus.

Her next bus was the 131, which departed every five minutes. It was a shorter journey to Albert Grove—twenty-five minutes. They passed uneventfully, and she was relieved to get off the juddering double-decker to walk through the streets to Merton Park tram station. Once inside the building, she topped up her Oyster Card at an automatic machine, feeding a twenty-pound note into its grasping slot. But she didn't resent spending that sum because she could move freely on the different types of transport with the trouble-free, easy-to-use system.

It was still towards the end of rush hour, so the first tram for Beckenham Junction was crowded. She clung to a yellow upright pole near the door and stared balefully, even threateningly, at a woman who was selfishly occupying a seat with her bulky shoulder bag. When the woman stood up by the door at Belgrave Walk, Bethany deliberately crushed her foot under her heavy boot when the tram came to a halt. She grinned wolfishly into the woman's face before she could object, before barging her out of the way so that she could sit down. After all, what would you expect from a punk? She smiled at the thought. *You wouldn't expect to receive a posy of white daisies, would you?*

She luxuriated in the smoothness of tram travel, so unlike the airless, noisy, juddering underground trains, and complimented herself on her choice of killing scenario. Three-quarters of an hour later, she alighted at the Birkbeck stop, having considered and rejected the previous station at Harrington Road. As she looked around the short platform, she realised that Birkbeck was not as perfect as Avenue Road, because beyond the tram track was a railway line and past that, in turn, was the much longer platform of Birkbeck railway station. Still, if she took care not to be captured by the CCTV on that side, all would be well.

A cursory glance took in a shelter with a bench, which would be suitable for her research after she'd recce'd the outside of the station. The original railway station was a mid-Victorian brick construction, and a tall wall flanked the steep steps with an L-turn down to the main A214: Elmers End Road. She glanced up and down the road and noticed how it passed under the railway bridge to the right. This pavement was not a good place to leave a body. It was too exposed, and she felt the same way about the station above her.

Returning slowly to the station, she sat on the bench and noticed with satisfaction that there was nobody on either side of the railway line. She took out her notebook and ballpoint pen, wrote the time at the top of the page and waited. She'd done her research, so she knew that six trams per hour passed through on the way to the last stop at Beckenham Junction—there were three stops to the terminus after Birkbeck. A glance at the electronic timetable display at the end of the platform, about ten yards from where she was sitting, told her that the next tram would arrive in three minutes.

As the green nose of 2556 appeared, she wrote the time, 19.08, in the left margin of her notebook. Four people stepped out onto the platform; she jotted that down. The Stadler Variobahn tram had four compartments, and she scribbled down the approximate number of passengers in each one. She observed that they had already updated the illuminated display as the tram pulled away. The next one would arrive in ten minutes, at 19.18. When it squealed punctually to a halt, she delighted in the presence of fewer travellers. The successive 19.28 carried fewer still. With remarkable patience, she filled in the details of another three arrivals before taking the 19.58 to Beckenham Junction to travel back to the western terminus at Wimbledon.

On the return journey, she matured her plan by studying the tram's interior. The seats were laid out in groups of four, each pair facing the other so that two passengers could sit facing the direction of travel and two with their backs to it. The latter interested her because, given the low passenger affluence on the 19.48, she decided to strike onboard the tram. Also, people were creatures of habit, and the 19.48 had transported her profiled victim. Crucially, she timed the trip from Birkbeck to Harrington Road—precisely three minutes. It would be on that stretch that she would kill. When she arrived at Wimbledon, she studied the weekday tram departure times. The one she was interested in left Merton Park at 19.04, so she'd be there at that time the following day, equipped for the kill. Now for a good night's sleep.

Bethany had no trouble sleeping, especially when she had a clear plan. She decided to stick with the Goth disguise for her second murder. She couldn't wait! Having the power to snuff out a life made her feel almost omnipotent and, somehow, performing in a costume added *theatre* to her killing.

Bethany was a perfectionist, so the tram departing exactly at 19.04 put her in a splendid mood. *What could go wrong?* The flux of passengers tallied with her notes from the previous day, but there was a moment of anxiety. She had studied the compartments, looking for her victim, a white male in his mid-twenties, but there was no sign of him. Of course, there were twenty-one stops for him to board before Birkbeck, so the percentage chance of him having boarded at the only two previous stations was slight. After a dozen stops and still no appearance, she began to worry.

The scenario for murder was ideal at Reeves Corner, where she and an elderly woman had the compartment to themselves. The old lady hobbled off the tram at Centrale, so Bethany had the compartment to herself for one stop. Five people, including her target, entered at the busy West Croydon Station. She chuckled to herself and positively glowed, but there were too many witnesses. Three alighted at East Croydon, and nobody boarded; another passenger left at Sandilands, and no one entered their compartment. As the tram pulled away, she changed her plan. They were alone in the carriage, so why not now, without witnesses? Why wait for Harrington Road? But she had not recce'd the intermediate stations. She didn't like the unexpected. What if he altered his routine and got off before Harrington Road? *Damn it! I must take this chance.*

She moved silently to sit behind him, reached for the phial, pulled it out of her pocket and adjusted her position on the seat so that she could reach behind his head. She took a deep breath under her Adidas face mask, unstopped the phial and poured the blue liquid. It soaked the cotton wad, and, holding her breath, she moved like a cat, pressing the pad over the man's mouth and nose. Luckily, he had lowered his face mask under his chin, probably reckoning that there was no danger of viral infection in an almost empty carriage. But he had calculated without the greater peril. He seized her arm in a futile dying attempt to prise the wad away from his face. She resisted his counterpressure and felt him slump exanimate in his seat. She'd just had time to do the deed when the train pulled into Addiscombe station.

Moving like a puma—how appropriate that she was dressed entirely in black—she slunk out of the tram. She watched it glide away with pleasure, primarily because her victim remained in a sitting position, somewhat slumped against the window. So, she'd got away with another crime. The cotton wad in her pocket would come in useful for M3—as her brother would have called *murder three* in his notes; she smiled at the thought. She was going to surpass him. She needed to check for CCTV cameras because there was one detail to attend to before the 19.39 tram drew up. She had five minutes to spray **9-2=7** on the wall over there. But she didn't want to be filmed doing it.

Once again, the circumstances underlined the importance of thorough reconnaissance. She found a wall not covered by a prying camera and, taking the can from her bag, sprayed the formula. The police would find the body on the tram. Should she have spritzed the message on the back of a seat? No, this would be her little surprise for the fuzz. Unlike Arnold, no poetry was forthcoming from her, but the substance was more important than the form. Her lithe frame shook with suppressed laughter. Ah, here comes the tram! What a delightfully smooth means of transport!

CHAPTER 7

SCOTLAND YARD, VICTORIA EMBANKMENT, LONDON, UK

SHEPHERD LOOKED IN DISBELIEF AT HER FELLOW DETECTIVE inspector. "Come on, Jacob, you don't seriously consider this death to be by natural causes?" Vance didn't. He was playing devil's advocate; also, he enjoyed challenging Brittany's certainties.

"Doctor Tremethyk was quite clear that there is no scientific evidence of foul play."

"Jacob, you've built your career on the principle of not believing in coincidences. This death is rife with them—"

"Go on."

"The victim matches the Tebbit profile, mid-twenties, white, office worker. He died of a heart attack, and we know that is what hydrogen cyanide poisoning provokes."

"Hydrogen cyanide, of which there was no trace in his blood."

"Only because the body remained undiscovered for too long. And look, they found it on the same tram branch line as the first victim. Also, the timing of the death. We were expecting a murder yesterday, and here it is!"

"There do seem to be many coincidences, I'll give you that,

Shep, but it is our duty to consider the evidence, and that says a heart attack."

"There are nine stops on that branch. The body turned up at Beckenham Junction when a routine inspection of the compartment came across it. I'm going over there to question the guard who discovered him. I'm not prepared to write this off, Jacob."

Tired of his role-play, Vance relaxed. "Good for you, partner. Of course it's murder. My gut feeling goes with your instinct. But until we have some evidence, it's a heart attack!"

They discussed the death for a few minutes until Vance's phone rang. A constable on the switchboard had a member of the public on the line who wished to speak to a CID officer.

"He says it's important, sir. Putting him through."

Jacob listened intently to the hoarse, excited voice before taking action. He dictated his mobile number to the caller and said, "You can send a snap of it if you would be so kind, sir. Thank you, you've been most helpful."

"What was that about?" Shepherd's curiosity was piqued since Vance would not give out his personal number lightly.

"A passenger on the tramline who fancies himself as a bit of a sleuth. He followed the Tebbit case closely and knew about the messages left on the bodies and so on. All of that came out after the trial, if you remember. Anyway, he was waiting for his tram at Addiscombe Station when he spotted a formula in black paint sprayed on the wall, to get to the point. He recognised it at once as the Tebbit calling card."

"Let me guess: **9-2=7**, right?" Shepherd said excitedly.

"Right! Which means—"

"That my brain's as sharp as ever, and it confirms a murder that probably took place at or near Addiscombe," Shepherd finished for him, as the ping from his mobile notified him of the incoming photo.

"Thank you, Mr Phelan. Well spotted! Look here, Brit. A perfect match for the first killing at Avenue Road. I'd say it was sprayed by the same person. Let's get over to Addiscombe Station. We might just get lucky."

In the car, Vance's ringtone filled the interior with Schubert's *Rosamunde* as he groped in his pocket. He glanced at the display and said, "Tremethyk!" Then, "Hello, Doc, what's up?" He listened carefully, trying to memorise the scientific jargon to report to Brittany. When the call had finished, he said, "When will I learn to use the speakerphone? My brain hurts with all this medical terminology."

"Do your best, partner." Shepherd couldn't conceal her smirk. She'd been on at Vance to use his speakerphone for years.

"It seems that the good doctor wasn't taken in by the heart attack theory, so he hurried across the city to where they have more sophisticated equipment. It appears, and I quote, that one can 'determine cyanide in blood by head-space gas chromatography with electron capture detector'—"

"Gobbledygook! But our Cornish Pasty discovered cyanide poisoning, didn't he?"

"Yes, he did! And never let him hear you call him that! He's the best in the business and deserves your respect, Detective Inspector."

"Yes, sir! Strange, isn't it?"

"What?"

"Arnold Tibbet fell over himself to leave all sorts of clues. This bloody Bethany is copycatting, leaving nothing except the sprayed calling card. I reckon she's a much tougher nut to crack than her brother was—and he was bad enough! Take her method, for instance. His poison was much more complicated to process, and he had to employ a syringe. Hers comes ready-made, and it must be easier to use than a needle. Then there's none of that poetry nonsense."

"Arnold Tibbet was proving that he was cultured, to hit back at the Commissioner's insult. Bethany, or Melanie, whoever she is, just wants revenge for Arnold's death."

"Well, maybe she should start with the paedo who killed

him. He's still in the psychiatric prison. Why take it out on innocent people?"

"Daft question. Because she's a psychopath, like her brother.
She's probably enjoying every minute of this."

———

Bethany was indeed enjoying herself, across the city in her
cramped bedsit, planning M3. She had now convinced the police
that her killing ground was on the branch line to Beckenham.
The cops were sure to flood the trams with plain-clothed detectives in the foreseeable future. In any case, she had always
considered changing location for M3. Hadn't Arnold done the
same? She could transfer her work to the New Addington
branch, but maybe that was too obvious, and if the Old Bill rode
the line, she would have to share a compartment as far as Sandilands, which was too risky. Until her chance discovery last night,
the alternative had been the western end of the line at Wimbledon, but, as to that, she could raise the same objection.

She stared with glee at the booklet she had picked up the
evening before, discarded on a seat. Bethany had been an avid
reader from infancy. Going to the toilet without something to
read was inconceivable to her. If she hadn't found this on the
tram, she'd have compulsively read the fixed adverts above the
passengers' seating on the vehicle's ceiling. As it was, it
provided unexpected inspiration. Idly turning its pages,
ignoring the various theatrical productions and music concerts,
she came to a revelation.

Bethany knew that the City of London had retired its trams in
July 1952. Still, she had no idea of the existence of the Kingsway
station in Holborn, which they had sealed off to Londoners since
it was closed in that year, when the capital's once-extensive tram
system fell out of favour with commuters who preferred the
London Underground. She was thrilled to read that it was set to
open to the public for the first time in almost seventy years.

From July 9, members of the public would be able to take a guided tour of the tunnel for £45 per person. For £90, she could make a reconnaissance tour the following day and then strike the day after. The timing was right, too. Hadn't Arnold killed the estate agent early in the morning at White Horse Yard? The space between M2 and M3 would be the same, give or take an hour or two. Her main problem would be to find a forty-year-old male on the guided tour. She hated being limited in this way, but was comforted by the thought that a middle-aged to elderly group of tourists would be more likely to visit such a site than a more youthful party.

This time, she would wear her tracksuit. It seemed appropriate for underground exploration; besides—she studied her reflection—she looked very sexy in this outfit. But no, not for her preliminary survey; she could not afford to let the guide see the same persona on consecutive days, so she would remain a Goth for one more day. Attention to detail, that was her watchword!

Tickets for the guided tour of the Kingsway subway were available from the London Transport Museum, so she happily paid her £45 and presented herself at the meeting point. The purpose of the ramp down into the gloom—in the middle of Southampton Row where it intersects with Theobalds Road— had long puzzled her. Now she knew. She stared at the gaping entrance of the Grade II-listed subway, which ran directly above part of the new Crossrail route, and which they expanded in 1929 to allow it to accommodate double-decker trams. Adrenaline kicked in to set her heart racing. This would be the perfect setting for M3. She surveyed the eager faces of her fellow tourists. Some were Asian visitors, but there were sufficient middle-aged Englishmen to whet her appetite, and she noticed how many of the men were ogling her in her punk outfit. She would be wearing her even sexier gear the next day. She wondered if the guide would be the same person. A lanky character with long, dank hair and round glasses over an aquiline nose, he, too, kept shooting lascivious glances at her trim body.

She wouldn't mind him being victim three, but knew that to be impossible.

The guide led them down the steep gradient to the tunnel mouth and treated them to charming anecdotes about the famous flag-waving Freddy, a colourful personage. He brought London traffic to a halt with his red flag in favour of the lumbering trams for many years in the 1920s. If she hadn't had murder on her mind, Bethany might have indulged her love of tramways more by listening less distractedly to the guide, who knew his stuff. "The Kingsway subway took passengers from Holborn as far as Waterloo Bridge, linking the north and south tram networks together," he declared.

She came out of her reverie to hear him state, "In 1953—the year after it was closed for good—the tunnel was used by London Transport to store one hundred and twenty buses and coaches in case they were needed for the Queen's Coronation. Part of the southern end of the tunnel was then opened to road traffic as the Strand Underpass in 1964."

Now they were down in the bowels of the earth, and the guide pointed out the vestiges of the old Holborn tram station. There were the remnants of some lettered tiles to admire, and the platform where passengers stepped onto the old trams was visible. It didn't need much imagination to picture the rustling skirts, frock coats and top hats of a bygone era. Her attention was caught by a gloomy steep flight of steps off to her right that led up to a distant chink of daylight. A plan rapidly formed in her head and it was a buoyant Bethany who strode out of the Kingsway tram subway. She could hardly wait for the following afternoon.

At about the same time, Vance and Shepherd were questioning the operative who had found the body at Beckenham Junction.

"It's my job to check the compartments before a tram is withdrawn for the evening. 2251 had completed its last run, so before going to the depot, I had to give the all-clear. That's my normal routine, but last night, instead of just clearing litter and looking for lost property—it's surprising how people can be forgetful—I found him. I knew at once, of course. The stillness gave him away. No snoring, head resting against the window, no movement; I just knew, if you get what I mean. I didn't touch him, apart from shaking a shoulder, but there was no response, so I called the police."

"Did you see or smell anything strange?" Shepherd asked.

"In London, the first thought these days is that it was a knife crime, but there was no blood. I reckon nobody did him in, probably a heart attack, poor devil! Smell? That's a rum thing to ask. No, there wasn't a smell about him. He wasn't a tramp, if that's what you mean. Kind of well-dressed fellow. Can't say as I noticed any scent or anything like that, though, sorry."

"Was this the seat where you found the body, sir?" Vance asked.

"Aye, it was." The guard sat there to act the part, slumping down a little, and resting his head against the glass. "Like this, he was."

"Stay like that a moment, would you?" Shepherd hurried to the seat that backed onto his. She sat and twisted so that she could reach behind the guard's head. Try as she might, she couldn't stretch her hand in front of his face, so she hopped up, knelt on the upholstery and leant forward. Then, it became easy to pass her hand over his nose and mouth. "That's how she did it," she hissed. "Thank you, sir, you can stand now."

"Is there CCTV on this tram?" Vance asked.

"There's a forward-facing camera from the driver's cab and one at the back filming the rear view, and several cameras inside the trams for customer safety and security. But the first thing the railway police did was to check it out, and they found it wasn't working."

"Why was that?"

"Dunno, you'll have to ask the driver. Maybe the system's faulty."

"Bloody typical!" Shepherd muttered.

They weren't going to learn more from the guard or the tram, so they decided to drive to Addiscombe Station to check out the graffiti and the CCTV situation. Seeing the spray on the wall didn't add to the impression gained from Mr Phelan's photograph, but it gave them the perspective of the station from that spot. The killer had taken the risk of being seen at work with the can, so she must have been sure of herself, Vance concluded. His expert gaze sought out CCTV cameras, but when he saw one, his shoulders sagged. The damned thing was pointing along the opposite platform, and this one didn't have a camera trained on it. Their killer must have come to the same conclusion.

Interestingly, they were on the westbound platform, "She was on her way back to wherever she lives," he told Shepherd. "Look, this tram's heading for Wimbledon." The destination was illuminated with a large number 3 next to it. "Let's get back to base. I want to read Doctor Tremethyk's report."

Bethany, who would have been delighted at how little the detectives had discovered, was back in her bedsit, running over the details of her plan for the following afternoon. To complete her scheme, she needed to do some shopping. What a nuisance! She had a serviceable printer in her riverside flat, but she guessed that the apartment would be under police surveillance. Too risky to go there, so she'd buy an inkjet printer since there was no point in purchasing a more expensive laser model when she had a perfectly good one in Fulham. The basic black ink model would suffice—no need for coloured inks. *I'm not Arnold, the poor devil!* She laughed hysterically at the thought of his *colourful murders*; it was a release from pre-killing tension and nobody could hear her, shut away in this pokey hovel.

On her way back with her acquisition, she bought a first-class postage stamp and a pack of envelopes. She had already purchased a ream of A4 paper. In the bedsit, she typed out the letter and printed it off via a cable connection. No question of a wi-fi router in Ms Kelly's dump. Now she was ready to go ahead with her murderous scheme. *Thank you, Arnold, for giving me this idea.*

The following afternoon, dressed in her tight-fitting tracksuit, and having taken extra care with her make-up and hair, Bethany waited at the meeting point, ticket at the ready. She had chosen her victim, a tall, dark-haired fellow in his forties, who she had caught staring at her. She opened her eyes wide and smiled at him. The poor fool grinned cheerfully back. Before long, he had sidled close and his opening gambit was, "I'm looking forward to this tour, aren't you? It'll be like stepping back in time."

Bethany was ready for any approach. "Mixed feelings, to tell the truth." She tried her little-girl-lost expression on him. "I suffer from claustrophobia and I'm beginning to think of skipping this tour."

"That would be a shame, after paying £45 for a ticket."

"It was an impulse. What if I panic down there?"

"Don't worry, you'll be all right. I'll stick by you to give you moral support."

She gave him what she believed was her most seductive smile. "Oh, would you? That's reassuring, Mr—"

"Welsby, Peter Welsby, Pete to you."

"Thank you, Pete. Bethany Earnshaw." She tended to avoid the name Tibbet after Arnold's excesses. She stuck out her hand and he took it, squeezing gently.

They talked about trams for a few minutes, their benefits and how both appreciated the Tramlink from Wimbledon to Beckenham. Bethany remembered some of the guide's spiel from the day before, so she displayed her knowledge of the Holborn tram station. She could see that she impressed her intended victim and exulted inwardly. He was lost!

The guide ran through his patter of the previous day, and

Bethany waited impatiently for him to move on down the ramp. She didn't follow but bent down to tie her shoelace that she had deliberately left loose so that she could stall. Obligingly, Pete waited for her so that they were at the back of the group as they entered the gaping tunnel mouth. Bethany began her act, clinging onto the arm of her surprised escort. "You don't mind, do you, Pete? Don't think me forward, but it makes me feel safer down here."

"Uh, not at all," he said, enjoying the sensation of her soft body pressed to his arm. She deliberately slowed their pace so that they fell behind the others. It didn't matter, as they could still hear the ringing voice of the guide. The rumble of traffic was so muffled as not to be an obscuring factor.

"Look!" Bethany whispered, steering Pete towards the steps she had spotted the previous day. She checked to see that nobody had missed them. "I'd love to see where they lead." She kept her voice low.

They piqued his interest, but he was a gentleman. "They are rather narrow. Aren't you claustrophobic?"

"It's a challenge to overcome my stupid nerves. Please! I dare you to go up forty steps. Then," she gave him a coquettish smile, "you'll get your reward." She ran the tip of her tongue along her lips. He gave her a knowing grin, turned and began counting, "One, two, three—" They were quite a way up when he said, "Forty!" Triumphantly, he spun round, legs akimbo and spread his arms wide for his imagined recompense.

Bethany, who had thought of everything, had allowed for his height, her being petite and standing on a lower step, so she launched herself forward head first, with all her might. Her blonde head struck him between the legs. Caught by surprise and off-balance, he cried out in pain and fell backwards, hitting his head on a stone step. He lay stunned and motionless. That stroke of fortune was better than she had hoped for. She quickly pulled on her face mask, poured the lethal liquid onto the cotton wad and, moving like a lynx, placed it over his mouth and nose.

The tourist group were standing on the old platform judging by the guide's words, so she had time to hold the pad longer than necessary. Her protector's promised reward was well and truly given, *Poor Sir Galahad!* she chuckled inwardly, then, thrusting the empty phial and the cotton into her handbag and carefully putting her face mask into her tracksuit pocket, she stealthily slunk back down the steps. Stopping only for a moment to retrieve her paint can from her voluminous bag to leave her calling card, she sprayed a black **9-3=6** on the side wall.

Safely back down and integrated into the rear of the tourist group, Bethany exulted. Nobody suspected anything. Pete Welsby might as well have been invisible, for no one had noticed him missing. Her plan had worked superbly. As they retraced their steps to the ramp and broad daylight, Bethany cast a fearful glance towards the narrow tunnel escape flight. But she had calculated well, choosing forty steps. There was no sign of the body from their level, where the trams had once run. That number of steps, as she had supposed, had taken him high enough not to be seen from below.

Now for the last stage of her plan: returning to the bedsit via a pillar box to send her letter to Commissioner Phadkar. Without the letter, there was little chance of Welsby's corpse being found any time soon. That, of course, would never do. She laughed silently at the thought that detectives were riding the Tramlink in vain, searching for a petite blonde. Well, here she was, glorying in her latest achievement!

CHAPTER 8

NEW SCOTLAND YARD AND SILVERTOWN, LONDON

COMMISSIONER PHADKAR ADDRESSED THE ENTIRE SQUAD WORKING on what she labelled *the tram murders*. On her instructions, DCI Ridgeway had assembled his team in a communal area around a whiteboard, where Shepherd had written the salient points of the case with coloured arrows evidencing possible links. Vance gazed thoughtfully at the highest-ranking officer at Scotland Yard as she stated what disturbed him most.

"Ladies and gentlemen, history is repeating itself. We are dealing with a copycat murderer. Quite likely, it's someone intimately connected with Arnold Tibbet. This individual is not only sticking closely to the same series of victims but is aping the timings—and now this!" She flourished a letter that had arrived with the morning post. "Exactly like Arnold Tibbet, this person has sent a second minatory letter, again, making demands. The letter's timing is similar to that of Tibbet's, and it has the hallmarks of his arrogance. I will read it to you. She cleared her throat and, in her clear, measured voice, read:

Commissioner Phadkar,

How can I express my disappointment? You have wantonly allowed three people to die rather than admit the errors of the

Metropolitan police. To prevent six further deaths, you will have to issue a statement to the effect that the Met has reopened the Tibbet case to investigate a miscarriage of justice. There, would that be so difficult? Do that, and there will be a suspension of the tram executions. Yes, I mentioned three people. It will come as a surprise to you, but you still have not discovered the third body. Maybe a little assistance is called for? You will find Peter Welsby's corpse on the emergency escape steps of the Kingsway tram tunnel.

As you can see, I am only too willing to be reasonable. Why not reconsider your inflexibility, Commissioner? Your intransigence could be interpreted as weakness. Remember, the clock is ticking. Ting, ting! The next tram is due soon!

Regards from one whose name is writ in blood.

Read without hesitation or stumbling, the effect on the gathered officers was numbing. Although some of them exchanged glances and others raised eyebrows, nobody spoke until Miriam Walker, the profiler, coughed discreetly and said, "If I may make some observations?"

"Please do, Miriam," Phadkar said, disguising the eagerness she felt to obtain an expert opinion by making her tone nonchalant.

The psychologist placed a forefinger to her lips and held her pose pensively for a moment before beginning, "We heard the words of an educated person. There is no use of so-called *street language*, but an almost scientific command of vocabulary that indicates a postgraduate level of education. This confirms my earlier diagnosis that we're dealing with a deeply disturbed individual, whose behaviour has become psychopathic. If we are to prevent further killings and capture her—I believe it's a woman —we must make every effort to delve into her family background. I believe that it's there we'll find the clues to lead us to our killer. I suggest that the writer of this letter, an extremely intelligent subject, is trying to distract us from that precise operation by leading us to deduce that she knew the third victim personally. I consider that particular line of inquiry to be a blind alley—although, at this stage, it would be dangerous to exclude anything *a priori*."

The profiler fiddled with the top button of her cabled cardigan before adding, "Finally, you will have noticed the mocking tone at the end of the letter, which suggests that our assassin is supremely confident in her abilities. Thank you." She sat down and smiled prettily around the tense faces.

"Thank you, Miriam. I've sent body recovery team and forensics to the derelict Holborn Station. I expect them to report in soon. You heard Doctor Walker, ladies and gentlemen. Dig into Arnold Tibbet's family. Leave no stone unturned."

The gathering dispersed, and Vance strode up to his computer expert. "Max, I want you to find out whatever you can about Tibbet's mother's sisters and sisters-in-law. Go to it, at once."

"Yessir! Will do!"

Moments later, Doctor Sabrina Markham phoned Vance with bad news. "We found nothing helpful at the scene of crime, Jacob. Doctor Tremethyk has the body for autopsy. His off-the-cuff conclusion is that it's the same *modus operandi*. It looks like it, even if my impression is that the severe blow to the back of the head caused by falling backwards onto a rough stone step, might have been the cause of death. There was a lot of blood. The good doctor will have an answer for you on that score."

"One other thing, Sabrina. Am I right in thinking that trams no longer use that station?"

She laughed. "There have been no trams there since 1952, Jacob. What world do you live in? I'm amazed you haven't noticed the situation in Southampton Row. You should get out and about a little more!"

He joined in her laughter. He had a soft spot for the plain-talking forensics expert; especially now she was engaged to his computer boffin, who had asked him to be his best man. Thinking aloud, he said, "So, what matters to our killer is an association with trams, whether they are extant or derelict. I wonder why that is?" He made a mental note to mention his perplexity to Miriam Walker.

———

Meanwhile, having got up later than usual, the sleepy blonde, the subject of their conversation, was busily researching her fourth killing ground. She asked herself whether it was too soon to return to the Tramlink. Besides, her fourth victim was one she didn't particularly wish to lure onto the tramline. She would attract too much attention. Arnold's fifth victim was a prostitute, so her fourth would be, too; Arnold's fourth had been a female Korean tourist. It didn't matter if she inverted Arnold's victims *four and five* for her convenience. It might help confuse the cops.

There again, she couldn't return to the Kingsway subway. By now, the guide and the police would be on alert in that ideal site. She couldn't use it again. Instead, she researched the internet for London's derelict tramlines. After much frustration, she found what she was looking for. Her Korean target, postponed temporarily, would be well-suited to the Tramlink, so, after dispatching the whore, she would return to her first killing ground for the Korean. Enough time should have passed by then to confuse the police. With her new location, she'd have them spinning like tops! She laughed and began to sing an old Nick Cave song:

> *"When you search in vain to find*
> *Some law-abiding citizen*
> *Just remember that death is not the end."*

She grabbed a wooden spoon from the drainer and held it like a microphone in front of her face, singing the chorus, *"Just remember that death is not the end,"* over and over again.

The blonde consulted her notebook to remind herself how

much time she had to prepare for this murder. Arnold had indeed been busy! Too busy to leave his calling card at the scene of Matthew Spinks's murder. At least, she had done so with her **9-3=6** on the wall near Welsby's body. She congratulated herself —compared to Arnold, she was a genius!

There was no need for a particular disguise when she visited her selected location, so she would go dressed smart-casual.

Some time later, Melanie Bradshaw, also dressed similarly, having got up later than usual too, unscrewed her sterile contact lens case, gazed in the bathroom mirror and carefully positioned the Aquarella Sea Green lenses with a dark limbal ring. She stood back and blearily admired the prettiness of the effect. She scolded herself for poring over chemistry texts until the early hours of the morning. By careful application of make-up and eye drops, nobody would have said that her face betrayed her tired-ness. Weary as she felt that morning, she had to dash across the city to St Pancras. She must hurry to her appointment at the British Library, where she had applied for a Reader Card. Her mood was cheerful because she had obtained a fee-paying place on a part-time MSc degree course in Material Chemistry at St Mary College, and the BL would enable her to study in depth.

The range of books and periodicals available there was insu-perable. She had been awarded a first-class honours degree for her BSc and hoped and expected to do equally well with her postgraduate degree. She did not regret having left her research work at Porton Down because when she obtained her MSc within two or, at worst, three years, she would walk right back in there, armed with the justification of her master's degree.

She smiled to herself as she entered the fourteen-storey building at St Pancras. Her heart fluttered, conditioned by the hallowed structure that had seen every type of intellectual enter its doors. She was acutely aware of treading in famous footsteps. If laid end to end, the shelving would reach Aberdeen from

London. But Melanie refused to be cowed. She was a serious person. Her passion was chemistry, and she intended to become as renowned as Marie Curie, but in her chosen field.

She'd had to book a Reader Pass appointment to be accepted as a reader at St Pancras. Registration proved to be a formality. Of course, she had to provide her personal details, but Melanie had nothing to hide, so she provided them willingly. She signed the requisite forms, her signature endorsing a promise to maintain the rules and regulations, which tended to cover civil and courteous behaviour on the premises. She had no problem with that, regarding herself a model of propriety.

As soon as she'd completed the formalities, she hurried into the periodicals room and browsed through the overwhelming range of journals offered there. She picked up the latest issue of JACS—the Journal of the American Chemical Society, and, obligatory face mask in place, began to take down notes from an article entitled *Controlling Nucleation Pathways in Zeolite Crystallization: Seeding Conceptual Methodologies for Advanced Materials Design.* The article had nothing to do with her previous work at Porton Down, but was relevant to her course at St Mary College. This kind of up-to-the-minute research would ensure that she kept a step ahead of her fellow students and maybe even her professors. She smiled smugly; *I just need to keep my nose to the grindstone and not allow other distractions into my life,* she thought, closing her notebook and glancing at her watch. *Good heavens, how time flies! I've been here for two hours. I'd better go! There's shopping to do. Did I remember to bring the list? The fridge is almost empty.* Congratulating herself on being a model student, Melanie tucked her notebook in her large yellow shoulder bag and hurried off to find a supermarket in the area.

Bethany Tibbet decided to combine her shopping with reconnaissance for M4, as she called it. With this in mind, she took a train as far as Canning Town, where she located a promising supermarket. That done, she considered it sensible to delay the shopping until after her recce of the Tay Wharf area that she had chosen, as it would be pointless carrying laden bags around the streets. She found the place quickly enough and, much to her pleasure, discovered that the gates were unlikely to open because the jam factory that had previously occupied the site had closed as long ago as 1997. The area had a rundown appearance except for the part of the entrance that bore the name Tay Wharf in block capitals and the date 1900 in black numbers in the white pediment above, which had been restored to a high standard and listed for preservation.

Bethany crossed the road and came to the nearby sugar refinery. High on a wall outside the factory, hung a giant reproduction of a can of Tate and Lyles Golden Syrup. She remembered that her Aunt Felicity always had such a tin in the larder when Bethany was a little girl, with its fascinating depiction of a dead lion and the bees swarming around the carcass where they had made a hive. *"Out of the eater came forth meat, and out of the strong came forth sweetness."* She quoted Samson's riddle aloud, then looked around guiltily to confirm that she was unobserved. How she had loved loading a teaspoon with the sticky substance and rolling it around her tongue as a little girl. Perhaps she would buy a tin in the supermarket later.

Sadly, this once-thriving Victorian area between the Thames and the Royal Victoria Dock induced in her a sense of abandonment. She giggled, for it suited her purposes perfectly. But she'd seen enough, and it was time to get back to Canning Town and the shopping.

First, though, she must find a phone kiosk in this neighbourhood. The darned things were becoming rarer by the day, thanks to the advent of mobile phones. Even so, she found a classic red booth farther down the North Woolwich Road, containing, as she'd hoped, postcards placed there by prostitutes. She chose one depicting Kaylee Kuddles, particularly because this lady of the night promised lesbian encounters as well as threesomes among her variegated offerings. Bethany detached it and slipped the postcard into her handbag, muttering, "I'll be in touch soon, dearest Kaylee." She hurried out of the unwholesome air of the kiosk and directed her triumphant stride, giggling to herself the while, towards West Silvertown DLR Station—one stop from Canning Town.

Shopping completed, Bethany retraced her steps to Canning Town Station and headed for the tube, where she took the Jubilee line to change onto the Central line for Ealing Broadway. The journey took her three-quarters of an hour, in which she grumbled inwardly about the jostling underground train, comparing it negatively with the Tramlink—how she loved trams!

———

At Scotland Yard, Max Wright had drawn a blank with black Audi TTs, none of them traceable to a young woman owner. He had abandoned that line of inquiry in favour of researching Violet Tibbet's siblings. He discovered that she was one of eight children. Her position among the female children was last. DS Wright jotted down the names in order of seniority: Margaret, Felicity, Edith, Marion and Violet. He noted that the eldest three, like Violet, had died, but located an address for Marion at Penn Street in Shoreditch.

He hurried with this information to a somewhat testy DI Vance.

"No joy on the Audi TTs, sir, but there's a Marion Tibbet, the sole survivor of the Tibbet sisters. I have her address for you. She's in a one-bedroom flat over in Shoreditch—it's in rather a pleasant part of that district."

"At last! Something to sink our teeth into. Come on, Shep, let's call on Marion Tibbet. Good work, Max. Keep on searching. There may be sisters-in-law, too."

"Right you are!" Max Wright beat a hasty retreat. Vance had been polite, but the computer expert recognised the frustration bubbling beneath the surface. That tone, the inspector reserved for when cases were not going well, and he could explode into a rage at any moment.

The simmering detective slid into the passenger seat, as Shepherd automatically assumed that she would drive after years of working with him. She recognised that she had a better knowledge of the city streets than he, so she set off cheerfully northwards to Shoreditch. Two main roads took her quickly to Shoreditch Park and onto Penn Street. Marion Tibbet's flat was on the third floor of a seventeen-storey brick-built apartment block set in a smartly-paved pedestrian way. Vance pressed an entry phone button, and a voice, almost unintelligible thanks to the crackling, invited them to the third floor.

Marion Tibbet, unlike her slatternly sister Violet, kept a spotless flat where everything sparkled with polish. Nothing seemed out of place. The woman's appearance was equally neat; her grey hair, blue-rinsed, was pulled back into a Dutch Crown Braid, which Vance thought more suited to a thirty-year-old, not a pensioner like Marion. He appreciated her colour sense, however, both in her practical choice of clothing and in home décor.

"Ms Tibbet, we're sorry to disturb you, but we're carrying out a murder inquiry."

"Good Lord! Not again, not after what our Violet's lad got up to."

"I'm afraid so. We're investigating one of Arnold's sisters."

"Dear me! I always thought Beatrice would turn out bad."

"No, Ms Tibbet," Shepherd cut in gently, "as far as we know, Beatrice has done nothing wrong—"

"Call me Marion, my dear. But who then? The others are good girls."

Brittany smiled at the elderly lady's choice of word. *Girl* didn't apply to the two pleasant middle-aged mothers that she had interviewed. "No, Marion, not Beryl and Brenda; they are splendid, law-abiding citizens. We're trying to find out about Bethany."

Their hostess looked puzzled. "Bethany? There's no one of that name in our family—" She frowned and hesitated.

"What is it?" Brittany sat next to her on a two-seater sofa, taking her hand gently. "Have you remembered something?" She smiled encouragingly and Vance thought, not for the first time, *Shep's good at what she does.*

"I spoke to Felicity once about her situation. I bumped into her on Queensway. You see, she and her husband couldn't have children. She mentioned the possibility of adopting or fostering that day. Not that I know whether she did. I must have been distracted, and I rather lost touch with her after her marriage. She went to live over in Richmond, you see, Frank had a good job as a fitter or something like that. A pity he died a year after retiring. Then I heard that Felicity suffered a long illness before joining him and crossing over the rainbow bridge," she said quaintly. She sat staring into space for a moment, then added, "Our Violet kept having kids, and she didn't want the poor little mites. It's ironic, isn't it? Felicity wanted one and couldn't have one, and Violet was trying to get shut of them."

"And did she?" Shepherd urged.

"Well, I know that Vi tried to get Felix, that was our name for Felicity, to take Arnold when he was a toddler, but he was already such a mischievous imp that she flatly refused, saying she'd rather take a baby. Well, if there was another babe that I know nothing about, you'll have to ask the girls to be sure. I can't say as I remember a Bethany, but there's a chance, with the name beginning with a B—Violet was strange like that. She always said she didn't like girls and that they weren't A-class, like the boys. You see, all the boys' names began with an A and the girls' names with a B. As if she treated them first-class! It's a real pity she wasn't a better mother. Maybe Arnold might not—" She sobbed and sniffed, hanging her head.

Shepherd put her arm around her shoulder. "Don't take on,

Marion; what's past is done, and you've been a great help to us. Would you like me to make you a cup of tea before we go?"

After joining the kindly woman for the beverage, the officers left a more cheerful soul than they had found.

"She's lonely, the poor dear," Shepherd explained, "we probably made her day by calling in on her."

"It's a possibility worth exploring." Vance, as he often did, made no connection with what his partner had just said. "I'll get Max to find out whatever he can about Felicity Tibbet and, in particular, her life in Richmond upon Thames."

CHAPTER 9

NEW SCOTLAND YARD AND BELGRAVIA, LONDON

BACK AT HEADQUARTERS, VANCE PASSED MAX WRIGHT'S WORK station and enquired casually, "Any progress, pal?"

"I've made contact with the Registrar's Office in Richmond upon Thames, sir. They are digitalising their archives, so they're not open to me at the moment. I spoke with a very helpful clerk, though, and asked her a set of questions that she's prepared to answer as and when she can."

"I hope that you impressed on her how urgent our investigation is. That *as and when* sounds too lackadaisical for my liking."

"I'm sure she'll do her best. She seemed very pleasant on the phone."

"Give her half an hour. If she hasn't got back to you by then, threaten her with obstructing a murder inquiry. That should put a rocket up her proverbial! If need be, I'll get a search warrant."

Max Wright rolled his eyes at someone behind the detective and grinned. Vance spun around to stare into the pleasant, beaming features of Miriam Walker.

"Our killer would be delighted to see you so tense, Detective Inspector."

"Damn it, Doc, we have three dead and six deaths pending, and we've made almost no progress!"

"Jacob, you know better than I, a case like this often hinges on the smallest mistake on the part of the perpetrator or an apparently unimportant detail, either of which could give you the breakthrough you need."

"I sincerely hope so, Miriam. I was just on my way to ring you for your opinion. Have you got a few minutes?"

"Of course."

"Good. Max, allow no more than half an hour for that registrar woman, got it?"

"If I haven't heard from her," he glanced at the clock on his desktop, "by 12.32, I'll call her, sir."

Vance smiled at the psychologist. "Must have been his potty training," he quipped obscurely. "Come on, we'll have a chat in my office over a coffee."

Vance switched on the coffee machine in his room, opened a biscuit tin where he kept the espresso capsules and grumbled, "I can't believe it! Only six. I'd better place an order straight away. Excuse me a minute, Doc. We have two priorities in this department: solving murders and maintaining coffee supplies."

She chuckled and shot back, "I guess that the two are inseparably intertwined."

"Too true! There are criminals behind bars who would be walking free today, but for our little friend here. He patted the machine and inserted a capsule, positioning a cup to receive the steady brown flow of liquid. "Sugar?"

"Never! The only way to appreciate coffee is to drink it bitter."

"Ah, a woman after my own heart! Shepherd heaps the stuff into her coffee—undrinkable!" He shuddered and, as soon as he'd tossed the cardboard cups into his bin, made a call, an apologetic expression on his face. "DI Vance, New Scotland Yard. Yes, the usual three hundred capsules. See you later." He replaced the receiver almost reverentially in its cradle, in stark contrast to when he was in a bad mood. Ordering coffee always cheered him.

"Three hundred? That should last you a couple of days, Jacob!" the psychologist teased.

A few years ago, Vance would have been incapable of socialising with a profiler. The very word, *profiler*, would have set his teeth on edge, but he had mellowed and now enjoyed the company of the psychologist, quite apart from appreciating her valuable insights. He admired her dry sense of humour, but above all, how she kept an open mind, considering every circumstance from every perspective.

"Miriam, I wondered what you thought about this third killing? I find the scenario unsettling. Surely, it must give us some insight into the way our murderer's mind works?"

"I've given it considerable thought and I agree, it does. As I said earlier, we are dealing with a clever person. She changed location from Tramlink to escape detection. At the same time, she insisted on her chosen theme. That intrigues me, Detective Inspector." The calm, grey eyes stared at him for a moment, inviting his reaction.

"Me too. Why trams in particular?"

The profiler fiddled with the top button of her cardigan. Vance had noticed her do that before when anyone put her on the spot. "When we consider the nature of the crimes, so meticulously planned that she hardly leaves a trace of her deeds, in conjunction with her two messages, a picture begins to form of another Arnold Tebbit. This killer shares many of his—erm, *attributes*, seems too positive a word—let's say *traits*. They both reveal psychosis. Like Arnold, she appears to show symptoms of dissociative identity disorder."

"Hang on, Doc! Are you saying that, like Arnold, she is guided by voices in her head?"

"I wouldn't exclude it, but the illness can manifest itself in other ways. She might even assume the persona of Arnold Tibbet."

"Heaven preserve us! So, you wouldn't rule out the possibility of our killer being his sister?"

"Not at all. As I said, there are so many shared behavioural traits. Take the idea of thematic murder. Why not just kill and be done with it? Arnold was obsessed with his colours, French artwork, and poetry. She is equally fixated with trams. At the moment, we don't know why. You know my motto—*take nothing at face value*. But it's hard to overlook the connection between the theme and the psychosis. With this type of disturbance, often associated with highly intelligent individuals, by the way, we have to look into traumas in childhood. When did Tramlink open, Jacob?"

"I'm not certain. I'd hazard around the beginning of the century. Max will tell us for sure."

"Let's speculate that as a child of seven in 2000, our suspect underwent a trauma on a tram, which would make her around thirty years old today. Seven is a very impressionable age. That would fit with our suspicions that the killer is Arnold's younger sister. She could be two years his junior. Of course, Jacob, I'm clutching at straws without more to work on."

"Don't worry about that, Doc; your suggestions are invaluable and tally nicely with our suspicions." He glanced at his watch. It showed 12.25 and still nothing from DS Wright. "Thank you for your time, Miriam. If you'll excuse me, I'd better go and chase up our geek!"

Vance found the computer specialist making notes whilst speaking with someone on the phone. The detective waited patiently, even taking a seat. At last, Wright ended the call and looked at his superior officer with a meaningful expression on his face.

"What?"

"That was Olive in Richmond. She's dug out some interesting morsels for your consumption, sir."

"Talking about consumption, I quite like olives, especially with a dry Martini." Vance gave his sergeant a cheerful grin. "Let's have it, then, Max."

The computer wizard, relieved that his boss was in a better

mood, tapped one forefinger with the other as if about to tick off a list. "Most importantly, Marion Tibbet's husband, the fitter, was called Frank Bradshaw." Having delivered his bombshell, Max waited for a reaction.

It came more slowly than he had expected, but then, as if a light bulb illuminated above his head, Vance exclaimed, "Bradshaw! Melanie Bradshaw! That would explain a lot—if only we had the other missing pieces to fit together."

"Maybe we have, sir, but I'll have to work on it. Olive told me with certainty that Marion and Frank had a daughter named Melanie. It's all in the files. You see, they didn't move to Richmond until 2009. Before that, they lived in Wimbledon. Olive gave me an address in Wimbledon, so, with your authorisation, I mean to chase up the registry office there, too."

"Good lad, get onto it straight away. I have a gut feeling that this might be the breakthrough we've been waiting for. Melanie Bradshaw, eh? Intimately related to Arnold Tibbet's family, well, well! Ah, Max, a quickie for you. When was London Tramlink opened?"

"That's easy," he clicked on several icons and links and within a minute said, "May 10, 2000, sir."

"Perfect!" He smirked at his friend without explaining and set off for another coffee, calling over his shoulder, "Get me something from Wimbledon as soon as you can, Max."

He had only the time to switch on the coffee-maker when a polite knock came on his door. The robust figure of Doctor Tremethyk, the Chief Medical Examiner, entered.

"Morning, me-dear, or should that be afternoon? One tends to lose track of time with all this gadding about."

"Coffee, Doc?"

"Don't mind if I do, dear boy."

"So, what brings you to these far-flung reaches of your empire?"

The middle-aged doctor's face creased with pleasure. He

loved visiting Vance if only for his witty exchanges, not to mention the best coffee for miles around.

"Not so, me-dear, I'd go as far as to say that the hub of the Empire is here, and my domain is but a too-far-flung vassal on its outskirts. Not that I'm complaining. One thing I can guarantee at the morgue is peace and quiet."

With his back to the pathologist as he organised the drinks, Vance involuntarily shuddered at the thought of Tremethyk's realm with its stomach-turning odours and sights unfit for a healthy detective inspector to endure.

"I thought you would be cross with me, Jacob. I've kept you waiting for your report this time and felt the least I could do would be to bring it in person." He glanced down at the briefcase he had placed next to his chair.

"What delayed you, this time, Doc? Too much work on? Bodies fished from the Thames?"

"Good Lord, no! It was this case of yours. You see, it was hard to determine the cause of death, but I've concluded that if Mr Welsby didn't die by the violent striking of his head on the stone step, it would have been a close-run thing as to whether our killer's hydrogen cyanide fumes put him out of his agony. In the end, as you'll see from my report, I believe that the poison was the *coup de grâce*. He must still have been breathing, however shallowly, for the substance to enter his bloodstream. Again, I had to trot over to more sophisticated facilities to confirm the presence of the toxin in his blood—"

"Ah, the famous gas chromatography technique!" Vance looked smug.

The pathologist laughed. "That's what I like about you, me-dear, you're as sharp as a carving knife. Once you learn something, you never forget it, am I right?"

"I wish that were true, Doc. If I could remember everything I'd learnt, I'd be a real brainbox. As it is, I sometimes forget the most obvious facts. But I'd say there's more to your visit than meets the eye."

"Sharp, as I said. Your lovely colleague mentioned a petite blonde, so I can't help but wonder how on earth she knocked over a well-set fellow like Welsby when presumably she was standing on the steps below him."

"She must have caught him off guard; otherwise, it would be impossible for a woman of her stature. And, by the way, it's looking increasingly likely that the killer is indeed our petite blonde."

"Do you want my opinion?"

"Absolutely, I want nothing more than your expert verdict."

"You honour me, me-dear. Well, in that case, I'd say she had no alternative but to strike his centre of balance, which in a man of his stature would be about here," the expert stood and rather comically pointed to his genitals.

"Are you saying that she nutted him in the balls?"

"Somewhat crudely expressed, Detective Inspector, but aye, that's what I believe happened. Let's say our little blonde bombshell, by surprise, launched herself there headfirst; it would take one heck of a gladiator to remain rock-firm on two feet."

"I see what you mean and, as poor Welsby was no Spartacus, he fell backwards, striking his head so violently that the impact almost killed him. I suppose that he was in no condition to fight off his assailant at that point?"

"Definitely not. My feeling is that the blow would have rendered him unconscious, making the little missy's task very easy. I dare say that she'd figured out and planned how to overpower her companion. I have to ask myself how she convinced him to take those steps with her—probably played the siren, at a guess. The poor fellow most likely fell for her charms and fancied something far more pleasant than striking his head on a stone step."

"It's a compelling picture you portray, Doc. I wonder if Cornwall suspects that it has lost a prime investigative detective and London has gained the best pathologist in the land?"

"Dear boy, your appreciation is as excellent as your coffee.

Here's my report. I must return with all haste to my base in Dacia." He stood again, bent to retrieve his briefcase, opened it, took out a manila folder and slid it across the desk to Vance.

Remembering their earlier exchange, Vance quipped, "Wouldn't Hibernia be a more appropriate province? Last time I called in on you, you were to the west, not the east, of us, Julius Caesar."

Tremethyk roared with laughter. "I almost wish the authorities would open a morgue in this building. I enjoy crossing swords with you, DI Vance."

"I don't mind swords, but I sincerely hope you won't be using your scalpel on me, Doc!" Vance crossed his fingers behind his back and exchanged farewells.

Next, he paid DS Wright another visit.

"Ah, I waited for Doctor Tremethyk to finish before disturbing you, boss."

"So, did you get something from Wimbledon?"

"I did. More than I hoped for. It seems that Frank Bradshaw was a practising Catholic and an altogether model citizen. The couple adopted Melanie in 2002 when she was four years old. Of course, you know how it is with adoptions, privacy and all that. I was unable to confirm that Melanie's mother was Violet Tibbet, but it remains a strong possibility."

"Aye, it does. Shep is convinced that Bethany and Melanie are the same person. We have to keep an open mind on that score."

"There's more. As I said, Frank was a Catholic, so he enrolled his little girl into the Oratory Roman Catholic School in Belgravia."

"Hang on! Isn't Belgrave Walk a stop on the London Tramlink?"

"It's the fifth station from Wimbledon, so by tram, it must be a ten-minute ride. It doesn't take much imagination to picture the little Melanie going to school all neat and pretty in a bottle green uniform, and white blouse. The girls wear the school tie, too: green and old-gold stripes. Wouldn't that just delight a paedophile?"

"I see what you're getting at. Well done, Max. Anything else?"

"Not at the moment, sir. Would you like me to check out Melanie's school record?"

"No, I think DI Shepherd and I can do that. We'll pay the headmaster a visit."

"Headmistress, sir. The Head is a lady teacher."

Vance snorted; he should have realised that, after all, most primary heads were female. "Where is DI Shepherd, anyway?"

"Last I heard, she was off to interview Beatrice Tibbet."

"Ah, fair enough. I'll wait for her to get back. I have Doctor Tremethyk's autopsy report to read. A little light reading, you might say!"

It was Wright's turn to snort. His lip curled as he thought how lucky he was that his computer work kept him away from the morgue and its goriest details.

When Shepherd returned, she quickly updated her partner about her interview with Beatrice Harris, née Tibbet. "Nothing concrete to work with, Jacob, but she came over as more possibilistic this time regarding the existence of a younger sister. When I asked her about her Aunt Felicity, she started gushing about the long weekends she'd spent there aged four or five. She says she has fond memories of her aunt. Always treats like treacle tart, jelly and pies."

Vance dropped his bomb. "Felicity Tibbet married Frank Bradshaw, and adopted Melanie when she was four." Before Shepherd could intervene, he hurriedly updated her on the latest developments.

When he'd finished, Shepherd stared hard at him. "I've always felt that Bethany and Melanie were the same person. Are you sure we can't find out who Melanie's natural mother was?"

"The Commissioner might be able to lean on someone, but it's notoriously difficult to breach that kind of privacy. If the

Swan plays the murder inquiry card, she might get results. I'll try her now."

A rapid phone call and equally quick explanation later, Vance put down the receiver with a satisfied expression on his face. "The Big Boss says she'll pull a few strings. It would be a neat solution to our case. Fingers crossed."

"Except, partner, there's no trace of either Bethany or Melanie."

"Let's get on the trail of Melanie. It strikes me as a more amenable task."

"Where do we begin?"

"At her primary school. Come on!"

They drove to Belgravia and soon found Cale Street. The Oratory RC Primary School, an impressive three-storey building, stood on the corner of the street, as squat and solid as a medieval fortress.

"Let me do the talking, Jacob. You know, woman-to-woman." Shepherd said this as she rang the bell on the green door surrounded by its elaborate white stone architraves and under a small statue of the Virgin and Child in the pediment. After inspecting their warrant cards, a pleasant secretary with an Irish brogue invited them inside.

"I hope nothing has happened to one of our little angels," the secretary said anxiously.

"Nothing like that," Shepherd said gently. "No need to fret; we wanted to ask your headmistress about one of your former pupils. Has the Headmistress been here long?"

"A lifetime, no less, and a more dedicated teacher than Miss Browning, you'll not find within these shores, so you won't!"

Vance smiled approvingly. He admired loyalty in a person. "There are too few people with a vocation these days. It's sad," he said.

"Well now, Miss Browning has a vocation, and that's a fact, so it is! But please come with me. I'll see if we can disturb her."

The secretary led them to the head's study. The school was

like a ghost town, with lessons temporarily suspended due to a new variant of a virus sweeping the city. As Vance adjusted his face mask, he thought that the temporary closure might help his cause since the Head would be under less pressure than usual.

The headmistress welcomed them with what Vance identified as an Essex accent, given that he had a good ear for regional variations. She was probably on the verge of retirement, he considered. Shepherd began, "Ms Browning—"

"Oh no, dear, that will never do for an old stick like me! I'm no feminist, you know. Please call me *Miss* Browning. I'm quite happy with being a spinster." Her somewhat podgy face lit up as she peered at the pretty policewoman, secretly envying her oval face and turned-up nose. If the good Lord had blessed her with this officer's looks, she wouldn't have remained unmarried, for sure. But it had been God's will for her to dedicate herself to her little charges for forty years.

"Ah, yes, Miss Browning, how long have you been at the Oratory Primary School?"

Vance was staring at an image of the Sacred Heart of Jesus, and it brought back unpleasant memories of Tremethyk's morgue. A picture like that of a heart outside the chest must terrify little children, he thought.

"I was a deputy head in Brentwood in 1990, when I came here to take up this position. Good Heavens! More than thirty years ago—how time flies!"

"That's what I wanted to hear, Miss Browning. You see, we're trying to obtain some background on one of your former pupils: a certain Melanie Bradshaw."

"Ah, Melanie, I remember her well. Let me see. Um, she was here for her junior years until her parents moved to Richmond, I think it was. But she would have been going on to secondary education, in any case. Lovely family and a dear child. Never a minute's trouble from her. I often thought she would make something of herself. Such a clever little girl and so pretty! I wonder what became of her?"

"I can help you there, Miss Browning." Shepherd's tone was obliging. "You can be proud of the solid base your school gave her, because Melanie went on to obtain a first-class honours degree in Chemistry from Imperial College."

"Did she? Bless my soul! Who'd have thought it? So, might I ask why you are inquiring about the girl? I mean woman, of course, she must be nearing thirty now."

"We were hoping to eliminate her from our inquiries. There was some suggestion that she might be involved in a case we are working on. Anything you can remember about her might be helpful, Miss Browning."

"Just a moment, officer, I'll have her file brought. It might help jog my memory." She pressed a button on an intercom. "Bernadette, please bring me a file: Melanie Bradshaw." She smiled at Vance, thinking, what a pity he's wearing a mask, I'll bet under that he's a handsome fellow. "We have a little stockroom dedicated to our filing system. There's a folder for every boy and girl who came to the Oratory School. I know you think we're old relics, Detective Inspector, but it's remarkably efficient, as you'll see. I'm only three years from retirement. I'll let some new broom deal with computerising. Is that the right word?"

The Irish secretary knocked politely, entered, and handed a buff manila folder to her boss before beating a hasty and discreet retreat.

"Bernadette's a jewel. I don't know what I'd do without her."

"She speaks very highly of you, too, Miss Browning," Shepherd said.

"Does she, bless her," the headmistress replied distractedly, adjusting her glasses up her nose with her forefinger to peer at the yellowing paper within. "Melanie came to join Class 1 when she was five in September 2003 and left to go to Richmond in 2009. I suppose she went to the St Richard Reynolds High School. That's an excellent school and I believe it takes girls. I have no idea which school, though. I expect it will have been a

Catholic secondary of some type." She looked inquiringly at Brittany.

"I'm afraid we know so little about Melanie," Shepherd said. "Is there anything that leaps out from the file, Miss Browning? We'll keep everything confidential. Bullying? Sexual deviation?"

The staid headmistress nearly fell off her seat. "Good heavens no, nothing of the sort! Of course, bullying does go on even here, especially among the boys. I don't suppose there's a school in the land immune from it. I come down hard on that kind of behaviour, I can tell you." She suddenly looked so fierce that Vance had to smile under his mask.

"Is there a hint of any unpleasantness that might have occurred on Melanie's way into school? On the tram, for instance? It can be a risk to send a little child on public transport, even for just a few stops."

The schoolteacher scowled at the papers, scanning and turning the sheets deliberately one by one. At last, she looked up. "No, Detective Inspector. In any case, I distinctly remember Melanie's mother accompanying her every day to the front door. She did that religiously right through her entire time here. Of course, she might have missed the odd day for influenza or something like that, but I recall Mrs Bradshaw very well. A kindly, affectionate sort, and Melanie was always immaculately turned out, not like the thankfully small minority of the poor mites we get here, although, on the whole, we draw from a very affluent catchment area."

In the car, Shepherd puffed out her cheeks and blew out to express her frustration.

"That's not what we were hoping for. Melanie turns out to be Little Miss Perfect and not even a victim of sexual interference."

"Unless, of course, you're wrong, and Melanie and Bethany are two different people. Melanie might be the angel to Bethany's devil."

"Do you know, half of me hopes you are right. Melanie Bradshaw might be a loss to society, but if Bethany is anything like her brother, the best place for her is locked away in a psychiatric hospital."

Vance grunted noncommittally but promised himself he'd contact the Catholic secondary schools in Richmond as soon as he got back to New Scotland Yard.

CHAPTER 10
TAY WHARF, EAST END AND NEW SCOTLAND YARD, LONDON

THE MISTY REFLECTION IN THE STEAMED-UP BATHROOM MIRROR grinned back at Bethany for having triumphed over adversity after applying her eye shadow. She had good reason to be cheerful, since her preparations for an early afternoon encounter with Kaylee Kuddles had gone superbly well. She smiled as she recalled the phone conversation. How well she had duped the prostitute into thinking that *she*, Bethany, was gay. Making it clear to the whore that she had made her choice thanks to her name, she convinced Kaylee that she didn't seek anything other than straight and cuddlesome sex.

"Do you like vodka, sweetie?" she had asked. "I'll need some Dutch courage because I'm not used to trysts like this." She played the false innocent, although, to be fair, her limited sexual exploits had never involved her own gender.

The liquor was part of her plan. From establishing that she would provide a bottle, it was an easy step to fixing the meeting place under the giant treacle tin. Bethany wiped the mirror with a towel to check her appearance. "Mmm, if Kaylee truly likes girlies, she'll like what she sees here," she murmured and pouted a kiss at her slightly smeared image.

Having made the trip to West Silvertown on reconnaissance,

it was easy for Bethany to get her timing right. She loved punctuality and precision in all things, so when she approached the sugar refinery and spied the figure in a decency-defying black leather mini-skirt, she trembled with anticipation of the kill. Kaylee Kuddles was an attractive woman in her late twenties. Above the belt-like skirt, her cleavage, enhanced by a push-up bra, beckoned white and full of promise, battling to escape from a pink frilly blouse. Bethany stopped a good twenty paces from her target, unscrewed the vodka bottle and took a swig. She was role-playing. With a smirk, she advanced on Kaylee, deliberately swinging her hips encased in skin-tight low-cut jeans that showed her trim waist and belly button to perfection under her tube top. Bethany had made every effort to look irresistible to the lesbian eye.

"Hiya!" She leered at the prostitute. "I'm Bethany. I can see I've chosen well. We're going to have a good time, girl! Here," she extended the vodka and watched, gratified, as Kaylee swilled down what must have been a triple measure at a bar.

She screwed the cap on the bottle and stored it in her bag before she made a special request. "See across the road, that gate farther down there? Well, there's a cute little monument I like. Will you oblige and take a selfie with my phone? Then, my lovely Kaylee, I'll have something to remember you by during my lonely nights."

"You're a weird little tart, aren't you? But, yeah, I don't see why not. Come on then. Let's not waste time. I can't wait to peel those jeans off your cute little arse."

Bethany pretended to shudder with delight and, having done her homework, lied, "Don't worry, babe, you won't have long to wait. I've booked a double at the Travelodge Hotel. It's not far from here."

"Cool! I know it well."

They crossed the road, and Bethany had to hurry to keep pace with Kaylee's long, shapely legs. *What a shame she's a whore. I'm sure she could do much better for herself than this line of work.*

Except it's too late, she has no prospects now! Bethany thought as she reached in her handbag for her mobile. She stopped under the monumental upright with its block lettering and date.

"I didn't tell you I'm an architecture student. I'll take one for my files, and then you can do the selfie, sweetie." She wanted to make the scenario seem as realistic as possible.

Passing the phone to Kaylee, she said, "Try and get your pretty face and the writing into the picture." She knew that it would be difficult, so she added, "Take your time, remember it has to be a turn-on for me." Whilst Kaylee struggled valiantly to oblige, well and truly distracted, Bethany poured her blue liquid onto the cotton wad and, not having a second of evaporation time to waste, sprang at the unsuspecting poseur, knocking aside the phone and covering her victim's nose and mouth. A moment of futile thrashing about, a muffled cry, and the large eyeballs rolled upwards as the whore slumped against the wall. Mercilessly, Bethany pressed the wad harder against the young woman's face. The prostitute's legs gave way, and Bethany had to lower the dead weight of her body to the pavement. Carefully, she heaved the corpse into a sitting position against the column.

She stood back and shot a fearful glance up and down the road. As expected, there was no movement—for the moment—as she had chosen early afternoon deliberately. *The dead hours of the day,* she chuckled inwardly. No time to waste! She rearranged Kaylee's long legs so that her white knickers were no longer visible. *Shame, I'll bet sex with her would have been glorious!* Next, she wiped the glass to remove her fingerprints, then pulled on latex gloves to sprinkle vodka over her victim's lips and chin before setting the bottle into the woman's left hand, taking care that it remained upright in a pseudo-grip. *That should do. If a car comes past, the driver will see a whore sleeping off her excesses.* Again, she reached into her voluminous handbag, took out the black paint spray can, shook it, and spritzed **9-4=5** on the column above the body. Ramming the can back in her shoulder bag, she thought, *now, I'm ready for the Korean.*

She glanced at the derelict tram tracks still visible in front of the gate, the reason for her choice of location. Then she peered along the road in both directions, saying, "Bye-bye, sweetie!" and hurried away to catch the train for the short trip to Canning Town, where she would take the tube to return to her temporary base.

On the journey, she wondered about the police for the hundredth time. Would they have concluded that Arnold's sister was responsible for the murders? She had to assume so. In that case, how long would it be before, if ever, she could occupy her lovely riverside flat? Trying to sell it would set the hounds on her trail, too. Thank goodness, she had the considerable sum that Arnold had left to her. Before embarking on her killing spree, her wisest move had been to transfer her legacy into a Swiss account. The cops couldn't trace her through her transactions, and she'd never be short of cash. Feeling eyes on her, she glared across the swaying compartment at a middle-aged man ogling her. He looked embarrassed and shifted his gaze to the overhead underground map.

For a fleeting second, prompted by the antipathy of the man opposite, she felt remorse for Kaylee Kuddles. Okay, she was a whore, but a pretty one with a likeable disposition, in stark contrast to human trash like the fellow across the carriage. If anything, he deserved Kaylee's fate. She refused to dwell on her victim, though. As usual, Bethany didn't have feelings for them, as they were mere pawns in her chess game with the law. The cops had check-mated her incompetent brother, admittedly a fine player, but she was a Grand Master—or should that be, *Grand Mistress!* She sniggered and thought no more of Kaylee Kuddles, deleting the whore's selfie from her phone and, with rather more regret, the photo of the listed monument at Tay Wharf. Better to take no chances. The cops might catch up with her before long, and she would have to wriggle free on the grounds of no evidence against her.

By the time she reached Ealing Broadway Station, Bethany's

head was tired of so many considerations, so she decided to relax. The earlier sip of vodka had given her the taste for alcohol, so she wandered into the Shanakee pub near the station and strolled up to the bar with its red panelling.

"A vodka and lime, please."

The barman grinned at her. "Do you like our statue, then?"

He had noticed her gazing up at the effigy above the bar, dressed in a green skirt with a white apron over it, the figure clasping a book to its chest.

"Yeah, what's it supposed to be?" she asked, removing her facemask and paying for the drink.

"I can tell you're not Irish, although you could pass as a pretty colleen. The pub's *The Shanakee*, see. And that's Irish for a storyteller. The statue portrays a shanakee." He grinned at her with the satisfied expression of a knowledgeable twerp.

"Beware of the pretty colleens," Bethany said through clenched teeth, but she began to sing:

"For they'll fill you with whisky and porter
Till you are unable to stand
And the very next thing that you know, me lads
You've landed in Van Diemen's Land."

"Hey! You've got a smashing voice. Hang on a minute." He disappeared through a door behind the bar, reappearing with a guitar in hand. "Here, this one's on the house." He poured her another generous vodka and splashed green cordial into it.

He fiddled about for a while, tuning his guitar then, grinning at her, said, "From the beginning now, and sang in a pleasant baritone:

"In a neat little town they called Belfast
Apprentice to trade I was bound..."

He had a delightful voice and knew how to finger-pick, so

she joined in willingly to sing along to her favourite Dubliners song. There were only two other lonesome drinkers in the bar at this hour, and they sang the catchy chorus lustily.

When he had finished, the barman stuck out a hand. "Mark," he said, "but you can call me Mark."

"Ha-ha! Very droll. Bethany."

"House of figs? Odd sort of name."

Bethany glared at him, but her scowl was mixed with admiration. "You're not just a musician, but also a Hebrew scholar! Not many people know the meaning of my name."

"Just a well-brung up Catholic boy," he joked, faking an Irish accent. "Fancy getting to know me better?"

She looked at his soulful brown eyes regretfully. "Sorry," she said, not wholly untruthfully, "I'm just on my way back from a gay encounter. It didn't end well, but I'm not quite ready to branch out. Maybe another time."

"I'll be here waiting for my pretty colleen," he said engagingly.

Bethany walked out to return to her bedsit. *I like him. But better not get involved with anyone until I've finished my killing campaign.* She smiled at the memory of their song, thinking it a pity that he'd given priority to chatting her up instead of singing another ballad. She sighed and decided to go back to the Shanakee when she was ready, after victim number nine—The Big One.

———

Acting on Miss Browning's suggestion, at headquarters, Vance struck lucky with the St Richard Reynolds High School. A well-spoken secretary remembered Melanie Bradshaw as a polite, well-behaved student who achieved outstanding A-level results. "Three straight A's, Detective Inspector. Let's say it was expected, and her teachers remarked that it was a foregone conclusion. No, as far as I'm aware, she hasn't returned to the school since then. Only a few students do that."

When pressed on the subject of sexual molestation, the secretary became flustered and denied any knowledge of any such eventuality. Vance thanked her for her kind cooperation and hastily ended the call. He chewed his lower lip. Again, the secondary school had confirmed the primary headmistress's assessment, that Melanie Bradshaw was in all respects a model pupil. Previously, he had gone along with Shepherd's instincts, but the more they uncovered Melanie's background, the less likely it appeared that she and Bethany were the same person. It seemed to him increasingly unlikely that she was the perpetrator of three heinous murders. Vance decided that their inquiries should now concentrate on Bethany Tibbet.

Despite the detective's intentions, Wright supplied him with new information about Melanie that provided his pursuit of the chemist with fresh impetus. The Detective Sergeant called his name as he strolled along the corridor. "DS Vance, have you got a minute? I have something for you."

"What is it, Max?"

"I followed up a hunch this morning, and it paid off. I thought that someone like Melanie wouldn't just disappear after leaving Porton Down. So, I checked the largest chemical companies in the area, who all denied knowledge of a Melanie Bradshaw. I changed tactics, asking myself whether she might have decided to pursue further education. That's where I hit the jackpot! There are a limited number of institutions in Greater London that offer postgraduate qualifications in Chemistry."

"I haven't got all day, Max, get to the point."

"Sorry, sir. Bradshaw has enrolled in a fee-paying place on a part-time MSc degree course in Material Chemistry at St Mary College. I followed up by checking the British Library, and guess what? She signed up as a reader at St Pancras only a few days ago. So, we have a double chance of pulling her in for questioning."

"Brilliant work, Max. I'll get Mark and Ellen onto it right away. I don't think Ms Bradshaw will slip through our net this time."

As luck would have it, Mark Allen and Ellen Rhodes were working independently but in tandem on the Tramlink. Ellen was on the eastbound line and Mark on the westbound, stopping every petite blonde over twenty and under fifty and asking each one to furnish ID. They had drawn a resounding blank and were only too eager to return to headquarters after a day of hearing, "You can't ask me that," or similar. British people, not just petite blondes, do not like being asked for ID, and many make a fuss. ID cards do not exist in the country. Still, the majority of adults possess a driving licence and, as Mark Allen and Ellen Rhodes insisted, "Yes, ma'am, we can ask you, and even arrest you for obstructing police inquiries if you refuse to cooperate." This threat was enough to produce, usually, a driving licence, or a library card, in Mark's case. Someone showed Ellen her credit and debit card, another, her passport. Their controls did not find a Bethany or a Melanie.

Vance didn't need to be a detective to infer the tousle-headed Mark Allen's mood. Not that the sergeant would ever have been short with his inspector, whom he idolised.

"Bad day, Sarge?"

"Does it show, sir? It's just that it feels like I've wasted the last six hours harassing little women."

"Some of them deserve the hassle," Rhodes said grumpily. "Talk about resenting the police. They'd be the first to yell for help in an emergency. I mean, sir, you ask someone for ID, and it's like you're stealing their liberty. And I'll bet most of them are signed up to the social media, or that Google even knows when and how often they go to the loo. Some of them should've experienced a fascist regime, and then they might appreciate how we go about our business."

"Calm down, Rhodesy, I take your point, but it's all in a day's work in this job." Vance tried to sound sympathetic, but he, too, was stressed by this case and its lack of progress. He also felt that he could do with more time with his lovely wife, Helena, not to mention more time for a few pints of London Pride. Now, he smiled in the fraught silence that followed his words and said, "Cheer up, the pair of you. I've got something concrete for you to work on."

He proceeded to explain Wright's breakthrough on the whereabouts of Melanie Bradshaw.

"Mark, find yourself a constable and take the British Library. We can't be sure that Bradshaw is the murderer, but it's better to be safe than sorry if she is. Ellen, you too, go over to St Mary College with a constable." He addressed them both, "We don't know her schedule, so once again, it's a question of biding your time and checking the petite blondes, although, Ellen, in your case, it might be easier. There will be chemistry staff to ask about her scheduled tutorials and lectures.

"Mark, you'll be doing more of the Tramlink-style surveillance stuff. Sorry about that, but at least we know she's just signed up at the library. Good luck, both of you. Bring her in for questioning."

CHAPTER 11
THE BRITISH LIBRARY AND NEW SCOTLAND YARD, LONDON

THE BEAUTIFUL, SUNNY MORNING INSPIRED MELANIE, AND SHE WAS determined to take the time to admire her surroundings on her second visit to the British Library. With this in mind, she strode into the piazza with its two-tone pavement designed in squares. From there, she surveyed the building's red bricks on the outside, which blended in seamlessly with the neighbouring St Pancras Station and the Renaissance Hotel. She took a few photographs with her smartphone. The building, seen from one angle, almost seemed to resemble a great ship. She was right, although she didn't know that the famous Sir Colin St. John Wilson was a naval lieutenant before becoming an architect.

She strolled over to a stone bench against the low brick wall separating the piazza from an ornamental garden. Sitting with her back to it, Melanie raised her phone camera again and took a snap of a bronze statue of a man bent over, measuring with a pair of dividers. She was adjusting the light and contrast of the image when a pleasant male voice addressed her.

"Excuse me, miss, Metropolitan Police." She looked up at the tousle-haired, smiling policeman, with a puzzled but not remotely guilty expression, he observed. Her gaze transferred to the extended warrant card, and she smiled brightly. "How can I help you, Detective Sergeant?"

"Do you have any ID on you, miss?"

She frowned, put her phone in her yellow shoulder bag, and pulled out her purse. "I've got a few things with my name on, officer. Will my driving licence be alright?"

As he studied it, she noticed another well-set man standing a few paces away, pretending to survey the architecture idly. He was probably another policeman, she decided. Since she had nothing to hide or to worry about, she remained unruffled, merely wondering what this was about. She asked politely, "Are you investigating a crime?" She smiled innocently.

DS Allen handed back her license but didn't answer her question, stating, "Ms Melanie Bradshaw? We have reason to believe that you can assist us in our inquiries. I have to ask you to accompany us to the police station."

"Good heavens! But I haven't done anything wrong, Detective."

"There's no charge, miss. You might have information that doesn't seem important to you but could be vital to our investigation."

"In that case," she said brightly, springing to her feet and slinging her shoulder bag into position, "I'm only too happy to help. Let's go!"

Allen exchanged glances with Constable Brightwell. Neither man had expected such polite cooperation. So, they headed to the ornamental gate that served as the entrance from Euston Road, where they had left the car. Brightwell drove them to New Scotland Yard.

"How exciting! I've never been here before," Melanie chirruped, "of course, I've often walked past and wondered what was inside."

I'll eat my hat if she's guilty, Allen thought. *I'll put in a good word for her with Vance.* They led her to DI Vance's room, where Allen told her to wait outside a moment with Brightwell.

"We've got Melanie Bradshaw outside, sir."

Vance looked up from documents he was scouring, his expression one of pleasure, followed by a mixture of irritation and perplexity.

"Why isn't she in one of the interview rooms, DS Allen?"

Allen looked abashed. He had been expecting praise. "Fact is, sir, she strikes me as a charming and cooperative person. I'd be surprised if she's our killer. Not for one moment did she come over as guilt-ridden."

"Don't you think I'm better qualified to judge that, Sarge? Always stick to procedure."

Allen's face turned fiery red. "Sorry, sir, I'll take her down to Interview Room 1 right away."

"You mustn't take anyone on face value, Mark. Remember, she's a very bright young woman and for all we know, she might be a consummate actress."

The young detective looked so crestfallen that Vance felt sorry for him. After all, he had apprehended Bradshaw in record time. "Good work though, Sarge, you didn't waste any time catching up with her." He gave his promising officer an encouraging smile. "Take her down there and leave her alone to stew for ten minutes, then I'll join you. Stand behind the one-way mirror glass. Whilst she's in there, don't take your eyes off her. We don't want her self-harming or attacking anyone with hydrogen cyanide."

Melanie Bradshaw sat in silence in the interview room, telling herself there was nothing to worry about. The nice policeman who had brought her in had been remarkably polite and reassuring. He had relieved her of her shoulder bag, explaining that it was routine practice *to cover ourselves*. She had smiled when he pointed out that some people self-harmed. Why would she do that? He had beamed back with a lovely smile—she quite fancied him, but he had been inflexible; no, he couldn't even leave her her mobile to surf the internet. She was supposed to sit and wait quietly. Well, she could do that, but now she was becoming a little bored, so she tried to repeat the third line of the periodic table from memory, K, Ca, SC, Ti, V...she continued unhesitatingly and, she thought, without erring, as far as atomic number 33, As, Sc, Br and 36, $Kr-$ "Krypton!" she cried out loud, triumphantly, just as Vance and Shepherd entered the room silently.

He heard her and, taking a seat opposite hers, smiled and said, "Ms Bradshaw, I'm DI Vance, and this is my colleague, DI Shepherd. We have a few questions to ask you informally. I'll make it clear that you are not charged with anything, but this recording," he nodded to awards a small black box, "is merely routine. It helps my poor old memory later on." Melanie smiled sweetly.

"First question, why did you shout *Krypton* when we came in?"

She giggled; Vance noted that it was a joyful, unforced sound. "Oh, that! I was bored with nothing to read, so I repeated the periodic table line three. It ends with Krypton, you see."

"I see. Your memory must be better than mine. If I remember rightly from my school days, there are quite a lot of elements on the third row."

"Yes, eighteen. I think I got them all in the right order: K, Ca, SC, Ti, V," she recited confidently.

Vance smiled at her and, noting what a pretty young woman he was interviewing, he said, "Impressive. So, with such a good memory, you'll have no trouble remembering what you were doing three evenings ago." He watched her reaction closely—no sign of guilt or anxiety.

"None at all, Detective Inspector. That was the day I signed up for my Reader Card at the British Library. I stayed there until about six-thirty and then went shopping in a nearby supermarket. It was Sainsbury's on the corner of Great Portland Street. I collect the Nectar points there. I picked up another twelve," she smiled winningly. "Then, I walked back to The Angel underground station and took the tube to Moorgate where I share digs with two other students, Janice and Ram—that's Ramona, by the way." She giggled again. "We ate a curry that Janice prepared and then we watched a film on Netflix. It was about Guatemala Bay and a miscarriage of justice. A bit of a harrowing movie. It's called *The Mauritanian*; I can recommend it." She smiled at Shepherd, who stared stonily at her.

"Tell me about your mother," Shepherd fired. She'd seen how Vance looked at the pretty woman, so she had no choice; it was her turn to play the bad cop.

"My mum died four years ago. Cancer. Her name was Felicity, and she was always cheerful, at least," the lovely face clouded and the green eyes brimmed with tears, "until Daddy passed from a heart attack. It was so sudden. I think that's what triggered her illness. I'm convinced the cancer was linked to stress and unhappiness."

"Did your mother have brothers and sisters?"

"Yes, she did, but I think she lost touch with them. You see, we lived in Wimbledon and then in Richmond upon Thames. She always said that they were in other parts of the city, and it was best that way." Melanie frowned. "I asked her what she meant by that once, and she went all secretive on me. It was clear she didn't want to talk. I got the feeling she might have been ashamed of them."

"With good reason," Shepherd snapped.

Melanie looked confused and hurt. "Excuse me, what do you mean, detective?"

"Come on, Bradshaw, don't take us for fools!" The green eyes widened. "You must have known your mother's maiden name."

"Of course. Walker."

Shepherd slammed her hand on the table. "You're a smart one. I'll give you that!"

"I don't know what you're getting at, Detective. Did my mother do anything wrong?"

Vance raised a finger at Shepherd and took over. "Melanie, did your mother tell you her surname was Walker?"

"Yes, she did."

"And didn't her sisters come to the funeral?"

"I had to make the arrangements, detective. I didn't have their addresses and couldn't find any Walkers in her address book."

"Did you find any Tibbets?"

"Sorry, I don't think so. Wait a minute! Wasn't Tibbet the name of that horrible serial killer?"

"Yes, your mother's brother," Shepherd shot.

"That can't be true! She never said anything—" She looked disconcerted. "Oh, she wouldn't, would she? Are you sure my mother was a Tibbet?"

"Didn't you ever see her birth certificate, Ms Bradshaw?" Vance asked gently.

"*You* can call me Melanie." She smiled weakly and glared instead at Shepherd. "Come to think of it, no. I organised all the important documents after her death, and I found it strange that I couldn't find her birth certificate or marriage certificate. But look, detective, you'll know better than I; you guys can soon trace these things. Please take my word for it, you've given me horrible news that my mother was sister to that monster. My mother was the kindest, loveliest soul you could wish to meet."

"I believe you, Ms Bradshaw." Vance stood, signalled to his colleague, who turned off the recorder. "Thank you for cooperating so fully." He extended a hand, and Melanie took it willingly. She liked Vance but made no effort to shake hands with the female police officer, who said, "Leave your address at the desk in the hall, we may need to contact you again. You can sign for your bag there."

"I have the Sainsbury's receipt in my purse if you want to see it. I keep them for the points total. It'll have the time and date on it."

For the first time, Shepherd smiled at her. "No need,

Melanie," she used the name pointedly. "As we said earlier, you are not under investigation," she lied. "We just needed to ask you a few questions. You can go now. Turn right in the corridor."

Shepherd and Vance went up to his room. He said, "Hold your fire, partner. I need to make a quick phone call to Monarch Chemicals." He found the number and tapped it out. *No bloody speakerphone again!* Shepherd scowled on hearing the faint ring tone. "Hello Stephanie, DI Vance here, put me through to David Brookes, would you?" He sat down slowly with the mobile attached to his ear. "Hi, Mr Brookes, just a quick question for you. Can you confirm that the Melanie Bradshaw we talked about had blue eyes? Yes. Are you quite certain? Indeed, I remember you saying that! Fine, just checking. No, that's all."

Vance turned to his colleague. "I had to clear that up. I remembered correctly. I might not be able to recite the periodic table, but I'm not senile yet! David Brookes said that Melanie's beautiful blue eyes attracted him initially. He confirmed the colour just now, but as we have just seen, Melanie Bradshaw has exquisite *green* eyes."

"Can't say I noticed," Shepherd snapped, her own lovely sapphire blue eyes blazing at her partner. She preferred to lie rather than agree that Melanie Bradshaw's eyes were heavenly.

"Well, she has! A man notices these things," he ignored Shepherd's snort, "which means that the Melanie Bradshaw who presented herself at Monarch was an imposter. I'll bet my last twenty pence that it was Bethany Tibbet."

"So, you don't think Melanie could win an Oscar for her acting ability, Jacob?"

"No, Brittany, years of police work have honed my skill in picking out a fraud. Melanie Bradshaw is a genuine Chemistry student. She was telling the truth throughout that interview. Her reactions were all normal, as far as I'm concerned."

"I have to agree," her tone was grudging, "bang goes my pet

theory, but this time, I have to go along with you, and we must concentrate our investigation on the elusive Bethany Tibbet."

"To make certain, I'll consult Miriam. She watched our interview alongside Mark Allen. Ah, by the way, put a call through to Rhodesy. I forgot to haul her in from St Mary College. Meanwhile, I'll get on to Miriam."

A few minutes later, Miriam Walker knocked.

She smiled at Shepherd and asked how she was before getting down to business. "Hi, Jacob, well, that was an object lesson in good cop-bad cop, I must say." She darted a complicit smile at Brittany. "If I didn't know you better, Brit, I'd say you were a right virago. Odds-on poor Melanie Bradshaw thinks just that!"

Shepherd muttered something incomprehensible under her breath, then shot clearly, "If you don't offer us a much-needed coffee, Jacob, my badness will reach new levels." They all laughed.

The caffeine consumption over, Miriam said, "I believe that Melanie is an intelligent, well-balanced young woman who misses her parents terribly. I feel she is truthful and her reactions and body language tell me that she's innocent of any crime."

"Thank you, Miriam. That confirms what we both think. We're concentrating on the elusive Bethany Tibbet from now on."

"Do you want my report in writing, Jacob?"

"If it's not too much trouble. We have to stick to the regulations, especially with Phadkar watching our every move like a famished hawk hunting vole."

"She has every reason to be anxious," Doctor Walker reminded them, her homely face breaking into a dimpled smile.

CHAPTER 12

MOORGATE, SILVERTOWN AND EALING, LONDON

THE DRIVER OF THE AUDI A6 DROVE PAST THE TAY WHARF GATE, caught sight of the attractive long legs of the drunken prostitute and slowed to a halt, checked his mirror and reversed to a stop near her. He was a successful businessman, a partner in a small marble and granite importing firm. Although he was married, his insatiable appetite for women involved occasionally paying for the services of a sex worker. Graham Elliott couldn't resist an easy target like a boozed-up whore. He decided to get some strong coffee into her, then take her to a nearby motel that he'd used for such occasions from time to time. He pressed a button, and his window slid down, allowing him to call to her, but he received no reply. *Looks like she's sleeping off a skinful of vodka.* Unhooking a face mask from an air freshener clipped into a vent on the dashboard, Graham pulled the elastic over his ears, got out of the car and stepped over to the young woman. She had a lovely figure. The pink blouse revealed as much, but something was wrong. Was she unconscious? He glanced at the vodka bottle. It was still half full.

Gently, he placed two fingers under the woman's chin and raised her unresponsive head. A glance at the waxen complexion, and Graham Elliott realised there was no helping this one.

Considerately, he closed the staring eyes and let the head loll forward again. Rising from his crouching position, he groped for his mobile to dial 999. Elliott waited, more responsibly than his usual behaviour, for the police and ambulance to arrive. When they came, the two squad cars' sirens tortured his eardrums, but the drivers had the gumption to turn off the wailing as they drew up.

Elliott was explaining to a red-haired uniformed policeman how he'd found the dead woman when a third ear-rending siren heralded the arrival of the ambulance. When the ambulance driver cut the siren, he continued, "I thought she was the worse for drink, officer. I saw the bottle in her hand. I mean, that's what it looked like, but when I came to see if I could help, I realised she was a goner."

"Did you touch anything, sir?"

"No, I raised her head to look in her face—that's how I knew —oh, and I closed her staring eyes. It seemed like a decent thing to do. But that's all. Poor lass, I don't think she even made thirty by the look of her."

"What were you doing in this quarter? Did you have an appointment with her, sir?"

"Good Lord, no! I was on my way to work. I'd just finished my lunch hour at the pub in Canary Wharf. I often go to the Henry Addington because it's convenient for our place at Silvertown Quays—our company took advantage of the new regeneration incentives. Here's my card, officer." He handed over a visiting card that the policeman scanned.

"Thanks very much, Mr Elliott. I'm afraid I'll have to detain you a while longer until my superiors arrive. Oi, you!" The officer shouted at a paramedic, who approached the corpse. "Back off, pal. This is a crime scene." He turned to Elliott and explained, "I'd tape it off, but I'd have to close the road to do that." He was speaking his thoughts rather than conversing.

"Look, I'll sit in my car and make a couple of phone calls if that's alright."

"That's fine. Sorry to inconvenience you, sir."

An hour later, Vance received a call from the East End of London. He listened carefully for a few minutes, then interrupted. "So, what makes you think it's connected to our inquiry?... I see. That's interesting... Have you removed the body? No?... Keep the scene intact for as long as it takes me to get over to you. We're on our way."

Vance found Shepherd and hustled her out of the building with an authoritative, "I'll explain in the car."

"Where to, partner?"

"Tay Wharf, it's in Silvertown. Do you know the sugar refinery?"

"Tate and Lyle? Yes, I can take you to the giant treacle tin."

"Let's go then! That's near enough."

Shepherd listened to Vance's reconstruction of the phone call. "I get it! But aren't we missing a couple of things, Jacob?"

"Such as?"

"Wasn't Randy Mandy Tibbet's *fifth* victim? Unless I'm mistaken, we have three. I don't suppose the fourth didn't turn up. Wasn't it a Japanese tourist?"

"No, Korean—but you're right, that poor girl was Arnold Tibbet's fourth victim. The sex worker was his fifth, as you say."

"Odd, isn't it? Also, why would Bethany Tibbet strike so far from the Tramlink?"

"That's what I wanted to know when they called it in. Damn, another red light!"

The traffic lights seemed synchronised to slow their progress across the city. It wasn't so far along the river to Silvertown, but for the traffic and associated restrictions. "We should have had the river cops take us by boat! It'd be a darned sight faster," Shepherd jested. She returned to her argument. "So, why would she?"

"That's just it; she didn't. It appears that there are derelict tramlines about ten feet from the body. That part of dockland is often deserted these days. Why risk killing on the busy

Tramlink when you can make your point in comparative safety?"

Shepherd's hands beat the steering wheel in irritation as the lights remained stubbornly red.

"That won't make them change any faster, Brit."

"Come on! Come on! About bloody time!" She almost shunted the car in front in her frustration to get away.

Vance knew when to say nothing, preferring to dwell on Bethany Tibbet's cunning.

While the detectives were studying the crime scene, Melanie Bradshaw was speaking urgently with her flatmates back in Moorgate.

"They took me into New Scotland Yard for questioning. I mean, I didn't know that my uncle was a notorious serial killer, and it's hardly my fault, is it?"

"Bloody harassment, that's what I call it!" It took little to set Ramona off against the police. Like her single mother, who had brought her up in the tough quarter of Brixton, Ram was a paid-up member of the Workers Revolutionary Party. "When the proletariat triumph," she snarled, "we'll replace the pigs with a workers militia." Ramona might have been pretty if it wasn't for her cropped hair, that looked as if she'd taken secateurs to it herself, the cheap aluminium nose piercing and the almost permanent pugnacious expression.

On the other hand, Janice was from a council estate in Putney, an unassuming, recent academy sixth-form scholar who had difficulty in believing that she was the university material that she patently was. Ram's railing against the system, to her frustration, hit a rubber wall with Jan, who believed that society was perfectly all right as it was. She compensated for her mousy hair by adding light brown highlights and, although she was not a good-looker like Mel, she made the most of her appearance with a bright complexion and clean hair, not to mention her make-up skills. Next to Jan, Ram looked what she was, careless of her aspect.

"I was completely truthful with the police," Melanie was saying, "except for one minor detail, so if they come checking, I want you to back me up, girls. Will you do that?"

"Damn right we will!" Ram growled, glaring at Janice. "What do you want us to say?"

"Well, remember a few nights back, when you made that delicious prawn curry? I told the cops that we watched *The Mauritanian* after it."

"So what? We did!"

"Yeah, Ram, I know, but you told me about it in the morning, get it? See, I went to bed with a bad headache, so I haven't got an alibi for my whereabouts."

"And *were* you in bed," Ram asked suspiciously, narrowing her eyes, "or were you out doing a Jack the Ripper?"

"Bloody hell, Ram! Not you as well! Of course I was in bed, but as far as the police are concerned, I was watching that DVD with you, right? Anyway, they might not even come and check if they believed me."

"You can count on us, Mel, can't she, Jan?"

"Eh? Oh, yeah, sure."

Melanie relaxed and said, "I knew I could count on you two. Now, I'm off to a tutorial. I'd better get a move on, I'm running late."

"You'll damage that brain of yours by overworking it, sister." Ram often used that form of address for solidarity. "You're hardly ever here. Always bloody studying—and it's not as if you're like us two, you've already got a degree, you little brainbox!"

Melanie smiled; she had missed this sort of companionship at Porton Down. Student life was completely different. "I can pop into Sainsbury's on my way back if you need anything." She looked meaningfully at Ram, who had taken on the role of cook, in exchange for the other two washing and cleaning.

"We're almost out of toilet paper, and I could use some

Worcester sauce for a recipe I want to test on two willing guinea pigs!" she grinned provocatively.

"You got it! See you later." Melanie hurried away to catch the first tube train to make her tutorial in time. As she rode in the almost empty compartment, she sat back and closed her eyes. She had told the police the truth, except for that small detail, and it had bothered her ever since. But now she'd dealt with it, she could relax and concentrate on her chemical studies.

———

Returning to base, Shepherd did not notice the sequence of green traffic lights that eased her progress. Not one to count her blessings, Brittany's character contained an element of siege mentality that enabled her to succeed against any adversity, which tribulations inevitably she was quick to complain about. Not that she felt like protesting against anything in particular at that moment, but her instincts wouldn't give her any peace.

"Jacob, I can't help thinking that this Bethany is like a ghost. My mind keeps going back to that day at Tibbet's cremation. She appeared like a spectre among the gravestones, looking for all the world like Melanie Bradshaw."

Vance groaned. "Not again, Brit, give it a rest! You've got a bee in your bonnet."

"All I'm saying is that you've drummed into me countless times that you don't believe in coincidences. We know from her diary that a petite blonde stalked Gundega Krūmina. Melanie Bradshaw and Bethany Tibbet fit that description. I still say that they could be the same person."

"Listen, Shep, we agreed that Melanie was telling the truth, and then there's the fact that one has green eyes, the other, blue."

"Mmm, well, I still think we should check up on Little Miss Perfect's alibi. We're on the road, so why don't we turn off here and nip over to Moorgate?"

Vance acquiesced with a sinking feeling but had to confess that they were no nearer to catching up with bloody Bethany Tibbet, whereas Melanie Bradshaw was accessible to them. That alone made him think that Bethany was the killer and Melanie the chemistry student she claimed to be. Brittany Shepherd's instincts had cracked many a case when he'd been chasing shadows, so he gave her free rein now. She was troublingly right about coincidences, too.

"I'll do the talking, partner. Two young female students might be impressionable," Shepherd said, unaware of the character she was about to meet. She presented her warrant card to a sullen Ramona Clayton.

"Yeah, you can come in, but I haven't got all day."

Shepherd's trained eye immediately picked out the copy of *The News Line* daily paper carelessly tossed on the divan with its headlines: *PM PUTS NAVY IN CHARGE OF REPELLING REFUGEE DINGHIES.*

"Are you a commie, then, Ms Clayton?" the detective asked.

"Trotskyist, to be precise. What's it to you?"

"Nothing, just as long as you don't go breaking the law."

"You mean your capitalist laws designed to oppress the honest working classes?" Ramona's face had contorted into spiteful aggression that made Shepherd want to slap her hard.

Vance decided that allowing Shepherd to continue was counter-productive. His deep, calm voice intervened. "Come on, ladies, let's not argue. We're only here for a couple of quick questions, and then we'll let Ms Clayton get on with her life."

"OK, I'll talk to *you*." Ramona glared at Shepherd. "What questions?"

"Do you share the flat with Melanie Bradshaw?"

"Yeah, and with Janice Moore, they've both gone to uni. Mel's got a tutorial at St Mary College, and Jan's got a lecture at Imperial."

"And you've got bugger all!" Shepherd couldn't resist.

"As a matter of fact, although it's none of your business, copper, I happen to have a free morning on Wednesdays, and if you weren't interrupting my studies, I'd be poring over an original Herodotus text."

Vance, sensing another Punic War in the offing, intervened swiftly.

"Classics, and you can read Greek, too. My compliments!"

Ramona Clayton's taut expression softened slightly, if he wasn't mistaken. "I'll be frank with you, miss; we brought in your flatmate to help us in our inquiries on a murder case. It's our duty to follow up on what she told us. Melanie strikes me as an honest young woman. Can you tell me where she was three evenings ago?"

"Good cop, bad cop," Ramona said, glaring at Shepherd again. "Let's see, three evenings? Last night I cooked cottage pie, whilst two nights ago it was cod steaks in an Italian sauce with olives; before that, we had a prawn curry—yes, that would have been Sunday evening, right?" She looked for confirmation at Vance, who nodded. "OK, well, after dinner, we watched a bloody good film about oppressive capitalist methods. You should watch it, Detective." She scowled at Shepherd again. "Did you know that the Americans are torturing innocent people in concentration camps?"

"You should look at what the Russians are up to, Alexandra Kollontai," Shepherd snapped, showing a remarkable knowledge of the Russian Revolution that Vance couldn't match.

"Ah, so, you *do* know something worthwhile, copper."

"Please, you two, give it a rest, let's get back to business! So, you watched *The Mauritanian* together, all three?"

"Yes, Jan, Mel, and me. But I reckon it was wasted on our Janice; she stuck up for the Americans, silly cow!"

Shepherd let off steam in the car, berating the left-wing student in vulgar terms that not even Vance had heard her use before. When the storm blew itself out, Vance added quietly, "I take it you're not too keen on young Ramona."

Recognising that his calculated understatement was meant to defuse tension, Shepherd smiled and said, "Whether we like her or not, she confirmed Melanie's alibi, and so, we have to conclude that Melanie is not our killer. Where that leaves us in the hunt for Bethany is anyone's guess. I admit, I don't know where to start. Her family have no idea of her whereabouts, and the Fulham apartment seems to be deserted for now. Any suggestions, O wise one?"

"The murderer made a mistake, Shep. She left the dead woman's mobile in her pocket, and I've copied the recent numbers. By elimination, we should find Bethany's among them. Then, I'll put a trace on her phone. If she uses it, we'll catch her in no time."

"That's unlike her, don't you think? These Tibbets are so damned cunning."

"I must say, I was surprised at the oversight."

Over in Ealing, so was Bethany. She had an after-lunch rest, spooking herself by reading a book called *A Study in Red* that entered into the mind of the notorious Victorian Ripper. Momentarily distracted from her book, Bethany mentally ran back over the Kaylee killing, comparing her handiwork to Jack's. *Much cleaner and less risky, although forensics weren't up to much back then. Nowadays, you can't be too careful. Oh, soddin' hell!* She sat up violently and looked at her mobile on the bedside cabinet. With fumbling fingers, she opened the Sim Card slot and extracted the incriminating piece of plastic. *Dammit, I'll have to destroy it, or I'll have the cops all over me. How thick can I be?*

She considered the tiny object in her palm and the implications of losing it. Her list of contacts was irrelevant. She had no close friends or family. Perhaps she could bear parting with the few photos she'd taken—nothing that struck her as indispensable. She rolled out of bed and flushed the chip down the toilet. Relieved that the card didn't reappear after the cistern had filled again, she grinned at her reflection in the mirror, saying out loud, "You're still on your game, girl!"

Whilst she lived in this bedsit, the police hadn't a clue where she was. Her mobile was little more than a tool for the occasional call, so she would venture out and sign up for a new SIM card and number later; there was no hurry. Let the cops put a trace on her old number: they would draw a blank. She grinned in triumph at the mirror and twirled her long blonde hair around her forefinger, blowing herself a kiss.

Vance was in the bathroom when Dr Tremethyk's call set his desk phone ringing and vibrating, so Shepherd answered. She listened intently to what the CME had to say about Kaylee Kuddles so that she could pass the information on to her partner. He promised her that Vance would receive the full written report for their case files in due course. When the Detective Inspector returned to his office, Shepherd, omitting a subject, said, "She wasn't drunk, you know."

"Who?"

"Kaylee, the sex worker. I've had Doc Tremethyk on the blower, and he says the BAC was only 0.05. In his words, *the poor lassie wasn't drunk, but maybe loose and less self-conscious, me-dear.*" Shepherd giggled. "As if a prossie would be self-conscious in the first place! Our Cornish Pasty lives in a different world, Jacob— he's so old-school, it's unbelievable."

"Francis is a damned good pathologist, and don't you forget it, sassy little Mancunian that you are."

"Oh, I'm not disputing his abilities. This tells us that the vodka was a prop for our killer. I guess that she used it to give herself more time to vacate the scene. An ordinary passing motorist was supposed to see a drunken slag sleeping off her binge drinking. As I see it, it took a punter who fancied availing himself of her services to discover the truth that Kaylee was dead. As expected, the good doctor confirms the cause of death as hydrogen cyanide. In his words, *you know that already from the message on the wall and the tramlines, but I thought I'd spell it out for you, me-dear.* Shepherd managed a passable Cornish accent as she mimicked the pathologist.

Vance had to smile, but this case was no laughing matter. His voice revealed the tension gripping him. "The fact remains, we're stumbling around in the dark, and I don't like it, Brittany."

CHAPTER 13

NEW SCOTLAND YARD AND ADDISCOMBE, LONDON

BRITTANY SHEPHERD GAZED UNDER HER LONG LASHES AT JACOB Vance without letting him notice. She had seen him in this mood in the past when a particularly complicated case frustrated him, but never to this extent. Shepherd mused that it was thanks to Vance that she had found her niche in life. He was easily the best boss she had worked for, a man who listened and valued the opinions and input of his colleagues without ever pulling rank. Since he had such an incisive mind, he resented being unable to crack this case.

He broke into her reflections in a voice heavy with annoyance. "Maybe we're approaching these murders from the wrong angle, Shep. We have three victims on our hands and not a trace of Bethany Tibbet. Perhaps we should go back and start over."

"So, where do we begin, Jacob? I have to say, as to that, I'm no wiser than you."

"What strikes me most about Bethany is that she can't be found. So, we're dealing with the invisible woman, or we're looking in the wrong places. It's a fact that the two Tibbet siblings we've dealt with are exceptionally devious, but come on, in twenty-first century Britain, a person can't just vanish without a trace. Our starting point has to be with the late Violet Tibbet and the birth of Bethany. I want everyone in the team on this. It doesn't help that Violet is deceased, but there must be records. We have to be systematic. Whatever is out there, Max Wright will find it. I know that we've taken surveillance off the Fulham apartment, but Big Mal has given me the option of more men. He said he could let me have a dozen uniforms right away and more if necessary, so, you see, I think he's feeling the pressure from above."

"That's understandable if the Tibbet woman is copycatting her brother. The planned ninth victim is sure to be the Commissioner's nephew—oh, bloody Hell!"

"What?" Vance picked up on Shepherd's shocked anxiety.

"If she's copycatting, we'd better find her pretty damned quickly!"

"What's on your mind, Brit?"

Shepherd rubbed her knuckles against her forehead as if cudgelling her brain. "Why did she invert the killings? Or have we not had reports of a missing or dead Korean tourist? In either case, you know who's next on the hit list, don't you?"

The colour drained from Vance's face. "Shit!" He hadn't previously given it any thought. "The victim after the prostitute was DC Williams—damn it, Shep, we're not going to lose one of our chaps!"

"I'm going to get on to the Korean tourist. There must be ways of learning whether anyone's missing. Or what if the inversion of victims four and five was to confuse us? Not that I could be any more confused than I am right now!"

"Or, it might be part of Tibbet's cunning," Vance thought aloud. "Choosing Silvertown, where we weren't expecting her to strike, at a time when we were intensifying our patrols on the Tramline was, let's face it, a pretty smart move. I'll put Mark Allen on checking all vestiges of the old tramways in the capital. Bethany has a harder task than Arnold. Colours constrained him, but as we know, the city is full of streets with colours in the name. Apart from the Tramlink, she's decidedly more limited."

"The Tramlink has thirty-seven stations, Jacob. That's plenty of options for her. I suggest we deploy our extra uniforms there as well as watching the Riverside apartment twenty-four-seven. Look, I'll take charge of deploying the recruits if you don't mind. It'll be good experience for me."

"Good thinking. To work, then!"

Elsewhere, air in the water pipes made a howling sound—*like a jackal in distress,* thought Bethany, fed up with living in her fifth-rate squalid bedsit. She asked herself why she didn't pack up and leave the city, because she could afford a luxurious home in another attractive area of the country. Lower Slaughter in the Cotswolds, for example, lovely part of the country, and how she loved that name! She knew that there was an Upper Slaughter, too, but despite her learning, she didn't know that the names had nothing to do with killings but came from the Old English *Slohtre,* which means muddy place. If ever she left the metropolis, it would be for Upper Slaughter because her killings were superior in every way, which brought her back to the matter in hand that was becoming an obsession. How to find and kill a female Korean tourist?

It was alright for Arnold; he had only had to find a backwater street with black in the name. Her problem was harder since she had exhausted quiet corners of the capital with derelict tram-lines. With a sigh, she returned to the quandary of how to murder a young woman in full sight of other travellers whilst the cops were sure to have intensified their search for her. She pulled the map of the Tramlink closer and pored over it for the hundredth time. There were thirty-seven stations to choose from, but most of them were too risky. She needed to return to the prototype of her first murder. She smiled at the recollection of how easy it was to pounce in the Avenue Road subway. The difference between then and now lay in the time factor. Then, she had planned the operation for weeks. Her careful preparations had paid off with the almost perfect murder. Now, she had a matter of days if she wished to stick to her self-imposed, or should that be *Arnold-imposed*, schedule? The water pipes grumbled and vibrated again and Bethany swore under her breath. How was she supposed to concentrate?

The bedsit didn't have wi-fi, and its absence limited her research. She wanted to know whether there was CCTV at Elmers End, one of the two eastern termini of the Tramlink. The internet would supply the answer in three clicks; instead, she had to do on-the-ground research, though in some ways that was better, because a successful murder implied careful attention to detail. Elmers End attracted her because it was a terminus, but how many Korean tourists would go there? Her best hope for a selected target would be a busy station, but that would make her task much more complicated. Ending her mental turmoil, she dismissed the idea and returned to her idea of Elmers End. Was it the second part of the name that appealed to her? She laughed out loud; it would be the *End* for a Korean if she got this right. Koreans? Why did young Koreans come to London? To learn the language, of course! This insight gave her another idea.

"Next stop Elmers End," Bethany told her grinning reflection. *Should I cut my hair short? These long blonde locks are a giveaway. I can't bear to part with them, though.* She drew her hair back into a chignon. She glanced out of the window. Today, the wind was whipping around the buildings across the road, strong enough to oscillate the unfixed cable of the opposite house's satellite dish. "Ideal weather for my woollen knit beanie," she told her mirror image.

She cursed at the dump of a bedsit again when the top drawer of her chest of drawers jammed half-open. By aggressive jiggling of the offending compartment, she managed to reach inside to retrieve the chunky, baggy grey hat with its fancy detachable pompom. For a moment, she considered whether to remove the adornment, but on looking at the effect in the pathetic wardrobe mirror, she decided to leave it, as it countered the overly-slouchy look. The important thing was that she had covered her baby-blonde locks.

Bethany enjoyed the feeling of being whisked along smoothly in a tramcar. She had timed her departure to coincide with the first journey after the rush hour peak. This choice meant that, whereas she was sure to find a seat, she would still have most of the morning for her survey of Elmers End. At least, that was her plan because how could she foretell that she wouldn't reach the end of the line? As usual, she got on the tram at Merton Park and at once took a seat in the second compartment. There were only a few unoccupied places, but hardly anyone was strap-hanging. Bethany disliked standing on public transport even if the tram was not as jerky and unpleasant as the tube or the famous red buses.

She took her copy of *A Study in Red* out of her handbag and returned to the tale about the leather-aproned handiwork of the Ripper. Her fascination with the Victorian serial killer of poor Whitechapel girls began to transfer vicariously as she studied newcomers boarding the tram at various stops. One young woman hastily broke eye contact with the strangely-lit stare of Bethany's blue eyes. Had she known that the petite woman was contemplating what Jack would have done to her body, the innocent traveller would have screamed the tram to a halt.

Immersed in her book and the mind of the Ripper, Bethany returned to twenty-first-century reality when the tram squealed to a stop at a station. After her initial interest in the boarding passengers, she had become consumed by her reading, so she didn't know which station they were at. Peering outside, she caught sight of the nameboard: Sandilands. This junction was where the eastbound routes separated for one of three different termini. She had chosen the Elmers End tram, that saved her from having to change to reach her destination.

Her plans altered at the next halt: Addiscombe. Onto the tram stepped a young woman of Far Eastern aspect, quite possibly a Korean, judging by her lineaments. Bethany had no

difficulty distinguishing Chinese people from Japanese and each
of those from Koreans. In general, the Korean face has a more
prominent jaw and higher cheekbones. The young woman sat
opposite Bethany. She was perhaps about nineteen and smiled
timidly. Bethany treated her to a flashing smile and a nod. She
was thrilled to encounter a Korean, just as she had hoped. By the
time the tram slid into Blackhorse Lane, Bethany felt she had
garnered knowledge about her Asian fellow traveller. The girl
had a ridged transparent carry case with a red handle on her lap.
A sticker on the case bore the logo of an English language school
and, glimpsed through the plastic when she moved her hands
away, she had read *English Grammar in Use* in yellow lettering on
the dark-blue cover.

The next stop, Woodside, was two from the end of the line.
The Korean stood, smiled and waved her right hand shyly at
Bethany. In a split second, the recipient of the gesture decided to
follow her intended victim. After all, she was the only passenger
who had matched her desired profile on the entire journey. After
the briefest hesitation, Bethany sprang forward; to a casual
observer, it would have seemed that she'd just realised this was
her stop. Gazing down the platform, she spied the diminutive
form of the Korean hurrying towards what looked like a disused
former railway building. Indeed, it was boarded up and covered
in graffiti. With three other travellers, the English language
student turned into a flight of steps, which led down to street
level.

Bethany was disorientated, never having been to this part of
the city. She desperately wanted to see the Korean's destination.
As she descended them, she considered the steep steps as a
possible killing ground. Under the right circumstances, it could
be, she mused. Her thoughts returned to that day with Peter
Welsby. She shivered with pleasure, but those steps were
deserted and disused, whereas these probably received passengers every fifteen minutes. On those grounds, she rejected them

as a possibility; she could do better, and that was what she was here for: reconnaissance.

At the end of the steps, she surveyed a busy main road. The student was striding along as if late for a lesson. Methodically, Bethany checked the time on her phone's digital display—09.52. She wondered, and indeed, hoped, that the girl had a daily routine. Bethany broke into a jog when she saw the Korean turn right into a narrow lane; she didn't want to lose sight of her prey. She passed a red brick church, its notice board informing her that this was the Parish Church of St Luke. Again, the hurrying figure vanished into a close, and Bethany was in time to see her enter a building. On closer inspection, she found a sign: IELTS Champions School.

Not knowing what the acronym stood for, Bethany checked the strength of the signal on her smartphone. It showed maximum bars, so she opened her browser and typed the letters and got the immediate response *International English Language Testing System*. "Great!" she said aloud and boldly entered the building to stride up to reception. A receptionist, probably of Mediterranean origin judging by her olive complexion and lush black hair, smiled at her. "Can I help you?" She had no noticeable accent; maybe second generation then.

"Yes, I'm English, but my Korean friend just came in. I was wondering what time she finished? Should I wait for her or come back later?"

"That would be Lee Jeong-Hui; she just came in. Lovely girl! Have you known her long?"

With a flash of inspiration, Bethany said, "No, we met in a café in Addiscombe last week."

"Ah, yes, she's staying in the Aparthotel there. Let me check her timetable. Ah, Lower Intermediate, here we are! I'm afraid she's in lessons until half-past one. You could catch her in her lunch break later. This afternoon, she has a conversation class from two o'clock until four and then she's finished for the day."

"What about tomorrow?" Bethany tried to keep her eagerness from reaching her voice.

"The same as today and Friday, too."

Bethany considered her next question carefully. She didn't
want to alert the receptionist, Carla, going by her name tab, to
anything that might strike her as slightly off.

"Does Jeong-Hui come to all her classes? I thought her
English was pretty good."

"She's very punctual. Today she was a few minutes early for
class. I'm glad her English is getting better; her shyness doesn't
help." She checked a register. "Her attendance is one hundred
per cent. You can bet she'll be in tomorrow."

"I'll catch her then. Don't mention I was asking after her,
please. I want to surprise her. My name's Beryl," she lied to be
friendly, stretching out a hand that was grasped by a better-
manicured one. Everything about Carla was glamorous. Bethany
said goodbye; the less conversation she indulged in, the better.

She retraced her route with only one thing on her mind—the
search for a suitable killing spot. It was a fruitless survey. There
didn't seem to be anything that met her standards. As she
climbed the steps to the platform, to her dismay, other passengers preceded and followed her, so that location was out of the
question, too. The westbound platform didn't offer any possibilities, either. An idea came to her while scouring the station
layout. *It's no good forcing the issue; Woodside is all wrong. Jeong-
Hui got on at Addiscombe. I've got all day, so I'll check out the possibilities there.*

A few minutes later, the green-nosed tram, with Wimbledon
in large white letters over the driver's cab, squealed to a halt.
Only two stops, and she was there. A cursory glance around the
station told her that there was no suitable place for a killing.
Suddenly, she felt pessimistic. When things went right, they
were as though preordained. But nothing leapt at her today.
Would she have to revise her plans?

She made her way out of the station to a busy main road

intersected by the tramlines. A level crossing without gates, but with traffic light controls, incorporated a pedestrian crossing. She gazed past the moving vehicles to the other side of the road, where a grey-green shopfront caught her attention. It was a café. A frisson of excitement made her heart beat faster when she read the bold white lettering over the window: THE TRAM STOP. She would *kill* for a coffee—*almost literally*; she chuckled at her private joke.

She made her way inside the spotless room with its glass-fronted food displays and ordered a cappuccino, noting a black-board with a breakfast menu chalked up. She decided to come the following day for toast, scrambled egg, and coffee. The milky drink with cocoa sprinkled on top went down a treat, and her optimism returned. She took the name of the café to be a good omen. Outside, she studied the scene. Between the café and the level crossing was a stretch of overgrown verge. Her lip curled into a semblance of a wicked sneer. She could do this!

Bethany returned to the platform and scanned the timetable on the platform, not for her soon-to-be trip to Wimbledon but for departures to Woodside the following morning. Jeong-Hui must take the 09.44 to reach the IELTS school before 10.00 am. Presumably, she could intercept her some minutes before that. Hadn't Carla specified that the Korean was a punctual young woman who resided at the Aparthotel here in Addiscombe?

The next morning, Bethany positioned herself near the pedestrian crossing at 09.30. Sure enough, she spotted the Korean girl approaching, hurrying along Lower Addiscombe Road, the street where her accommodation was located. To reach Bethany, she had to cross the pedestrian crossing, its illuminated green man brightly showing that it was safe to traverse the tramlines.

"Hello again!" She smiled at the girl, who had recognised her from the day before. "Come on, let me offer you a coffee or something. We can take the tram together."

Almost all Korean people are extremely polite, and Jeong-Hui was no exception. She may have been surprised, but she

accepted readily in precise but halting English. Bethany estab-
lished that her chosen victim liked cappuccino and ordered one,
plus an espresso for herself. She looked hungrily at the food on
offer but ignored her rumbling stomach. Her breakfast plan had
gone by the board because her stomach had clenched. After all,
she intended to commit murder.

She managed a little chit-chat about the girl's Seoul origins
whilst Jeong-Hui finished her cappuccino, and they both
laughed at the milky moustache the drink had left on the Korean's upper lip. The girl attended to that with a tissue whilst
Bethany paid for the drinks, after which they left the café.

Bethany had run over her plan so many times that it now
seemed to her like déjà vu. The heavy traffic wasn't a problem as
she saw it; drivers concentrating on the level crossing, in a
worst-case scenario, would suppose they were seeing two young
women affectionately embracing, not grappling.

She had the tools of her trade ready in her pocket and,
allowing Jeong-Hui to stride a pace ahead, withdrew the lethal
substance, poured it into the cotton wad and, springing forward,
clasped it over the unsuspecting girl's mouth and nose. In
moments, she was able to spin her round in a hug and, looking
over her head, study the traffic. It was a continuous flow, but she
didn't care. Deftly, she frogmarched the Korean to the weed-
covered verge, swung her hip and sent the dead weight toppling
into the dense undergrowth. A glance revealed that the passing
drivers hadn't seen anything, so, confidently, she tore at some
plants and covered the legs of her victim until nothing showed.
As she finished, a man exited the café, coming in her direction.
With a composure that belied her racing heart, she moved casually to the kerb and looked along the road in both directions.

A brief break in the traffic flow allowed her to hurry across to
gain the far pavement leading to the tram station. The thun-
dering footsteps running behind her for the briefest moment,
panicked her. Had she been found out? No, like her, the man
from the café was hurrying for a tram. By coincidence, the next

tram for Merton Park was also at 09.44 am, so she took a seat, exulting once again in a job perfectly executed. She smiled secretly at that last word—*executed*. For a brief instant, she had the vision of the laughing face of the shy Korean as she pointed out the milky brown moustache, but she ascribed it to maudlin sentimentalism and dismissed it. More important was that she was outwitting the police on Arnold's schedule of murders—but, *oh, damn and blast!* Because of the difficulty of retreating from this one and its exposed location, she hadn't been able to leave her calling card.

She checked the compartment. Nobody was sitting near her, or across the aisle. This was an off-peak tram with low crowding. She couldn't see a CCTV camera, so, slowly and carefully, she took out her black paint spray and bent forward, unseen, to leave her signature on the carriage wall: **9-5=4**. Hopefully, someone would understand its meaning and report it to the police. For the moment, she would keep it covered by her jeans-clad leg until she got off. The important thing was to replace her spray can in her handbag and finally relax.

She closed her eyes for a few minutes but opened them suddenly with the worrying thought that her next scheduled victim had to be a policeman. In one sense, it would be the most justifiable of her killings, but, at the same time, the most difficult. The coppers would know that a policeman was next in line. Arnold's advantage was that his victim cop had received no forewarning. Still, she had faith in her abilities. She closed her eyes again and her mouth formed into a sinister, self-satisfied smile.

CHAPTER 14

NEW SCOTLAND YARD, AND
WIMBLEDON TRAM STATION, LONDON

THE COMMUNAL AREA WHERE DI SHEPHERD GATHERED HER uniformed contingent of recruits had rarely been so crowded. The police officers' attention was focussed on a map of the thirty-seven Tramlink stations, positioned at the centre of a whiteboard and from which coloured marker arrows led to photographs of the victims found so far. News of the latest addition to the death roll had come into headquarters fifty minutes before the meeting began. Another dog-walker had phoned 999 to report a body the animal had discovered in the undergrowth near the Tram Stop café in Addiscombe. The death of the Korean student continued the series of copycat killings, even if somewhat out of sequence. A green arrow led from Addiscombe Station to a space reserved for the photo of Lee Jeong-Hui, which the Lambeth pathologists would provide in due course. Shepherd was particularly interested in the time of death. There was still the chance that Tibbet hadn't inverted M4 and M5.

"That's five people our killer has murdered," Shepherd continued her spiel, "and if that wasn't enough, ladies and gentlemen, we have to assume that unless our assassin changes the pattern again, the next victim will be a police officer. Our task is to apprehend the woman before she can perpetrate another outrage. You all have a copy of the description of chief suspect, Bethany Tibbet, and the details of her *modus operandi*. Sadly, we are working with too many incognitos. We have no leads as to her whereabouts or the slightest trace of any social connections. I have already chosen four of your number to work in shifts to keep a careful watch on her known address in Fulham. I will allocate the rest of you to stations along the Tram-link line.

"As you can see from the printed brief, and also here, and here, on the board," she pointed with a baton to the two anomalies, one in Silvertown and the other in Holborn, "we can't exclude the possibility of further strikes in places other than the Tramlink, but still associated with tram transport. I have an officer looking into that aspect as I speak. Now, before I assign you to your work*stations*—literally, this time—" her weak joke elicited smiles and chuckles among the audience, "I'd like to ask for your input and give you the chance to state any preference you might have."

She waited patiently, allowing time for exchanges of views, realising that many of those present might be a little overawed in the presence of half of the renowned Vance and Shepherd partnership. She told herself their reticence was understandable, but she needed staff to show initiative on this particularly challenging case. So, impatiently, after waiting longer than she liked, she rapped the whiteboard with the pointer, cutting off the murmur of conversation. "Well? I have twenty officers. Has nobody anything to say to me?"

A sergeant in the back row stood slowly and introduced himself. "Sergeant Russell Simons, ma'am, from the West Hampstead station." He spoke with a pleasant baritone that matched his tall stature to perfection. Shepherd couldn't prevent herself from smiling inanely at the handsome, dark-haired man.

Among the staff at Scotland Yard, the detective inspector had a reputation for rebuffing in short measure those officers brave enough to attempt chatting her up. She had never once succumbed to their approaches. So, she marvelled inwardly at her reaction to this unknown character from North London. "It's probably a wild theory," he continued, "but looking at the locations where the victims were found, I notice they are all concentrated in East London. My suspicious mind leads me to think that a killer as devious as this one would plan her strikes far from her residence. I'd like to volunteer to take the western terminus."

"It's a theory, Sergeant Simons and shows me that you are thinking about the movements and psyche of the perpetrator." She smiled encouragingly at him and noticed that he didn't once break eye contact. "I'm assigning you to the Wimbledon Tramlink terminus. Since it is one of the busiest stations on the line, you'll need a colleague. Is there anyone here that you would like to work with?"

"Apart from you, ma'am?" He said it so suggestively that it provoked a titter from one or two of the female officers present. To cover his daring comment, he adopted a serious face and spoke decisively, "In fact, there is, ma'am." He pointed to a constable sitting two seats in front of him. "PC Victor Carter works with me in Hampstead, and he's as good a cop as any I've known. I'd appreciate working with him."

"Is that OK with you, PC Carter?" Shepherd asked.

"Yes, ma'am, we've worked together for years. I'm more than happy with that."

Shepherd picked up on the friendship and, appreciating that a similar situation had enhanced her own career, she seized the opportunity to say, "That's settled then; Simons and Carter are assigned to Wimbledon." Gratified to see the exchange of grins between the two colleagues, she pressed on with her task. "If anyone else has a preferred partner, I need pairs to work at the busiest stations, which are: East and West Croydon, Sandilands,

Mitcham Junction," her pointer beat a tattoo on the map on the board, "Ampere Way, Church Street, and George Street, not forgetting, of course, the eastern terminus at New Addington. Any takers?"

Hands shot up, preferences were stated and couples allocated, until Shepherd noted with satisfaction that she had assigned jobs to every one of the uniformed personnel.

"Ladies and gentlemen, a final word. I'm delighted to have you onboard for this investigation, which is proving exceedingly difficult. I hardly need remind you to be on the alert. We are dealing with a merciless killer, and we know that the next target will be one of us."

She paused a moment to let that chilling statement sink in, then added, "Appearances can be deceptive. You should remember that this woman, slight of build, has killed a well-set man of over six feet tall. So, proceed with extreme caution. If you can apprehend the suspect, do so, but first call on reinforcements. Good luck. To work, now! Report to me at the end of every shift. Sergeant Simons, a word, please." She wanted to thank and encourage him, but most of all wanted to be near to him.

At close quarters, Russell Simons proved even more attractive. She liked him as early as this first encounter. He had dark, wavy hair, which he wore quite long, making a pleasant change from the ubiquitous short, shaved look so popular among her male colleagues. She breathed in a delightful combination of soap and cologne and stared up into two intense brown eyes.

Today, she was wearing a pearl grey cotton shirt with half sleeves, and a wide, shiny black belt enclosed her trim waist. Skinny-fit black trousers completed her ensemble that showed her curves off to perfection. His ready smile and firm handshake pleased her, but not as much as his admiring glances. She couldn't help but tease him. "Seen enough, Sarge?" She grinned at Simons, who immediately became red-faced.

"Sorry, ma'am. It's just such a privilege to work with the famous DI Shepherd. I didn't expect anyone so entrancing."

"I forgive you." Shepherd grinned. "It's not every day a girl gets called *entrancing*, not on my watch, anyway. Most of the lads here haven't got your courage."

"Or, they're not as stupid as me. Maybe that's why they work here, and I plod around Hampstead."

"I wouldn't say you were dim at all, Sarge; I called you over to thank you for your intelligent contribution. It got the show on the road for me."

"My pleasure, ma'am." He looked genuinely pleased. "As to that, I've had another thought..." He hesitated. "I know our priority is sifting through the travellers in Wimbledon, but it was something you said earlier." He paused again.

"What's on your mind?" Her instinct told her that fresh ideas might open up new possibilities.

"You said the suspect owned a luxury apartment that she's cunningly steering clear of. That suggests two things to me: either she has family accomplices, but from what we know, that seems unlikely, or she's paying for temporary accommodation. In the latter case, following on my earlier thought, she could be to the north or west of Wimbledon, probably in a cheap let. I doubt she'll want to spend a fortune on lodgings when she owns a flat I'd give an arm for. We might be able to trace her through her digs."

"Good thinking, but I can't spare anyone to chase it up, with our urgent priority being to stop her killing sequence." She wanted to call him Russell but decided on formality. "Sergeant Simons, I think your colleague is getting restless." She nodded towards the whiteboard, where PC Carter pretended to study the contents, but Shepherd had noted the frequent glances in their direction.

"Right, ma'am, we ought to get to work, then." His right hand moved upwards as if he was about to offer it again but had thought better of it. Instead, he nodded, put on his hat and joined his colleague.

Outside the building, on their way to the nearest underground station, Carter quipped, "You don't waste time, Russ. A bit of a smasher is DI Shepherd, as you've noticed. I'll bet you an evening of drinks that you can't manage a date with her."

"I'm not going to risk your infinite capacity for alcohol intake, matey, on a lost cause."

"Oh, I wouldn't say that from the way she was simpering at you."

"DI Shepherd doesn't do *simpers*, cretin!" but the provocation urged him on. "OK, you're on." Simons accepted the bet and sent Carter staggering two paces ahead with a mighty clap on the back. The wager was what he needed to give him the courage to ask out a superior officer. In his heart, though, he felt he had no chance with her.

They took the District Line and didn't need to change for Wimbledon. The line branched at Earl's Court down to their destination. Simons counted off the stops impatiently—a reverse countdown from thirteen. He hated using the underground but accepted that it was the easiest way to get around the sprawling metropolis.

"Look." He nodded towards a slightly-built blonde farther down the compartment. "She could be our killer. I'll keep my eye on you. Go, and ask to see some ID. It'll be good practice for you."

"What? Now? Here on this train?" Carter protested.

"Yes, why not? She might be on her way to Wimbledon for all we know."

"But we can't stop every slim blonde in London, Sarge."

"We can, and we must. That's the task assigned to us. We're not at Wimbledon yet. Why not catch her by surprise? Keep an eye on what she has in her hands, and you'll be alright."

"I'm on my way." He returned three minutes later, looking more relaxed. "She's a shop assistant on her way to work. She showed me her driving licence, in the name of Angela Prescott. Pretty girl with a lovely smile; she works at Moka in the Centre Court Shopping Centre. I told her I'd go for a snack there in my lunch break."

"Why? Did she *simper* at you, Vic?" Simons couldn't resist getting his own back. "On to serious matters. When we get to the Tramlink, I'll take the eastbound platform, and you take the incoming."

"That's not fair!"

"What do you mean?"

Carter scowled. "You think our killer travels east from Wimbledon. Why would she be arriving at the terminus?"

"On the way back from killing one of our colleagues, maybe, *dummkopf*."

"Gone all Gestapo on me, have you, mate?"

Simons grinned wickedly, then, in his best SS voice, he barked, "Last time I checked on my sleeve, there were three stripes. I'm taking the westbound platform, and you the east-bound. That's an order!"

Back at New Scotland Yard, Brittany Shepherd was catching up on the latest killing with DI Vance. Her chat with him began by explaining how she had organised the uniformed brigade. She made no mention of Simons by name but referred to one excep-tionally bright sergeant who had impressed her with his enthu-siasm and thinking. She particularly liked his idea about lodgings.

Vance agreed. "I'll get Mark Allen to look into the potential areas to the north and west of Wimbledon. Mind you, it won't be easy. Not all landlords go through agencies. Some of the cheaper ones, owners of flea-pits, probably stick a postcard in a corner shop window."

Vance quickly updated her on the finding of Miss Lee, the Korean student. He assured Brittany that this was the fifth murder as the CME had given time of death as the early morning around 9 am. He described the location and the incoming report. Before contemplating the autopsy, Dr Tremethyk had rushed a blood sample to his trusted laboratory for the gas chromatography test. The result was conclusive; once again, the murder substance was hydrogen cyanide. "She never varies, does she? If only Bethany Tibbet would push someone under a tram, we'd have more chance of capturing her."

"But that would be a more painful end. Doc Tremethyk told us this technique leads to almost instant death," Shepherd said. "Truth is, Tibbet is efficient and ruthless. We have to stop her as soon as possible. I'm going back to square one." She stood and moved to the door. "I'll see what Max has for me." She wasn't entirely honest with her partner because she had another reason for seeing the computer wizard.

"Max, what have you got for me?" she asked brightly as she arrived at his work station.

He smiled up into the pretty oval face of the woman he had always carried a torch for, that is until he had got engaged to Dr Markham.

"Well, I can tell you that there *is* a Bethany Tibbet. I have a scanned copy of her birth certificate from Peckham Road Register Office. I remembered that Arnold Tebbit grew up in Southwark. She's twenty-nine years old. She was baptised in St Agnes Church, near Kennington Park. Her full name is Bethany Ann Tebbit. I'm still working on it, Shep, and I think the next step is to look into her schooling in the area. I've also been checking out disused tram relics in the city for Sergeant Allen— it's no easy task, especially since Bethany has chosen the two most prominent ones for her killings. I found an overgrown, disused Level crossing gate, and Mark will drive over to check it out, but it strikes me as a long shot. I think she'll return to the Tramlink."

"Talking about which, Max, I've put a score of uniforms on the said Tramlink. There's one in particular, who seems promising…" She moulded the truth. "Would you be kind enough to see what, if anything, you can dig up on Sergeant Russell Simons? He's currently with the West Hampstead station."

"Will do. That's an easier task. I'll give you a bell when I'm genned up."

"Thanks a lot, Wrighty. I owe you a pint."

———

At Merton Park tram station, Bethany Tibbet searched for a ladies' toilet in vain. Usually, she used the bathroom before leaving home. This morning, she had felt no urge and had forgotten this basic routine. There was a nip in the air, and the cold wind made her bladder complain. She'd reached the jiggling stage and now, swearing under her breath, concluded that this station offered no such facility. Whilst she had ascertained there was no toilet on the westbound platform, either, a tram pulled in. Quick as a flash, even if it was headed in the opposite direction from her intended destination, she stepped aboard. First, she checked for a toilet on the tram but knew it was a waste of time since the trams didn't have one. But Wimbledon was only two stops away, and she could hold out. The terminus was also an underground station. There were bound to be toilets there.

Victor Carter saw a petite woman in a grey duffel coat get off the tram. He couldn't tell whether she had blonde hair because she wore a grey beanie with a pompom. Still, she fitted their profile, and he would take the risk of her being a brunette or a redhead. He strode after the woman, who was heading for the District Line steps. As he drew closer, he called, "Miss, stop! Police!"

She half-turned, saw him, cursed under her breath, realising from the sign that the toilets were just down the stairs. Any delay might lead to an embarrassing episode in public, so, despite her protesting, insistent bladder, she ran for the stairs.

Her flight confirmed to Carter that this was the suspect, so he radioed to Simons, "I've got her, Russ! I told her to stop, she looked me in the face, but then she did a runner for the District Line!"

The crackling reply came, "I'll join you in a minute. I'm following my own suspect. Don't lose sight of her, Vic, and *on no account* try to apprehend her on your own. Clear?"

"Yep! I'm after her! She's headed for the toilets."

The constable raced down the stairs just in time to see the figure in grey hurry into the public conveniences. In front of the stylised signs of a man, a woman and a wheelchair on different doors, he halted, deciding to wait until she came out. Meanwhile, he thought, Russell Simons might arrive to help him arrest the suspect.

At that moment, the sergeant was stopping a petite blonde who was heading towards the Way-Out sign.

"Excuse me, miss, could you show me some ID, please?"

"What is it with you people today? Another policeman asked to see my ID on the train."

The first doubts assailed Simons as the young woman took out her driving licence, an exasperated expression on her face. What had Victor said? *She showed me her driving licence, in the name of Angela Prescott. Pretty girl with a lovely smile; she works at Moka in the Centre Court Shopping Centre.* Now, here he was, reading the name Angela Prescott on the licence. He felt foolish but handed back the document, saluted, and said, "Thank you for your cooperation. You won't be troubled again, miss. Have a good day!" In return, he received the sweet smile that Carter had so admired.

He watched her hurry away, pressed the button on his radio and called, "Vic, come in. Vic, are you there?" With a sinking feeling, he made for the eastbound platform. Why was there no reply? And what had Victor said? *She's headed for the toilets,* so he hurried there, too.

Moments before Sergeant Simons halted Angela Prescott, Bethany Tibbet relieved her suffering bladder. As she urinated with a long sigh of relief, her mind was racing. A copper had tried to stop her on the tram platform. She knew he had followed her and was probably waiting outside this toilet compartment for her to emerge. She had planned to kill a cop today, and here was one delivered to her on a silver platter. She thought, *the strange workings of Fate!* There had been no time to study the layout of the toilet, but she had surprise on her side. Opening her handbag, she transferred the phial of blue liquid and the cotton wad into the deep, square pocket of her duffel coat. Working the stopper almost free, it would take a split second to remove entirely, then she could tip the hydrogen cyanide onto the bunched material with her left hand, all unseen by her unsuspecting victim.

Ready, she emerged from the toilet to come face to face with a tall policeman, holding out a warrant card. *Shit!* Like her, he was wearing a face mask.

Thinking quickly, she said, "Excuse me, how am I supposed to recognise you from the photo if you're wearing a mask?" Her left hand was working furiously in her pocket.

He laughed and removed the elastic behind one ear, so that the mask dangled from the other ear. She bent to feign studying the warrant card photo, then sprang like a lynx, ramming the wad into his face. Carter just had time to recognise that he was having a heart attack and to comprehend his error, but she followed his sagging body to the floor, insistently pressing the lethal substance into his face.

She, too, had a pounding heart, but hers was due to the fear that someone would enter or exit the toilets and catch her in the act of murder. Had anyone entered at the next moment, they would have found her spraying black paint on the wall. She shoved the can back into her bag and rushed out of the door, almost barging into a middle-aged woman with a shopping trolley. No question of running up the stairs to the trams at that point, she thought. *I'll just take the tube—to wherever takes my fancy on the District Line.*

She hurried through the automatic barrier, swiping her Oyster Card, then along the platform, and merged with the crowd waiting for the next eastbound train. According to the illuminated board, it was due in one minute. To her relief, she was able to board the carriage without being accosted. Her eyes roamed frantically, trying to identify a plain-clothed police officer, but she found no one matching her mental image of a sleuth.

As the stations passed, she knew that once again she had succeeded, but not without a huge slice of luck, and that was unacceptable to her, but *all's well that ends well*, she smirked, and got off at Monument.

She knew the area well, so she hurried along Eastcheap to Philpot Lane from the station with two things on her mind: first, her stomach, then, a change of clothing in case the copper had radioed a description of what she was wearing. She came to Prêt à Manger in the Lane, where she grabbed a croissant and ordered a cappuccino. As soon as she'd finished, she strode along to the end of the lane and into Fenchurch Street, where she spied Next and entered the boutique to swap her duffel coat for a new parka. She told the friendly assistant that she would keep the new item on and carry her duffel coat in the sales bag. The parka's hood covered her grey beanie, and she felt warm and snug but, above all, safe from detection. Now she had equalled Arnold's killings, and there was no further time pressure on her or profile to meet. She could lie low in her bedsit for days, or weeks if she chose. Her fool of a brother had got himself arrested after the sixth: she had not. So, copycatting ended here, except for the last obligatory killing, M9. She would press on to the Big One in time. Oh yes, there was a definite profile *there*!

· · ·

At about the same time as Bethany Tibbet boarded the tube train, Sergeant Russell Simons, approaching the toilets at Wimbledon Station, heard a woman scream and feared the worst. He burst into the conveniences, and his heart missed a beat. The supine figure of Victor Carter, his face bearing the unmistakable pallor of death, lay with his warrant card still in his hand. *Oh, God! Why didn't he do as I told him? This tragedy is my stupid fault!*

Blinking back tears of rage as much as sorrow, Simons radioed to headquarters for the necessary intervention. The middle-aged woman was fussing and her torrent of words made little sense to his troubled mind, but Simons managed to order her, as the first person to find the body, to wait for the arrival of his colleagues. He saw the graffiti on the wall **9-6=3** and swore. He stationed himself at the door and turned people away from the crime scene until, thankfully, his colleagues joined him and took over so that he could surrender to his grief.

He sat on a bench for a moment's reflection. He had let down his best mate on the Force. If only he had been more aware that the young woman was Angela Prescott, whom he had followed for futile identification when he should have been helping Vic. What kind of useless policeman was he? He would resign. Surely there was something else worthwhile he could do?

Back at headquarters, he sat with DI Shepherd and poured his heart out to her. Contritely, he took the blame, save that, as he said, "I told Vic on no account to confront her alone, and he did the opposite, Detective."

"I also warned everyone not to do that. So, you see, it's not your fault, Russell." Shepherd understood the raw desperation that the sergeant was feeling.

"It was!" He stifled a wail. "I can't understand how I could have been so distracted. Any half-decent copper would have recognised Angela Prescott as the fellow traveller Vic had already checked out. I'll never forgive myself!"

"Did Constable Carter give you a description of the killer?"

Simons thought for a minute. "No, he said she'd looked him in the face and run down to the toilets."

"Perhaps she needed the toilet," Shepherd mused. "It might explain why she was at Wimbledon when you expected her to be going in the opposite direction. Not many tram stations have public conveniences."

"It doesn't matter now." The brown eyes were glazed with tears, and Shepherd gazed at him with anguish. She had so much to tell this lovely man. But his next words closed around her heart like an icy grip.

"Detective Shepherd, I'm going to resign from the Force. Vic would be alive now but for me."

Desperately, she grabbed his arm and clung on. She peered into the tearful, dark-brown eyes. "Russell, listen to me, I'm not going to let you do that. You're a bloody good cop. I've looked into your record—" DS Wright had given her the lowdown— "and it's the grief talking right now. How about a little role reversal, Sarge? I'm asking you out to dinner. Do you like Japanese food? I have a friendly chef, who'll give us a meal like no other you've ever tasted! It'll stop you dwelling on what happened."

Sergeant Russell Simons, twice awarded commendations for bravery, gazed unbelievingly at the glamorous detective. "You're asking me out?" All he could think of was the bet that had been made whilst bantering with Carter—*an evening of drinks that you can't manage a date with her*—and, finally, the floodgates opened for the tears to flow freely.

"Is that a yes, then, Sarge?" she asked, taking him in her arms and hugging him close to her.

Just then, DI Vance came into the room. He coughed discreetly, and Shepherd reluctantly looked his way. Their eyes met. "I hope I'm not disturbing anything?"

"Jacob! The bitch has just killed his best mate," she said, as Simons pushed her gently away and wiped his eyes with his sleeve. "Sorry, sir!" he said, with a catch in his voice.

"Don't worry, Sarge, we'll get her soon, and she'll pay for her crimes," Vance said, with such force of conviction that even the bereaved sergeant managed a faint smile.

By God! I won't resign. I'll capture the bitch myself, and DI Shepherd has asked me out, to boot! I'm behaving like a wimp! I'd better not blow my chance; I'll try to be decent company for her. What must she think of me?

CHAPTER 15
NEW SCOTLAND YARD

BRITTANY SHEPHERD KEPT SERGEANT SIMONS UNDER HER WATCHFUL eye, assigning him some paperwork and analysis tasks. She felt giddy, like a schoolgirl in love. After all, four years had passed since her last serious relationship. Nothing but a cuddle of condolences had occurred between them, but she had felt the shared electricity. The evening date was something to look forward to, and not even the horror of the Bethany Tibbet case could take the gloss off it, although she worried about Russell's state of mind.

Her anxieties surfaced when the sergeant begged her for an interview with Doctor Tremethyk. "I have to know," he said hoarsely.

Since the Chief Medical Examiner was due to come over with the results of the two autopsies—the unlawful killing of Carter having followed rapidly on that of Lee—Shepherd acquiesced. Her concern was evident as she murmured, "OK, I'll set it up for you, Sarge."

She didn't leave Simons alone with the Cornish pathologist but hovered in the background, absorbing their conversation so that she, in her mind, when called on, could help him better come to terms with the loss of his friend.

"What would it have been like, Doc? What does this poison do?" Simons began.

The pathologist, used to dealing with bereaved families, recognised the grief in the sergeant's voice and, drawing on all his experience, replied, "With the high concentrations our killer uses, death would have been mercifully swift. The victim would have known very little of what happened. He'd have undergone a moment of hyperventilation, a sense of giddiness, throat constriction and confusion. In simple terms, me-dear, hydrogen cyanide blocks the oxygen pathway in the cells, so the heart would battle to function. Loss of consciousness would be almost immediate, the toxin most probably inducing a coma. Immediately before that, there would be an absence of corneal reflex and impaired vision with maybe pain in the back of the neck and chest," he glanced anxiously to see what effect his words were having, and hastily softened the impact with, "but as I said, it would have all been over in a trice, dear boy, your colleague didn't suffer in agony, be sure of that." The doctor reached across and patted the sergeant's arm.

"Thank God for that! But Vic was only thirty-two; he had his whole life before him. We have to stop the bastard before she can strike again." His baritone had rumbled into a growl for the last few words.

"We will get her, no doubt about that, Russ," Shepherd said, her voice determined. She was thrilled that she had used the diminutive of his name. As precise and detailed as ever, the pathologist's reports didn't contribute to a breakthrough, but once they could bring Tibbet to justice, they would provide vital evidence for the jury to absorb.

The day proceeded without uncovering any clue to Tibbet's whereabouts. Max Wright supplied negative information about the suspect's schooling, in the sense that he had been unable to find a trace of her primary or secondary education in the South-wark area. Widening his net into neighbouring quarters had produced the same lack of data. "It's as if the child, Bethany Ann

Tibbet, didn't exist. She became a ghost," he muttered, voice heavy with frustration. "I tried the local police station, and they checked their missing persons records. Again, no trace of Tibbet, so it seems unlikely that she was a runaway."

"Don't worry, Max, I'm not sure that her schooling would have shed much light on the case. Although Miriam Walker did say that dissociative identity disorder is usually the result of sexual or physical abuse in childhood and becomes a way to distance oneself from trauma. We believe that happened with Arnold, and I'll bet my last fiver it's the same with his crazy sister."

Max Wright, his brain as sharp as ever, had a momentary insight. "Her fixation with trams might be associated with a trauma sustained whilst travelling on one."

"Could be you're onto something there, Max. See if you can find any records of sexual harassment reported on the Tramlink since 2000."

"Will do."

A couple of hours later, Wright came to the temporary coordination centre that was Vance's office to report his findings. "I dug up a case of sexual interference with a schoolgirl that occurred between Belgrave Walk and Phipps Bridge in 2002. The girl was seven then, and being a minor, she could not be named for privacy reasons. The police were unable to make an arrest, so it's another dead end, I'm afraid."

"It might be, and there again, it could just be our Bethany was molested on that tram and is now behaving as a consequence. I'll talk to Miriam about it. Thanks."

Towards the close of the working day, around 7 pm, Shepherd was inundated with reports from her uniformed officers. They had checked the IDs of an average of eight women per officer. No suspicious character had emerged, although several of the female officers complained about the abuse they had received from irate travellers in the course of their duty. Shepherd decided that the intense campaign should continue for the following days. Even if it didn't lead to the arrest of Tibbet, it might act as a deterrent to her, at least on the Tramlink.

Mark Allen reported on his visit to the disused level crossing gate. "I can't see it as a potential location for Tibbet, ma'am, it's far too exposed, and there's constant traffic. I discovered that they took the gate itself away in 2007 and ripped up the exposed tram rails in 2012, so in a certain way, there can't be much attraction in the location for Tibbet. I mean, a casual observer would think the road had nothing to do with trams. But if you prefer, we could allocate one of our uniformed officers to surveillance there."

"Good thinking, Sarge. No, I'll back your judgement on this one. Our team is doing an excellent job on the trams, and I don't want to detach anyone at the moment, especially for something so nebulous."

Russell Simons insisted on returning to his flat in Hampstead. He needed to shower and change for the evening.

"You'll be a bit pressed for time, Russ. You can freshen up at my place if you want," Shepherd suggested.

"No, I'll make it in time, no sweat, if you'll forgive the pun. We can meet at Bond Street tube station. That'll be the nearest to Mayfair. I've never eaten a Japanese meal and certainly not with a Detective Inspector."

"I'll be outside the station at eight. Don't keep a lady waiting!"

He grinned, but she felt a rush of tenderness as she could see the underlying sorrow far too plainly. "And listen, Russ, don't go brooding as you travel home alone. I want our first date to be a success!"

He nodded and walked out of the office stiff-backed, buoyed by the fact that she'd said the words, *first date*. That implied others to follow, and that was what he wanted more than anything in the world, except for the arrest of bloody Bethany Tibbet.

DI Shepherd prized punctuality, so it was with pleasure that, glancing along Oxford Street, still busy with tourists at eight o'clock in the evening, she spotted Russell Simons grinning at her as he strode across the road. He had seen her first, hence the grin, which widened as he saw her check her watch at 7.58.

"I'm on time, I couldn't keep a superior officer waiting. At your orders, ma'am."

"That's enough of that!" she snapped. "You'd better call me Brittany or Brit this evening and that's my last order for tonight!"

"So, where are you taking me, Brit?"

"To meet Chef Tatsuo Narisawa, an acquaintance of mine from Osaka, a busy port on the island of Honshu."

"Have you been to Japan, then, Brit?"

"If only..." she sighed, "but come on, I'll tell you all about how I met the chef when we're sitting in his restaurant."

The waiter took their coats to a small wardrobe and returned to bow them to their seats. Shepherd noticed that the table for two was the only one with a vase of fresh orchids—a nice touch by the beaming Tatsuo, who advanced with a broad grin to their table. He bowed and spoke about the honour of having the esteemed presence of the Detective Sergeant and her companion.

"Detective *Inspector*, chef, you are out of date."

Amid repeated congratulations, he apologised effusively before speaking of food that meant nothing to Simons.

"This is my friend's first experience of Japanese cuisine, Chef Tatsuo, so I'll leave the menu entirely to you." The chef's ruggedly handsome features again lit up in a wide smile. He bowed and vanished into the kitchen.

Within moments, a *hassun* of bite-sized appetizers appeared with two *Shokuzen-shu* aperitifs. "The chef has decided on *Kaiseki ryori,*" Shepherd said knowledgeably, "it's traditional Japanese multi-course haute cuisine. We're in for a treat tonight."

"So, how did you meet this chef?"

Shepherd related the long story about Arnold Tibbet's use of pufferfish poison, tetrodotoxin, and the chef's unfortunate role in supplying it because of blackmail over his affair with the beautiful escort, Akina Aoyama.

Simons couldn't resist teasing his companion, "I wouldn't mind meeting Akina Aoyama." His wicked grin made his handsome features even more irresistible to Shepherd, but she was equal to his challenge.

"I am a black belt in *taiho-jutsu,* and that's the nearest you'll get to a Japanese embrace, my friend."

He laughed, became serious, necessary to change the dangerous subject, and said, "So, this chef owes you big-time. You could have ruined him by prosecuting."

"As you can see from the food, that would have been London's loss. Anyway, it was a joint decision with DI Vance." She broke off as the waiter replaced the *hassun* with bowls of *suimono*: a clear broth garnished with seafood.

"Delicious!" Simons sipped elegantly at the soup. Shepherd liked the way the sergeant adapted so well to the classy surroundings and, for him, novel cuisine. She couldn't fault his manners so far. She decided it was time to move their relationship forward.

"Russ, I hope you don't mind. I had Max Wright run a background check on you and your career."

"Mind? I have no secrets to hide."

Did she imagine it, or was his response prickly?

"I know about your sister, and I'm so sorry."

"Rachel? Yeah, that was years ago, but it left a deep scar. I haven't been to a shrink, but it's not difficult to realise how her rape and murder drove me to become a cop."

"If you don't want to talk about it, Russ, that's OK. I just wanted to say that I understand and what, with Victor as well, it must be hard to take."

"I was eight when Rachel died and I'm thirty-two now, Brit. I think I can cope. I'd rather chat about you, if you don't mind."

"What about me?"

"Well, relationships. Do you have a boyfriend?" His dark-brown eyes bored into hers. Could she detect anxiety in his voice?

She smiled, but it was tinged with sadness, "That's why I said I could understand your pain. I was engaged to a colleague four years ago. He was a rugby forward for the Met—quite the star of the team was my Mark."

"What happened?"

"He was an outdoor type, loved mountaineering, hiking and so on…" Her face clouded and she concentrated on her soup, but then laid down her spoon to stare into Russell's eyes; he adored their sapphire blue, but noticed with concern their wetness. "It was Easter and he and three friends decided to go up Helvellyn in the Lake District. He'd climbed it so many times, but on this occasion, the weather changed unexpectedly. It wasn't forecast. One minute it was sunny; the next, according to the survivor, Daniel, they were enveloped in freezing fog. As experienced climbers, they were well equipped and would have had no problem returning to the base using a map and compass, except for a stroke of bad luck."

Simons reached across the table and took Shepherd's hand; he had seen her lower lip tremble. He squeezed it, and she gave him a weak smile and continued her tragic account. "David Stirling, another rugby player, lost his footing and with it his balance. He plunged down the side of the mountain, so Mark had to play the hero and go down after him to fetch him back. But it cost him his life because he turned his ankle and couldn't get back to the other two. They decided to go down to alert the mountain rescue team. Daniel made it, but he was in a state when they got to him. The other guy, Steve, didn't; he succumbed to hyperthermia and exhaustion. They found Mark and David with a helicopter, but," her voice caught, and Russ squeezed her hand again, "it was too late. Mark was your age, Russ. We were going to get married that summer, but that's destiny for you."

She managed a brave smile, released her hand and took up her spoon. "It'll get cold, and it's a shame to waste it."

He admired the way she had fought back the tears. Tough cookie, DI Shepherd.

"The mountains can be treacherous, even for experienced climbers. A bit like the sea, it can be calm one minute and rough, the next," Simons said, then fell silent, staring at his empty bowl. He liked Japanese food.

Their conversation became less intense as they ate the delicious *sashimi, nimono and yakimono* courses. They spoke about their respective preferences in music and shared dislike of rap and heavy metal, but their tastes were otherwise eclectic. Shepherd underlined that the musical genre didn't bother her so long as it was good music. She confessed to a weakness for Eddie Vedder, so Simons made a mental note.

After the last course, the *sunomono*, consisting of octopus dressed in a vinegar sauce and vegetables, Chef Tatsuo Narisawa appeared, carrying a bottle of premium Dassai sake.

"May I join you? I'd like to offer my best sake. Three glasses," he snapped at the hovering waiter. "So, how was your meal, Detective Inspector?" He gained points in her mind for remembering her correct title. "What do you think of Japanese food?" he asked Simons about the first impact of the Nippon cuisine and sat back to receive a torrent of compliments to his skill, occasionally, pleased and flattered, raising his glass of the expensive sake in a toast.

Simons studied the sake label, but the characters were Japanese and he couldn't understand the symbols. "What does it say, Chef?"

Tatsuo smiled, took the bottle and squinted. "Let me translate for you, it says: the fragrance is a bouquet of flowers, delicate and loving. The flavour washes over your tongue like a gentle waterfall deep in a secluded forest, and trickles away into a long, satisfying finish."

Simons grinned, "That's very poetic, but I must say, I agree with the *satisfying finish*."

Later, out of curiosity, Shepherd, who had surreptitiously photographed the label, discovered it cost £800 a bottle. Nope, she wouldn't treat Russ to that particular brand.

Tatsuo Narisawa would not hear of them paying for the meal when they took their leave, but Shepherd appreciated the gesture when she saw Simons slip the waiter a £20 tip.

She called a taxi, and, settling in the back, informed Simons that he was coming with her to her place for a coffee. As the driver navigated through the city, Simons took Shepherd's hand and, leaning towards her, asked, "And after Mark?"

"Nobody, until tonight."

He squeezed then released her hand, but she snatched it back and held on until they reached her street. She leant forward, telling the driver, "Here's fine," and swatting aside Russell's hand, holding another £20. "I'll get this. Keep the change, pal," she told the driver

They bundled out of the taxi and she groped in her handbag for the house key.

She turned to take his coat, hanging it on a stand in the hallway behind the front door, joining it with hers and her scarf. "That was a lovely evening, Russ."

He stepped forward. "It was," and he took her in his arms and kissed her full on the lips. To his delight, there was no resistance but enthusiastic response. He pulled away and gazed into the sapphire-blue eyes, saying, "Do you know, I've discovered a liking for Japanese food and Mancunian detectives, all in one evening."

She laughed and put on a hurt expression. "Only a liking, Russ?"

He joined in the laughter. "Damn it, no, a love of—" he kept her waiting, "sake!" he said, and they both howled with laughter.

"I'm afraid there's no sake in my house, but come on through into the lounge. I've got scotch or cognac if you need a drink. Or, there again, the coffee was a genuine offer."

"Not too genuine, I hope." He winked at her, and her stomach fluttered.

"I'm having a single malt, you?"

He decided to join her, so she poured two glasses of Craggan-more and sat on the sofa, where he joined her.

"So, tell me, how can such a glamorous cop keep her red-blooded colleagues at arm's length?"

"First *entrancing*, now *glamorous*. You're a bit of a flatterer, aren't you, Sergeant Simons?"

"Not at all, I always tell the truth, Detective. You didn't answer the question."

"Simple, Russ. I didn't find any of them attractive until I met you."

"So, it's not just that you felt sorry for me, with Vic, and all?"

She pulled him forward by his tie and pressed her lips to his. When the lingering kiss ended, she said, "Don't be stupid. All I'll say is that I won't let you be on your own tonight. Besides, it's cold out there and warm in here."

"Very warm," he concurred, loosening his tie, giving her another cheeky grin.

"Sergeant Simons, I do believe you're making yourself at home. Finish your drink and follow me." She stood, downed her scotch in one gulp and extended a hand, heaving him, with his help, from the sofa. Still clasping his hand, she hurried to the stairs and, in a vision certain to delight any red-blooded male, letting go of his hand, preceded him to the landing.

The bedroom, papered with a powder pink and gold pattern, contained a queen-sized bed, its pink bedspread featuring roses.

"Lovely room!" Simons approved, appreciating its feminin-ity. "All that's lacking is the masculine touch." He spanked her bottom playfully but, quick as a flash, she grabbed the miscreant arm, swept his right leg up and pushed his upper body back with her left hand, whilst holding his right wrist, to throw him backwards onto the bed.

Swiftly, she straddled him, pressing her lips to his. As he fumbled with her shirt buttons, "*Taiho-jutsu* throw," she explained, helping with the fastenings and shrugging her shirt off. He unclipped her bra. "Too expertly," she grumbled. "It seems you've had a lot of practice with bras, Sergeant."

"Beginner's luck, Brit." He grinned up at her cheekily and struggled out of his shirt.

She was determined to keep his mind off his loss with the special therapy she could provide. He gasped as her naked breasts pressed against his bare chest, and they lay still savouring the moment: the quiet before the storm.

CHAPTER 16

MITCHAM JUNCTION TRAM STATION
AND NEW SCOTLAND YARD, LONDON

ROUND-EYED, MELANIE BRADSHAW STARED INTO JANICE'S concerned face. "I'm going to call the police," she said.

"Oh, come on, it's not worth it. The scumbag's as drunk as a skunk and about as smelly!"

Melanie, still traumatised from an event on this same line twenty years before, wasn't inclined to listen to her friend. Warily, she gazed at the swaying man by the door; his posture had nothing to do with the movements of the tram and everything to do with the three-quarters empty bottle of gin in his hand.

The pervert had been loud in his appreciation of Melanie's physical assets, his comments too racy and vulgar for any young woman to tolerate. When she had rebuffed him, he had whipped out his male organ; true, it had been a fleeting second, but it was that offensive gesture that elicited long-buried memories—she swore she'd make the bastard pay, drunk or not.

Janice was of a different opinion. She made a joke out of his pathetic appendage. "There's nowt to brag about in *his* pants. Did you see it? My thumb's longer than that, and I've got tiny hands." She nudged Melanie, sticking a thumb up, wiggling it and laughing, but her friend was still in a state of shock and couldn't appreciate the humour.

"Come on! This is Mitcham." Janice stood and vaguely registered that the drunk was getting off, too. They had travelled in the foremost compartment, and now they strode past the front of the tram, but the pest was there to intercept them. He made a beeline for Melanie and began his harassment again.

"Come on, babe, give us a kiss!" He thrust his face forward into Melanie's, his breath stinking of alcohol, his grin inane and annoying in the extreme.

"Get out of my face!" Melanie screamed. "I'll call the police."

"Fuck the cops! Give us a feel of those lovely titties!" He slurred so much that the unacceptable word was almost unrecognisable.

Melanie pushed him away, but as he came towards her again, Janice tugged at her arm, feeling her friend resist, hauling in the opposite direction. Melanie wanted to claw at her assailant's leering face. Janice could not cling on and, on releasing her, the impetus of her pulling shot the young woman forward, causing her to crash into the man with her left shoulder, full in the chest. Unstable on his feet, the drunk fell backwards onto the tramline, just as the tram started to pull away. Women screamed, while someone shouted and pointed. Melanie gazed in horror as the heavy tram sheared into the man's limbs, sending blood spurting in fountains, spraying everywhere. The tram screeched to a halt.

"Oh, my God! I didn't mean to kill him! Jan, call the police!"

There was no need, as part of DI Shepherd's Tramline allocation, a young constable, shouting into the radio that was clipped to his uniform, rushed up to Melanie. "I saw what happened, miss. I have to ask you to accompany me to the police station."

"Have you got this, Andy?" a female voice asked, as a uniformed woman constable came running to join them. "Are you all right, miss?" She put a comforting arm around Melanie, who was trembling, tears streaming down her cheeks. "It was an accident. I didn't mean to hurt him. I... is he *dead*?" she wailed the last word.

"Oh, he's dead, no doubt about that," the police officer said gently, tightening her embrace. "Come with us; you can provide a statement. Don't worry, try to calm down and remember what happened exactly." Her colleague was talking to bystanders, taking the contact numbers and addresses of those who had witnessed the tragedy.

"It was an accident," Janice said. "Maybe it was my fault."

"Who are you, miss?"

"Janice Moore, I'm an archaeology student, Mel's flatmate and her friend."

"You'd better come with us, Ms Moore. We'll need your statement, too."

Melanie stared under the tram as if in a trance, unable to wrench her eyes from the mangled form that had been the obnoxious, lurching pervert.

The police officer removed her arm from the woman's shoulders but slipped a reassuring hand into Melanie's to steer her away from the horrible sight.

"I didn't mean to," she repeated, her voice choking, "it was an accident," she sobbed.

"We'll go as soon as we can," the officer said gently, "but we'll have to wait until our colleagues and the ambulance arrives. I think you could do with a strong, sweet tea, don't you?"

Melanie nodded, unable to speak except to repeat that it was an accident.

PC Rose Blanchard understood the young woman was in shock, but her professional training also told her that the female she was detaining matched the description of the killer the Force was striving so hard to capture. She wondered whether this accident was another murder in the series of tram killings, although the girl seemed genuinely shocked and cooperative. In addition, the method was different from the others—if this was indeed a murder.

"Listen, Andy, stay here until our lads arrive. This young woman is in shock, and I'm taking her in the car to a café for a hot drink, then I'll come back for you."

The policeman was about to argue that it was against protocol for Blanchard to go alone with the suspect when sirens warned them that their colleagues had arrived. They handed over the scene to the newcomers and the ambulance staff, leaving them with the unpleasant task of retrieving the body parts. Their arrival solved the problem for the two constables.

"We're taking her to headquarters," Blanchard said to the sergeant in charge of the operation. Then, with a commendable presence of mind, she added, "Sarge, get hold of the CCTV footage." She pointed to the camera that must have captured the tragic event.

"Good thinking, Rose, leave it with me. See you later."

Blanchard drove the squad car away from Mitcham station, along Manchester Road, to the Cravings Café, which she knew was across the road from the Isle of Dogs police station.

She plied Melanie with strong, sugary tea and watched her charge closely, noting how she slowly but surely recovered her spirits. Janice Moore was gabbling non-stop to her colleague, PC Andy Beecham. She caught something about a flasher, but devoted her attention to Melanie. Only now that she felt sure that her detainee could cope, did she ask to see her ID. With some relief, she saw that the woman was Melanie Bradshaw and not Bethany Tibbet. That truly was a weight off her shoulders, and, in a more relaxed state of mind, she led them back to the squad car.

"Hey, I thought we were going to the police station." Janice Moore glanced across the road.

"We're going to headquarters. This matter is too serious for the local police," Andy Beecham said, half-turning in the front passenger seat.

"But it was an accident," Janice pleaded again.

"As you keep saying, miss. Don't worry; you can do all the explaining you want at New Scotland Yard."

"Scotland Yard," Janice moaned. "Anybody would think we're criminals."

Unimpressed by Beecham's lack of empathy, Rose spoke softly as she manoeuvred the steering wheel deftly. "Don't go upsetting yourselves. It's a question of routine. A man has died, and we have to get to the bottom of the circumstances. Luckily, there was closed-circuit television recording the movements on the platform, so whatever you say can be checked." She left this ambiguous statement to sink into the minds of the listening women.

When DI Shepherd heard that Melanie Bradshaw was in Interview Room 1, accused of pushing a man under a tram, she hurried downstairs to conduct the questioning. She had never entirely relinquished her pet theory that Melanie Bradshaw and Bethany Tibbet were the same person. Before entering the room —the delay a standard ploy by detectives to leave suspects alone to stew—she spoke with the arresting officer. She recognised him as one of the uniformed officers she had delegated to the Tram-link. "Constable Beecham, isn't it?"

"Yes, ma'am." His face lit up as he realised that the gorgeous detective had remembered his name. "I was first on the scene."

"Did you see the suspect commit the act, Constable?"

"No, ma'am, screams alerted me, but I did hear Ms Bradshaw shout to her friend to call the police. Also, she put up no resistance to the arrest. I'd say she was too shocked to use any initiative. Ma'am?" He saw the faraway look in the detective's stunning eyes.

"Yes?"

"I took the names of five eyewitnesses. They independently

stated that the dead man had been, *ahem*, sexually harassing Ms Bradshaw."

"Did they, indeed! Well, that's a plausible reason for murder, I'd say."

The constable looked shocked, "You don't think—" He bit off the rest of his sentence. In front of him stood the redoubtable DI Shepherd, whose career dazzled for its brilliance. Who was he to question her reasoning?

"What I think, Constable Beecham, is that it's time I spoke with Melanie Bradshaw so that we can get to the bottom of this matter."

He saluted and turned to go.

"No, wait, as the arresting officer, you can come in with me. It'll be a good experience for you. Feel free to make your contribution, as and when."

Suddenly, Constable Andrew Beecham felt ten feet tall. Also, it occurred to him that he believed Bradshaw to be innocent. Whatever had happened at Mitcham station, it certainly wasn't cold-blooded murder. Maybe he could help the young woman.

He watched on with interest as Shepherd explained to the hunched form of Melanie Bradshaw—already petite, she seemed to have shrunk into a tiny fairy-like figure—that she was not at present charged with anything. The detective clarified that this was an informal chat to ascertain facts. "You don't need a solicitor, Miss Bradshaw, unless and until you are officially charged with an offence. Is that clear? Now, I'm going to record our conversation to compensate for my poor memory. Do you have any objection to a recording?"

Bradshaw smiled weakly and shook her head.

"OK, you know Constable Beecham here. He brought you in. We have already met, you'll remember, Melanie."

She remembered all right: the bad cop! What a pity the nice one wasn't here to balance things in her favour a little.

"My first question, Melanie, is what were you and your

friend doing at Mitcham tram station? Isn't it off your beaten track?"

"Yes, you're right. Jan—I mean Janice Moore—studies archaeology at Imperial College, and she specialises in the Anglo-Saxon period. She's my flatmate. Her professor asked her to compile a project about the Anglo-Saxons in Mitcham. Jan told me that archaeologists had excavated two hundred and thirty-eight Saxon graves near Morden Road, so she asked me to come with her to photograph the present-day site. Jan's been to the Museum of London to view the grave goods, and she says there was weaponry, jewellery and other items from the eighth century."

"Does archaeology interest you, Melanie?"

"It's not really my field, but I went along to please Jan. I wish I hadn't." She bit her lower lip.

Constable Beecham glanced at the detective inspector, who picked up on his desire to intercede with the slightest nod. He asked, "Ms Bradshaw, some witnesses spoke about the deceased harassing you. Can you tell us about that?"

"It started before the tram stopped at Mitcham. There weren't many people in our compartment, but he…" she hesitated, and a strange expression as if she had smelled a foul odour crossed her face, "he was drunk. He'd almost swilled a whole bottle of gin. Anyway, he fixed his attention on me. At first, he started telling me that I was pretty, but then made pointed remarks about my breasts, legs, and bottom. Except that he used crude and vulgar words." She looked at Shepherd for moral support but only found hard blue eyes staring at her.

"You didn't lead him on in any way, did you?" The detective inspector's voice was harsh.

Bradshaw looked stricken. "Good Lord, no! Why would I? He was vile and stank of alcohol. When I told him to leave me alone, he became aggressive, saying I was a snooty bitch who needed a good shagging. You see, it brought it all back to me." Melanie began to cry and Constable Beecham took a packet of tissues from his pocket, removed one and passed it to her. She took it and dabbed her eyes.

The constable was about to say something, but Shepherd held up a warning finger to silence him. She knew the value of waiting. After a while, Bradshaw continued, "You see, when I was a schoolgirl, I was on that tram route. I was only seven and a man molested me. We wore a green school uniform, and I know that can excite some weird men. I tried to fight him off, but he kept touching me and told me he'd kill me if I screamed. When I got home, I was in a state and my mum took me around to the police station. They said that they'd investigate and put officers on the tram to make sure I'd be alright in the following weeks."

"And were you?" Shepherd asked.

"Nothing like that happened again, but it made me shy and introverted and I had nightmares for a long time."

Shepherd leant forward to peer into Melanie's green eyes. "Would you say that when this importunate drunk pestered you, it revived memories and made you want to kill him?"

"Yes, er, *no*. I mean, it brought back bad memories, but no, I just wanted to scratch his face to make him stop when he carried on tormenting me on the platform with his foul suggestions. He whipped out his thingy in the tram, too."

"Hang on! Are you saying he exposed himself on the tram?"

"Yes, Detective, he did."

Beecham felt it was time to intervene. "One of the witnesses said that your friend tried to drag you away from the confrontation. What happened? Why didn't you just walk away?"

Shepherd shot her colleague a grateful glance.

"Of course, I just wanted to go away, but he kept getting in my face and shouting obscenities. At that point," she turned to look at Shepherd, "I admit, I wanted to hurt him to make him leave me alone. But Jan was hauling on my arm and... you know, it stopped me from dodging away from his disgusting breath, so I became frantic, and pulled hard to free myself. I was tugging when Jan let go. It sent me reeling forwards and—" her voice broke, and she grabbed the crumpled tissue to wipe her eyes, "I crashed into him. It's not as if I threw myself at him to push him off the platform. I swear I had no control; please believe me!"

"We'll check that, Melanie. At the moment, I *do* believe you. Luckily, or unluckily, for you, we can study the CCTV images, and we'll collect several eyewitness statements. Putting those together will either corroborate or disprove your account. You realise, Melanie, that a man died directly from your actions, so there will have to be a Crown Court hearing. Take my advice, young lady, get yourself a good lawyer. What I'm going to do soon is charge you officially with manslaughter. Then I'll send my sergeant to take down your statement after the obligatory caution. Is that quite clear to you, Melanie? Feel free to ask any questions."

The weeping young woman asked three pertinent questions about procedure and what might happen to her, but each time was rebuffed with, "Good question. But I think your solicitor should answer that."

Shepherd brought the session to a close and reminded Melanie Bradshaw to find a lawyer.

In the corridor, Constable Beecham asked the detective, "You don't believe it was an accident, do you?"

"Do you know, Constable, I might be inclined to think so if we weren't dealing with a bloody cunning serial killer who specialises in tram killings. And your name?"

"Andrew, ma'am, Andy if you like."

"Well, Andy, prepare yourself, as the arresting officer, for a court appearance. They'll probably hold the trial in the Inner London Crown Court."

The constable looked startled. "I suppose so. All I'll have to do is state the facts as they happened, no problem."

Shepherd's expression changed from friendly to frustrated. "I wish I could use the words *no problem* about our case, Andy. I can't remember one quite so complicated."

"But surely, you don't think that this vulnerable young woman is your serial killer, Detective?" Beecham insisted.

"Listen, Andy, you are a young and up-and-coming police officer. I have a feeling that you'll make a decent career for yourself. So, the sooner you realise that in this business, things are never what they appear to be, the better it'll be for your progress."

"Thanks for the compliment and the advice, ma'am." He wisely kept his thoughts to himself. *But you're wrong about Melanie Bradshaw; it was an accident, and that's what I'll tell the judge,* he decided as he walked away.

CHAPTER 17
ACTON DISTRICT AND NEW SCOTLAND YARD, LONDON

In the suffused light of early morning, DI Shepherd lay with her head on Russell Simons's chest, which had become the natural order of things as they slept together every night. It had been a simple transition for both parties. Shepherd knew she was in love because being with Russ was so easy. She adored his sense of humour, and his effortless politeness spoke to her of a real gentleman. Now, she soaked in his regular breathing and the heartbeat underneath her ear whilst one bleary eye studied the hair on his chest. Like everything else about him, it was perfect: not too hairy to repel her, but just enough to aver his masculinity. In the past, on the beach, she had been repulsed by hirsute males who made her think, according to her mood, of apelike creatures or, if they were black-haired, of spiders. That might have been due to her arachnophobia. Shepherd had not quailed when facing an armed robber, but a creepy, hairy spider was another matter.

She sighed happily and thought back to their torrid lovemaking of last night and how her life had changed for the better in a mere few weeks. Soon, she hoped to share her happiness with her closest friends. What a joy it would be to see the expression on Jacob Vance's face when she told him. Caution had held her back. Somewhere in the recesses of her mind, she had convinced herself that she would be denied the good fortune familiar to so many of her contemporaries. Fate had snatched Mark away only weeks before wedding preparations were due to begin. All the more reason why she couldn't face anything going wrong with this romance. She closed her eyes again and continued her reflections. If only her professional life were going as well as her private one. This time, her sigh was heavy and unhappy.

The sound penetrated Russell's subconscious mind so that he stirred and opened his eyes. "Brit," he whispered, "are you awake? Everything OK?"

"Yes, more or less."

"I thought I heard you sigh. Are you sure everything is alright, darling?"

She sighed again. "Not really. It's the damned case. We're no nearer to capturing Bethany Tibbet, and now we have six innocent people poisoned by a bloody ghost. Unless—"

He waited a moment as the faraway look came into the sapphire eyes.

When she didn't say anything, he prompted, "*Unless?*"

"Nah! It's just me. Jacob doesn't think my theory holds water."

"Vance is a good cop with a lot of experience. I'd back him to know what he's talking about, but Brit, nobody's infallible. Give me a try. What's on your mind?"

"Remember the case of the woman who pushed that drunk under the tram?"

"A couple of weeks back? Yeah, but didn't you say that the CCTV and witness statements proved she was telling the truth?"

"I did. And that's why she's out on bail, pending trial for manslaughter. I think a competent barrister will get her off with a suspended sentence, given the harassment the poor woman had to put up with. But my instincts rarely let me down, Russ." She pushed herself up on one elbow and grinned down at him as his eyes moved to her breasts. "They haven't as far as you are concerned, for example."

He sat up to kiss her lips and murmured, "By all that's holy! You're so beautiful, but go on, what are those infallible instincts telling you?"

"It's when I put the coincidences together, see? Jacob drummed into me when I was a constable that there are no such things as coincidences in our job. This Melanie Bradshaw is a perfect physical fit for Bethany Tibbet, except Bethany has blue eyes and hers are green. Then, whilst she was in police custody, the killings stopped and still haven't resumed. Melanie gets herself into trouble by killing the drunken Phillip Winterburn. Where? Under a bloody tram! All Bethany's murders are associated with trams. Then there's the fact of her childhood trauma on a tram. That fits with our psychologist's profile of DID."

"Dissociative identity disorder? So, your instinct is telling you that Melanie Bradshaw is Bethany Tibbet."

"But my brain tells me it can't be so, not just because Vance disagrees, but because, this accident apart, Melanie is a model citizen and a brilliant chemistry student, as I'm sure her brief will point out. So, where the devil is Bethany Tibbet?"

"Listen, Brit, you're the boss, but I've been chafing at the bit. I'm begging you, take me off this pointless tram surveillance and let me follow up on my proposed search for her lodgings. I'll bring Bethany Bloody Tibbet to justice. I swear I will!"

"Can I be frank with you, Russ?"

"I hope you always will be, my love," his deep voice rumbled.

She bent forward to kiss his cheek. It was chaste, so he knew she had something profound to say. "I've thought about your suggestion a lot, and it's a brilliant idea, but after what happened to Victor, I can't risk anything happening to you."

"Vic was a good cop, and my friend, Brit, but he didn't follow protocol, and it cost him his life. There's nothing I want more than to bring his killer to justice. Your Bethany Tibbet won't be a ghost anymore. If you let me do this, I swear I'll fetch her in within the week. I'll need a new partner, though, if I'm to stick to regulations."

"I've got just the lad for you: the constable who brought Melanie Bradshaw in. His name is Beecham, Andy Beecham—hey!" She pushed his chest playfully. "What do you mean, there's nothing more you want—where does that leave me, then?"

Russell Simons looked deeply into his lover's eyes and suddenly pulled her down onto his chest again. Gently, he stroked her hair. "What do you say, Detective? Should we make our relationship official?"

She sat up, fibrillating, like a curious, wet-nosed cat that had just sniffed at an old-fashioned radio valve. "Are you asking me to marry you, Russell Simons?"

"Nope, I'm inviting you to announce our engagement. This isn't the time and the place for a full-blown proposal."

"I can't." She said this, delighting in his stricken expression.

"Why not?"

"Because I can't announce our engagement if I haven't got an engagement ring to flash."

He laughed. "Trashy little blackmailer! If you put me on the lodgings task, I might find a castaway curtain ring."

"Now who's blackmailing? Anyway, since when were curtain rings set with diamonds?"

"Sparklers and a *sapphire* to match your eyes."

"Now you're talking, Sarge! Did I mention that you're on the lodgings search tomorrow?"

She reached over and pulled her new fiancé onto her. "But tomorrow is another day," she murmured throatily.

Across the city, in Ealing, Bethany Tibbet pored over a map of the Tramlink. She was well aware of the extra police surveillance on the tramline and, therefore, racked her brains to find a method of killing victim number seven without riding the trams. *I'm not prepared to abandon my tram theme.* An idea formed, and she chuckled. *This damned bedsit! No wi-fi. I'll have to go to an internet café.*

She had identified all the tram stations that also contained an underground station—there were six. The one that attracted her most was on the branch line to Beckenham: Birkbeck, and she'd already surveyed it. The internet would tell her how to get there by tube and which buses ran to the intermediate stop of Harrington Road. She dared not risk taking a tram for the seventh murder. The beauty of M7 lay in her not having to match Arnold's profile. Not even the police knew who he'd intended to kill on the seventh occasion; they'd been aware only at that point that he was obsessed with Lapique's sky blue. *So, I can pounce on anyone I like. Someone who Destiny throws my way: old or young, male or female, sound-limbed or not—I'm just hoping for a Goth!* She laughed hysterically, unrestrained because she had no neighbours, no busybodies to pry into or interrupt her moments of abandon.

Within the hour, Bethany had gathered all the information she needed in an internet café for the outlay of £2, which she considered money well spent. As a result, she decided to check out Harrington Street tram stop without using the Tramlink to arrive. To do this, she boarded a tube train at Ealing Broadway, knowing that the cops were neglecting the underground and concentrating their search on the Tramlink. The Central Line took her to Tottenham Court Road, where she could change line and go one stop to Goodge Street or walk there in seven minutes. She decided on the latter. It would give her a better feel for the area.

She put away her A-Z of London streets in her handbag before getting off at Tottenham Court Road. When she arrived on foot outside the tube station, she immediately found the bus stop for route 29. The buses were scheduled every five minutes, so it came after only a brief wait. It took her to Silverdale, where she got off to walk the short distance to the Harrington Road tram station.

A surprise flashback to the Korean killing greeted her there. Access to the station was next to a level crossing in the road, a sort of déjà vu, similar to the Addiscombe crossing. She smiled grimly. *That murder went superbly well*, she told herself; maybe this was a good omen. Even better, when she strode onto the platform, she saw that this side was fringed with woodland, unlike the opposite one, which was fenced off. Whether this was the up-line or down-line didn't matter. In record time, she worked out how to commit the murder. *It's too easy to be true! Now, I'll get away from here. I don't want to be spotted hanging around by a copper on the next tram.* She blew a kiss at the large, grey, upright ticket dispenser; behind it lay her perfect hiding place for tomorrow evening.

Destiny alone would choose the last passenger to alight from the off-peak tram. *If I could choose, it would be a paedophile, like the one who killed our Arnold, or a bloody Goth, but beggars can't be choosers*, she thought, chuckling to herself as she hurried away from the station. A tram was due any minute and, in any case, she had the journey home to consider—if you could call that soulless dump home—and it would take forty minutes.

The following morning, DI Shepherd called her Chief Inspector, Malcolm Ridgeway, to update him on her deployment of Simons and Beecham. The constable had been delighted to be taken off surveillance and to be trusted with more important investigative work. Shepherd smiled at the memory of the young man's enthusiasm. If he'd been a dog, his tail would have wagged frantically. She mused on people's body language. For example, Vance had greeted her this morning with, "You look like the cat that's got the cream! Don't tell me that the department's ice maiden has found herself a boyfriend?"

She had fallen straight into his trap. "How did you know that?"

"I *am* a Detective Inspector, Brittany. So, who's the lucky fellow?"

"You'll be the first to know, but only when I've got a ring on my finger."

"Bloody Venus Flytrap!" he smirked, and dodged a stapler that she hurled at his grinning face. "I could have you for attempted grievous bodily harm," he quipped, retrieving the stapler and weighing it in his hand with a frown.

Ridgeway had wanted to see her in a quarter of an hour, so Shepherd took the stairs to his office. She knocked and waited for his call. On the command to enter, she adopted a curious slouching gait to disguise her body language; Vance's intuitions were more than enough for one day.

"Morning, Brittany, are you alright?"

"Fine, sir, thank you." She frowned because he'd misinterpreted her unsuccessful body language.

"Take a seat. You look exhausted. Now, what's going on with this case? Quite frankly, I'm being leaned on from above. I know you and Vance are working flat out, and I've tried to act as a deflector for you. But the Commissioner wants results. So, what were you saying about lodgings?"

"One of the uniformed lads, sir, a sergeant and a bright spark in my opinion, put forward the suggestion that he should target likely areas where Bethany Tibbet might be holed up in digs. I chose a promising constable to back him up and I hold out high hopes that they'll flush her out."

"If this sergeant succeeds, I'll see he gets a commendation. We could do with a bit more initiative and staffing on our murder squad—no disrespect to you and Jacob, I'm well aware that you're the best in the business!"

Brittany was thrilled at the idea of Russell joining their team but kept her thoughts and emotions under control. Big Mal, as she thought of him, continued, "You'll have taken the two uniforms off surveillance. Where were they operational?"

"One at Wimbledon, where his partner was murdered by Tibbet, sir. So, we have nobody there as of this morning, and the other was at Mitcham Junction."

"Right, I'll get you another six uniformed officers, and you can replace those and deploy another three as you see fit, maybe put them on the trams as passengers. Keep up the good work, Brittany. I can feel it in my bones. We'll soon capture her."

Russell Simons chose to end his working day at 7 pm. He had enjoyed partnering Beecham, whose knowledge of the various quarters proved indispensable and saved a lot of time and effort. As he said, "Your theory is interesting, Sarge, but the sort of lodgings you have in mind, you're more likely to find in Hackney or Newham. There's not much point in looking for cheap rentals in Hammersmith, as it's one of the four most expensive areas in the city. Nowadays, it's an artsy riverside area and rentals are sky-high."

The sergeant nodded his head wisely, deferring to the young constable who had grown up in the Shepherd's Bush area in the shadow of the Loftus Road stadium. As he pointed out, he knew all the districts north side of the river. That was why they began their search in Acton. Much to Simons's satisfaction, there was enough in this yuppie area to keep them on their toes without the task being as onerous as, for instance, Hackney would have been. They visited a dozen estate agents and interviewed an equal number of helpful assistants, ending up with a list of four-teen single women tenants. They had checked out nine of these scrupulously, although none rented in the name of Bethany Tibbet. Also, not one of the ladies could be remotely described as petite. Simons decided to call on the other five on Sunday morning when presumably they wouldn't be at work.

"That's more or less crossed Acton off our list of likely neigh-bourhoods. Tomorrow we'll do Ealing, Andy."

They arranged a meeting place for 9 am with Beecham setting off home whilst Simons went to headquarters, "...to report our day's work to DI Shepherd."

They went their separate ways without Beecham suspecting anything.

On his way to New Scotland Yard, Simons checked the side pocket of his uniform for at least the twentieth time that after-noon. His hand groped for and felt the velvety material of the small clip-box. He had sent Beecham to check out a corner shop for postcards advertising lodgings at the end of the street where he had found a jeweller. By the time the willing constable returned, Simons had made his purchase and was back on the pavement. He jerked a thumb at the shop and said, untruthfully, in case the constable had seen him emerge, "I asked in there if there are any lets locally, but the jeweller hadn't a clue. What about your shopkeeper?"

"Nothing doing, Sarge. I think we'll have more luck tomor-row; Ealing is just a little more downmarket."

Whistling a cheerful tune, Simons walked with a spring in his step into the forecourt of New Scotland Yard, past the revolving triangular sign. He remembered Beecham's cynical comment that morning on their way out of the building. "I wonder how much it costs to power that motor? Did you know that it revolves fourteen thousand times a day? Whatever it costs, they'll earn far more. Did you know the force charges TV programmes and filmmakers to use its image?"

As he strode jauntily past the iconic sign, sparing it an admiring glance, Simons wondered why Beecham stored so much trivial information inside his blond, curly-haired head. Tomorrow, he would tell the constable about his engagement. He had been secretive with him today because Brittany had to be the first to see the ring. Beecham would be sick at his news tomor-row, as it was patently obvious that the lad was star-struck by the glamorous detective. He only stopped whistling when he strode into the curved glass pavilion entrance, which always had a sobering effect on him because of its grandeur. His ebullience returned as soon as he set foot on the stairs that led up to where the love of his life waited for him.

Vance's room was too small for the number of uniformed officers crowding it to report on their day's work. Simons strode towards it, giving a cheery wave to Max Wright as he passed his computer. He slowed as police trooped out of Vance's office, some acknowledging him with a smile and a nod. He hoped that Brittany would be free now for them to have time together undisturbed. Frustratingly, he had no such luck. Six officers were still with her; like their colleagues who had just left the office, they had drawn another blank—Bethany Tibbet remained a ghost.

"Hi, Sarge," Brittany greeted him, betraying no emotion to the constables in the room or to Jacob Vance in his chair behind his desk, looking for all the world like a detective fed up with the invasion of his premises. But it was he, not Brittany, who enquired, "How did you get on with the lodgings, Sergeant? Any luck?

"We've more or less eliminated Acton from our investigation, sir." He explained about the remaining five women.

"Good idea to catch them on Sunday," Vance agreed.

Brittany chivvied the uniformed officers on their way with words of encouragement. It was clear that morale wasn't at its highest as the case had seemingly stalled beyond recovery.

"What was that about Sunday?" she asked brightly. Nothing could adversely affect her morale whilst Russell was near her. He explained patiently, adding, "Tomorrow, we'll cover Ealing. If she's there, we'll find her, no worries."

Vance wanted to know how the two officers were going about the task. The detective inspector's greatest virtue regarding personnel management was his ability to listen and not interrupt. When Simons had finished, he used his second paramount quality, which was to contribute valuable suggestions. "If Tibbet lives in the area, she'll need essentials from the local shops and supermarkets. Ask around the shop-keepers and assistants if they've seen a woman matching her description, without making it too obvious."

"Why didn't I think of that in Acton?" Simons looked despondent.

"You had enough on your plate, and you were just getting started," Shepherd sprang to his defence.

"I didn't waste any time in Acton, anyway. Look what I picked up." He slipped the small velvet box into her hand and somehow managed to wink at Vance at the same time.

Shepherd clicked open the box and gasped, "Oh, Russ, it's beautiful!" as she stared in wonder at the large solitaire sapphire encircled by tiny diamonds. "It must have set you back a packet!"

Vance spoke. "What's that ringing in my ears? Sounds like wedding bells to me! It's over the top; need I remind you that on Saturday we have Max and Sabrina's wedding? All these years in London and I've never been to Fulham Palace," he said wist-fully. "Two wedding cakes in one year are more than I can cope with!" Despite his fake objections, he was delighted for his former sergeant. He had worried about her constantly since Mark Turner's untimely death on Helvellyn.

"How on earth did you get the size right, Russ?" Shepherd asked, waving her hand around to admire the dazzling effect as the gems caught and reflected the light.

"I'm not a detective like you two, but I have powers of obser-vation, you know. I checked my pinkie against your ring finger yesterday, and look!" He placed his little finger along hers. "Lucky for you, I haven't got great big paws."

They laughed, but Vance interrupted, "Bloody hell, this is going to cost me a fortune! Two weddings in the department. I hope you'll let Max get wed first. It's only decent."

"We're in no rush," Russell said, to a disapproving scowl

from his fiancée. "To be honest, it's all so sudden. We haven't discussed a date yet." He looked anxiously at Brittany, who beamed a broad grin at him.

"I'm off to show Wrighty and the rest of Scotland Yard my ring."

When the door closed behind her, Vance said, "Congratulations, Sarge, you've got yourself a woman worth her weight in rubies—and I should know," he added mysteriously. "I don't eat cake, you know. I only eat it at weddings out of a sense of duty and solidarity. I'm relying on you to make it my first and last dessert of the year on Saturday," he groaned.

With Brittany safely out of the room, Simons said, "I'll play for time. We have to get to know each other better. Isn't that what engagements are all about, sir?"

"I can hardly remember, mine was so long ago and, anyway, Helena was an old-fashioned kind of lass. If I'd misbehaved, she would have made me suffer!" He laughed and reminisced for a moment that Simons respected. He almost felt that he belonged in New Scotland Yard.

CHAPTER 18

FULHAM PALACE, LONDON

THE LONG-EARED OWL SKIMMED LOW ACROSS THE WELL-TENDED lawn and soared at the last minute to perch on the gauntlet of Vance's outstretched arm. The detective bent his elbow and brought the bird closer to stare into the two marble-like orange eyes. In a strangely smug way, the detective inspector was pleased that the falconers had chosen him to receive an owl and not a hawk. This sentiment was born of a fallacy—the ridiculous notion that owls were wiser than other creatures. Since wisdom was the virtue that Vance most aspired to, his expression of mild superiority was understandable to himself if to no one else. He glanced across at the bride. The gyrfalcon perched on her wrist was tearing at its reward of raw meat. When their eyes met, Sabrina Markham, Head of Forensics, gave him a smile of radiant happiness.

The idea of falconry after the reception in the ancient walled garden had been hers. The couple had selected only eight privileged guests to abandon the others, as there were strict limits imposed on the event by the organisers. The ten participants, including the groom, Max Wright, would each receive an honorary certificate in falconry at the end of the mini-course.

Sabrina looked like a princess in her beautiful, ivory, strapless, knee-length silk dress, with a Chantilly lace bolero jacket over her gown. She had opted not to wear a bridal veil, preferring to display her auburn ringlets to full advantage. Still, she hadn't renounced a discreet tiara, which served the purpose of holding back her hair from her face while adding a further exquisite touch of class to her outfit. The four-inch stiletto peep-toed shoes matched her dress, but were not practical for walking on the grass with a raptor balanced on her arm.

Vance ascribed his sense of euphoria as much to the beauty of the historic venue as to his best man's speech being over. In truth, he had been terrified at the prospect of delivering it poorly, but needn't have worried, since the guests had received it well without him making a fool of himself, and his jokes had amused his audience, more thanks to their benevolence, inspired by the plush surroundings, than to any inherent humour. After all, the meeting of a computer geek with a forensic scientist was not in itself a reason for ribald mirth. Vance had done his best to make it so, his dry delivery provoking gales of laughter from the champagne-fuelled listeners.

Soon after Vance's speech, Sabrina's father, Neville Markham, a bigwig in the City, stood up and invited everyone to join him in Fulham Palace's chapel, built in the then fashionable Strawberry Hill Gothic style. Neville, a staunch practising Anglican, had been dismayed when his daughter had informed him that the wedding would be a civil union, albeit in a bishop's palace. He heartily approved of the ancient venue, home to the Bishops of London for centuries. The site, dating from 740 AD, was more than venerable enough for Mr Markham's taste and, truth be told, the short, but delicate ceremony in the august Tudor setting of the Great Hall had moved him. For him, the dark panelling and chandeliers had added a much-appreciated touch of dignity and class to the occasion.

However, he had gone behind the couple's backs to arrange for a priest to bless their union in the chapel. Somehow, he felt that the blessing by a churchman legitimised the civil ceremony.

Luckily, both Max and Sabrina were delighted by the surprise. The lovely three lights of the stained-glass windows, within the tracery of their pointed arch, provided a warm, embracing atmosphere of subdued light and highly polished wood in the elegant chapel.

After the blessing, the guests drifted back for the cutting of the wedding cake and more champagne but, in an additional twist, this occasion was held in a marquee in the palace gardens. The torture of eating wedding cake for Vance was only surpassed by what he had endured in the moments before delivering his best man's speech. Surreptitiously, he tried to hide his plate laden with sickly-sweet iced cake. Feeling less like a detective and more like a criminal, he slipped his plate behind an ornamental potted plant. Only Helena, his wife, saw him but she was complicit. After the tradition of devouring the cake, Max Wright announced the names of the few guests to accompany the couple into the walled garden. Nobody in the room except the bride and groom knew the arrangements for the outdoor interlude. So, it came as a pleasant surprise when the bride pulled a gauntlet over her elbow-length silk glove, and a gyrfalcon swooped down to perch there. The other nine people were suitably prepared with gloves to receive their feathered guests.

Polite laughter greeted Max Wright's intimidated cringe when a red kite arrived at great speed and mewed in his face, demanding its treat; instead, Brittany Shepherd was uncowed and delighted by the plumage of her elegant sparrowhawk.

The aim of the occasion was to display a variety of raptors to the small party, to sensitise the guests to their beauty and, in some cases, precarious survival. A percentage of what Mr Markham had paid for the event was destined for a charity to preserve these at-risk species.

Having handed their hawks back to the falconers, Russell Simons and Brittany took advantage of the offer to explore a little more of the gardens. They longed to be alone for a while, and the thirteen acres of walled garden offered them the seclusion they sought. Brittany looked splendid in her olive-green bridesmaid dress. She worried about her appearance, but Russ had assured her that, with her figure, complexion and hairstyle, she would look sensational even in an old flour sack when she asked him how she looked before they set off.

Alone at last, they sat on a sheltered bench out of the cool breeze and kissed and cuddled for a while. Russell admired the famous ancient pear tree in the walled garden until Brittany confided, "Russ, I don't think I could be any happier than I am today."

"That's bad. You're only the bridesmaid here; won't you be happier when you're the bride?"

"Of course, what I said was a kind of figure of speech. But honestly, I don't see how we can top this. God knows what Sabrina's dad paid to hire this palace, and the falconry, too. Hey, you know, I might take it up as a hobby."

"What, being a bridesmaid?"

"No, fool," she pummelled his chest, "falconry. I had the strangest sensation that I was reliving a former life."

"I'll bet you down-trod your share of peasants, Your Haughtiness."

"Can't you be serious for one minute, Russell Simons?"

He pulled a face and remained staring at the pear tree for two minutes. Determined not to break the quiet, Shepherd waited.

"That pear tree," he said at last, "think how many times its fruit will have supplied the bishop's table."

"Max told me that the Great Hall is the oldest part of the palace and dates from 1495."

"Did he? The pear tree can't be that old, though. Most pear trees don't go beyond fifty years. Mind you, America's oldest fruit tree is said to be a pear, and it's supposed to be five hundred years old," he said, expecting her to challenge him.

She didn't, but offered a gem of her own. "Like the oldest tree in these gardens. It's a holm oak with half a millennium to its name."

He kissed her forehead. "I know you wanted me to be serious, so how about this? Will you marry me, Brittany Shepherd?"

She looked startled. "Yes, but you've got it all wrong, Russ. You're supposed to go down on one knee and offer me the engagement ring."

"I can do that! Take it off," he said, leaping up, going down dramatically on one knee and holding out his hand to receive the ring.

"There, I told you." She kept her ring on her finger. "You can't be serious for more than a minute, can you? Get up, you oaf! I said yes, didn't I? So, what do you think? A spring, summer, autumn or winter wedding?"

"Being as we can't afford a walled garden and I'm impatient to have Mrs Simons by my side, I'd opt for a July wedding."

"I like the sound of that!" She threw her arms around him.

"What, July or Mrs Simons?"

"Aw, stop it! Both, of course."

Suddenly, Simons looked pensive, much to his fiancée's consternation.

"Russell, what is it?"

"Oh, nothing. I just thought that now I'll begin the search for Bethany Tibbet, and I'm convinced I'll find her. It means that we won't be working together once she's locked away, Brit." He looked thoroughly downcast.

"Trust you to talk shop on a day like today. But don't be daft. It won't change much, if anything, between us. We'll spend all our free time together and, you never know, you might get a brutal murder up in Hampstead that calls for our expertise."

"I won't be hoping for murder on my patch just to see a little more of you, Detective. But look out! Here comes another happy couple." He nodded towards Jacob and Helena Vance.

Although the detective had been known as Jake the Rake in his early days on the force because of his eye for attractive females, he'd recently celebrated his twentieth wedding anniversary with Helena, to whom he had been unswervingly faithful.

Helena loved her job as a clinical psychiatrist and enjoyed an excellent reputation for her counselling and therapy. When called upon by her husband, she would frequently offer advice and invaluable insights into his more challenging cases. Recently, speculation about Bethany Tibbet's psyche had dominated these conversations.

"Brittany darling, you look stunning." Helena beamed at her husband's colleague. "That colour suits you."

"Thank you. Of course, Sabrina chose the bridesmaids' dresses to go with her ivory outfit. I think it was an excellent choice, don't you?"

"I'd expect nothing but excellence from Doctor Markham. I'm so happy for her, and I've known Max for years," she said, "he's perfect for her. What a lovely place for a wedding! By the way, how remiss of me. Congratulations on your engagement, you two. I'm delighted for you, Brittany. Is that your engagement ring?"

The two women sat huddled together talking about wedding arrangements whilst Vance and Simons eased away, to escape and talk shop.

"Brittany told me you're tired of surveillance on the Tram-link, Sergeant."

"Not exactly, sir—"

"Call me Jacob when we're off duty, Russ. We're bound to become friends, given my special relationship with your fiancée."

"Will do, Jacob. Everyone on the Force talks about the Vance and Shepherd combo. But I was saying, I'm not fed up with surveillance; I just think that to capture Tibbet calls for a change of tactic."

"Mmm. Brit mentioned your idea. It's good, and I think it's worth a shot."

"I start tomorrow, and she's assigned a young constable to partner me. She says he's good, so he must be."

"Young Andy Beecham is a good choice, plus he was brought

up in central London. I read his file. I can't remember if he's from Hammersmith or Shepherd's Bush: one or the other. Either way, his local knowledge will be useful to you."

"I'll make the most of it, Jacob. I just have a gut feeling that our killer is at the western side of the city."

"It's always good to go with your intuition. It's a good sign that Brit agrees with you—her instincts are rarely wrong. God knows, we need a breakthrough and pretty damned soon. Each death is regrettable in itself, but one by one, she's closing in on what Arnold Tibbet called the Big One. Maybe you don't know about that, but the intended victim was the Commissioner's nephew. Given that Tibbet is copycatting, we have to assume that he will be her target, too. So, you see, Russ, why I'm sweating over this arrest. I want to fetch her in before she gets any nearer to her ninth victim."

"Don't worry, sir... er, Jacob. I'll make it my crusade to bring her to justice."

They were interrupted by Helena. "Hey, fellas, don't you think it's time we were getting back to the reception before they send out search parties?"

They didn't walk back as couples, but the two men walked ahead. Russell changed the subject of conversation only slightly.

"Vic Carter was my best friend, so I've got a vested interest in capturing the bitch who killed him. But that's not what I wanted to talk about, Jacob. Apart from Vic, I don't have any other close friends. I have two sisters and no brother. So, I wondered whether you might do a repeat performance of today, but for me in July. Be my best man."

Vance looked taken aback. "But I hardly know you, Russell."

"That's a good excuse to spend some evenings together over a few rounds. We have until July. That's nine months away. Apart from anything else, I know that Brittany will be delighted if you agree. We may not be good mates yet, but you two most certainly are."

"Well, if you put it like that, I can hardly refuse. It'll cost you a few pints of London Pride, mind you!" He grinned and nudged the smiling sergeant.

"It looks like those two are getting on like a house on fire," Helena said to Brittany.

"I hope so. Russ has been understandably down after our killer took out his best friend, Victor Carter." Helena caught the concern in Brittany's voice and gave her arm a reassuring squeeze.

Vance chewed his lip thoughtfully. What were the chances of him not making a fool of himself twice? He'd only just got used to the idea that he'd brilliantly overcome a massive hurdle today. Now, Max Wright was beckoning him from the courtyard. The computer wizard looked happier than Vance could remember ever seeing him. Maybe, then, he'd done the right thing in acceding to Russell Simons's request.

CHAPTER 19

EALING AND SOUTH KENSINGTON, LONDON

WHEN MISS KELLY DECIDED TO STEP OUTSIDE FOR A CIGARETTE while her client's dye took effect, little did she know that this moment of fortuity would be of fundamental importance to the Metropolitan Police. As she lit up, Bethany emerged from her door, smiled and waved a cheerful greeting to her landlady. The hairdresser glanced at her phone and noticed that it was four o'clock. She wondered vaguely where her tenant was bound; probably out for shopping, she concluded.

An hour later, Sergeant Simons and a good-looking young constable entered her salon. Men, not to mention *police*men, were unusual in her world, so it was understandable that the Irish-woman was on edge.

"I understand that you let a flat upstairs, Miss Kelly," Simons stated, rather than asked.

"And that I do, to be sure. But it's taken at the moment."

Simons smiled and said, choosing his words carefully making them sound casual, "Who's the lucky bloke?"

The hairdresser laughed. "Not a fellow, now it isn't, to be sure. She's a mere slip of a girl, that she is!"

"Does this young woman have long blonde hair?"

Miss Kelly pulled a comb through her client's hair and

reached for a pair of scissors. "Funny you should be asking that, because, as Mary's my witness, she does, and that's a fact. Now, why would you be asking that, Sergeant? Miss Nepal's no bother at all, at all. She's a lovely snip of a lass."

"Nepal? That's an odd name."

"Now, look here, Sergeant, I don't care if my tenant calls herself Nicole Kidman, just so long as she pays her rent. And that she does, always punctual, always polite and no long face, either."

"Is this Ms Nepal at home at the moment?"

"Is the wee thing in trouble, officer? I'll…" which she made sound like *oil,* "be hoping that she's in no bother."

"We think that she can help us with our inquiries, Miss Kelly. Now answer my question, please."

"She went out at four o'clock, and that's the gospel truth. I checked the time when she waved to me."

"Do you know when she'll be back?"

"On all that's holy, why would I know that? Betty doesn't tell me all her comings and goings, now, does she?"

Sergeant Simons realised that he would get nothing further of use from the hairdresser, who was now combing and snipping fiercely at her client's hair. "You've been a great help, Miss Kelly. Thank you for your time."

"When a soul can serve, Sergeant, so she must, to be sure. But don't you go troubling that poor mite."

Outside the salon, Simons turned to Constable Beecham. "After wasting our time this morning in Acton checking on those five women, we've hit the jackpot. We've found her hideaway, Andy. At last, we've got the murdering bitch!"

The constable looked perplexed and frowned. "How can you be so sure, Sarge?"

"Betty Nepal! Come on! Betty is as near as dammit to Bethany and Nepal—Tibet, as in Tibbet! —are both—"

"—in the Himalayas!"

"You've got it! You see, our deadly little blonde has a sense of humour, or at least, a way of remembering her false name."

"So, what are we going to do, Sarge?"

"We don't know what time she'll be back," he said, glancing warily up and down the road, "and we don't want to scare her off by spotting us lurking outside the hairdressers. I'm going to radio headquarters for support and advice."

When Simons explained the situation to Vance, the detective inspector requisitioned an unmarked black van with dark-tinted windows, obtained a search warrant through DCI Ridgeway and, together with the driver and Shepherd, hurried across the city to Ealing, where they parked a little way down from the hairdressing salon. The driver flashed his headlights so that Simons and Beecham joined them.

"I've brought flasks of coffee and sandwiches from the canteen," Shepherd said. "We might be in for a long wait. At least there's a semblance of comfort and it's warm in here. We'll move the van closer if it gets dark before she comes home. I doubt she'll even notice a parked black van."

"Good work, lads," Vance said. From his face, none of them could tell how relieved he was to receive news of a break-through. He'd almost convinced himself that this complicated case was causing him to develop a stomach ulcer. "Here's how we'll go about this…"

When he had finished, he grinned and said, "Betty Nepal, indeed! Our killer has imagination."

Buying shoes was Bethany's favourite pastime, apart from killing people. The woman with the kind of imagination the police might not have wanted to explore at that particular moment, was biding her time by trying on different pairs of shoes in a shop on Harrington Road. She kept the assistant onside by stating that she would buy one pair, which was now on the counter by the till. Since that promise, to pass the time, she had tried on six assorted pairs but found none to her liking, or so she said.

"Can I try those with the cork heel? Are they a size three?"

She rechecked the time. *It never passes when you want it to,* she thought. She blamed herself for over-eagerness, having set off from Ealing too early. It was important that the peak time for tram transport passed to reduce the risk of being seen hanging about. She rejected the cork-heeled model after turning her foot to different positions in front of the floor-level mirror. "I'll just try those brown shoes, Sally." She used the name on the assistant's badge to gain herself further goodwill. "You don't mind, do you? I know I'm a bit picky."

"Not at all. It's what I'm here for, madam, and you have to be satisfied with your choice." She smiled sweetly.

Bethany calculated that the next tram would be in five minutes, and she believed it would be the last busy one. Yesterday, she had observed that her platform of choice was the eastbound line. It suited her better because there were sure to be fewer people travelling in that direction. After due reflection and a further time check, she bought the brown shoes as well as the trainers she'd chosen earlier.

"Can you put them in a bag? Boxes are so awkward to carry." She marched out of the shop with the strange, unpronounceable name above the window and watched a tram, sounding its horn, glide through the level crossing. It was perfectly on time. *Right! The next one's mine, and the last person out of the tram is M7.* She giggled to herself and there was an insane glint in her blue eyes.

Carefully timing her arrival in the station to perfection, she ensured that both platforms were empty. Quite sure, she dodged behind the tall ticket dispenser to take up position and set down her bag of shoes, before humming an old Smith's song: *To die by your side, the pleasure and the privilege is mine.*

She stopped mid-verse to strain her ears, but couldn't be sure whether the next tram was approaching. Then, suddenly, she was convinced, so she readied her phial and cotton wad in her deep pocket. Now, it was a question of timing. First, she needed to be certain that the last person off the tram had unsuspectingly strolled five yards past her, then she would creep out to do the deed by springing upon her helpless victim. The front of the tram nosed past her, and the carriages squealed to a halt. Two men and a woman stepped out, then farther down the platform, another more petite figure emerged. Bethany fought to calm her breathing to slow down her heart rate. She started to work loose the cork in her phial, but something stopped her, and she rammed it firmly home again.

The last person off the tram was a schoolgirl, and the fact that she wore a green uniform saved her life. Bethany had worn a green uniform and travelled on a tram in her school days. *Damn it! Of all the people to be last off the tram, Fate chose you. Oh, come on, Bethany, you sentimental fool! If the last person off the next tram is a schoolgirl, I'll kill her anyway.*

She watched the unheeding recipient of the miracle leave the platform and began to hum again: *And if a double-decker bus crashes into us, to die by your side would be a heavenly way to die.* She loved Morrisey's languid voice and Johnny Marr's brilliant guitar riffs. But she cursed herself as she grew cold, waiting for the next tram. *Why didn't I just snuff out that kid?*

The trams were scheduled only ten minutes apart, so the time passed quickly enough before the next one slid to a halt. *Now, who will be my chosen one this time?* A pretty girl with a Jamaican-bounce hairstyle was first off, followed by a heavy-set man with bare, tattooed arms under a leather jerkin. But wait! From the last compartment, illuminated by the carriage lights, a woman dressed in black began to walk down the platform. *Here comes M7!* she thought jubilantly as she began to ease the cork from the phial.

From the arc of light cast by the lamp over the platform, she saw the white wimple band. *It's a bloody nun!* Her jubilation rocketed. *Great! I can get my own back on bloody Sister Joseph and all of her kind. Joseph! Weird, the lot of them! That's a man's name, isn't it?*

Sister Joseph had been a martinet at Bethany's school. She waited until the nun had passed the ticket-vending machine that screened her, then dodged silently on her thick-soled trainers to swipe the lethal wad across the sister's mouth and nose. The woman barely had time to twitch before she slumped onto the concrete platform. Making sure that she'd breathed her last, Bethany hurriedly grabbed the nun's ankles and dragged her behind the shelter that contained benches for waiting passengers. She panted with the exertion as she thought, *Good job she's skinny. If she'd been overweight like Sister Joseph, I'd never have managed. Anyway, better her than that schoolkid!*

Bethany returned to pick up her newly-purchased shoes, but there remained the last task to complete her evening's work. But drat it! She ducked back behind the ticket dispenser. The westbound tram approached the other platform, and nobody must see her. When it came to a halt, she peered around the edge of the metal vending machine and saw a uniformed police officer, a woman, sitting in the second compartment. Bethany chuckled; *it's no coincidence she's on that tram. But it shows how wise I was to avoid the Tramlink tonight.* She felt smug and invincible. *If you're watching, Arnold, I've beaten your death count. Just one more, and then, it's the Big One and I'll complete your failed mission.*

The tram pulled away in a dazzling flash of lights. Before she left the tram station, Tibbet took out her spray can. She looked at the splendid choice of unblemished grey-painted surfaces and opted for the litter bin, not far from the ticket dispenser. On the rectangular side of the bin, she sprayed the familiar **9-7=2** in black numerals. A glance in both directions confirmed that she was alone in the station, so she threw back her head and released the pent-up tension by laughing hysterically. Calm again, she replaced the spray can in her bag, retrieved the shoes she'd purchased and set off for her squalid bedsit.

On another, less taxing day, as she approached her accommodation, her antennae might have picked up an unmarked black van as a potential danger. She might have felt invulnerable, but maybe she should have used more caution when returning to her bedsit. Carefree and still humming *There Is a Light That Never Goes Out*, she failed to notice the van parked fifteen yards up the road from her flat. Tonight, weary but exhilarated, she didn't spare it a glance but strode up to the door, inserted the key in the Yale lock and briskly entered the building.

Inside the van, an excited Constable Beecham nudged his sergeant. "You'd never think that tiny sprog with a shopping bag is a serial killer. She looks for all the world like an innocent young woman going about her daily routine."

"Looks can be deceptive, Constable, one of the first rules of our profession," Vance said, almost in a whisper, handing a regulation Glock pistol to the constable with a suitable warning, "so keep on your toes, everybody."

Following Vance's instructions to the letter, Simons inserted a flexible plastic card behind the Yale latch bolt and a couple of thin metal probes into the lock. In moments, the door swung open and Beecham, followed by Shepherd, each with handguns in their fists, mounted the stairs silently. On the landing, Shepherd signalled to Simons, whose beefy shoulder barged the door to the bedsit open. Stretched out on her bed, Bethany screamed and swore at them. Her protests and expletives were in vain as she soon found herself with her arms cuffed behind her back.

"Bloody hell," Shepherd snapped, "it's Melanie Bradshaw! I knew it—you're Bethany."

"What? What are you saying? Who the hell's Melanie Bradshaw? I'm Bethany Tibbet."

"Don't give me that, Melanie. Aren't you Betty Nepal, too?" Shepherd sneered.

"What if I am? There's no law against using a different name to pay your rent."

"As a matter of fact—" the detective broke off as Vance whispered in her ear, "Look at her eyes!" There was no doubt

Bethany had striking *blue* eyes. Shepherd scrutinised the suspect and told herself, *she has the same little mole over her upper lip as Melanie. Either they're identical twins or the same person.*

"Hey! You've no right to go in my bathroom, it's private!" Bethany yelled, with a note of desperation in her voice that didn't escape Vance's notice.

"We have every right, Ms Tibbet," Vance said phlegmatically. "This is our search warrant, signed by none less than the Commissioner of the Metropolitan Police. I'm quite happy to show it to your solicitor."

Meanwhile, Shepherd, wearing latex gloves, poked around the room, lifting and looking under cushions. As she bent to look under the bed, she noticed Bethany Tibbet stiffen. So, she got down on her knees, stuck her head into the unpleasant dust- and fluff-filled space. Reaching, arm completely extended, she clasped a security case, muttering, "What have we here?" She wriggled backwards on her stomach, standing triumphantly with the case in her extended hand. "Where's the key to this, Bethany?"

"How would I know, I've never seen it before," came the sullen reply.

"It makes no difference. We'll find your fingerprints all over it and there are no locks that can defeat our experts in forensics."

Knowing that her incriminating notebook was inside the case, Bethany's shoulders sagged and her eyes filled with tears of frustrated rage. What she'd give to clamp her cotton wad over the bitch of a copper's face!

After a few minutes, punctuated by mixed sounds, including grunts of exertion from the bathroom, the sergeant reappeared with a triumphant grin on his face.

"Sir! Look at this!" Simons held up a wooden case with clip closure. "She hid it behind the bath panel, sir." He opened it in front of the detective inspector. The felt-lined carry case contained, he counted, thirteen phials of blue liquid. "My money's on hydrogen cyanide," Vance said laconically. "Bethany

Tibbet, I'm charging you with multiple murders. You do not have to say anything. But it may harm your defence if you do not mention when questioned something which you later rely on in court. Anything you do say may be given in evidence."

The caution over, Shepherd's gaze shifted to the carrier bag she had seen Tibbet carrying into the house. "Been shopping this evening, Bethany? Or is it Betty, or is it Melanie?"

"What of it? And I *told* you, it's Bethany."

"This is interesting." She pulled out a receipt and showed it to Vance. "Our little Miss What's-her-name bought these shoes at 6.40 pm at Harrington Road. Wait a minute! That's a tram station, Jacob. We'd better send a scene-of-crime team out there immediately." She reached for her phone and made the call. It didn't take her detective skills to see that Tibbet looked as guilty as a dog caught stealing a sausage from a worktop, or, as she thought in that moment, *she's like a skunk in a funk.* "I guess that we'll find her seventh victim there. Would you like to make life easier for us, Melanie?"

"Fuck off, copper! My name's *Bethany*, and you'll get no help from me. I've never seen those phials before now in my life."

"As my colleague said, we'll check against your fingerprints, but things are looking somewhat bleak for you, Bethany," Vance said calmly. "Give some thought to legal representation. I believe you're not short of a bob or two. Now, we're taking you into Scotland Yard. Remember, you have the right to make *one* phone call."

In the van to headquarters, Shepherd returned to her *idée fixe* as she stared at Bethany. "So, is Melanie Bradshaw your twin?"

Tibbet glared at the detective without answering. Shepherd insisted, "You are identical, except that Melanie has green eyes and you have blue."

Beecham coughed. "Excuse me, ma'am," he withdrew an evidence bag from his pocket, "I clean forgot, I took this from Ms Tibbet's bathroom cabinet." He passed over the square plastic envelope.

"What's this, Constable?"

"It's a contact lens soaking case. I reckon that you'll find the lenses create a green-eyed effect. An optician will soon tell you."

Tibbet glared at him. "OK, smartarse," she said. "I'm not going into details until I have a lawyer, but I *am* Melanie Bradshaw, and Melanie is innocent of any crimes, I'll tell you that. The pervert who died at Mitcham Junction was a complete accident."

The police officers stared at her open-mouthed, and she allowed herself a short-lived grin of triumph.

CHAPTER 20

NEW SCOTLAND YARD, LONDON

VANCE SHOWED SHEPHERD A GRAVE FACE BEFORE BREAKING INTO A broad grin. "Big Mal's been on the blower, and he's as happy as a tramp who's just found a tenner. And he's every right to be, Shep, we've brought Tibbet's murder spree to an end. Also, it seems that the Commissioner is taking a personal interest in your boyfriend's career. You can imagine how relieved the Swan is that the maniac didn't reach victim number nine."

"What's that about Russell? He's my fiancé, not my boyfriend —that sounds squalid at my age."

"Mal Ridgeway told me in the strictest confidence, which is why I'm kicking against the traces and telling you, my dear girl," he grinned roguishly. "Commissioner Phadkar is likely to move Sergeant Simons into our investigative murder squad and to award him with a commendation for his part in Tibbet's arrest."

"Yes!" Shepherd leapt to her feet, clapping her hands. "Russ will be a great addition to our team. But hang on, who will he be assigned to?"

Vance's solemn expression returned. "Not to you, Brit. As Mal said, it would be unwise to have a husband-and-wife team working together. Apart from anything else, it might lead to domestic friction. We want to keep you lovey-dovey for as long as possible. I like you better with that lovestruck grin on your dopey face."

"Bog off, Jacob!"

Quickly, to foil her impending rant or any stapler throwing, he added, "Besides, Russ himself said that we needed to hang out more if I'm going to be his best man. So, I'll have two excellent detective sergeants, Mark Allen and your finance."

"The word is *fiancé,* Jacob. Well," her expression softened, "I couldn't think of a better mentor for *my* Russell."

"Coffee? By the way, I called Miriam. I want her to observe our first interview with Tibbet."

"Good idea. She's one crazy mixed-up bitch, and I don't want her getting off with an insanity plea."

"Prepare for a tough time, Brittany, she's bringing in Myra Bailey."

"What! That warped Jamaican brief with a chip on her shoulder?"

Vance pursed his lips. "That's nowhere near politically correct, Shep. Her parents are from Jamaica, but Myra is as English as you or I. As for warped, that's debatable, just because she's a damned fine lawyer and has snatched one or two miscreants from the maw of the prison gates. As for a chip on her shoulder: as you should know, it's harder for women to make a decent career, and her a black woman at that."

"Yeah, glass ceiling and all that, you're probably right, Jacob, but don't expect me to invite Myra Bailey to my wedding. I just don't want her finding an escape route for that nun-killing crazed piece of sh—"

"Regarding that, our case against Bethany Tibbet just got stronger."

"It did?"

"Yes, Mark Allen rang in. He's interviewed the Harrington Road shoe shop assistant. She perfectly describes Bethany Tibbet and is happy to pick her out in an identity parade. The young lady is a practising Catholic and knew Sister Agnes well. She was distraught when she learnt that she'd sold shoes to the nun's killer and will do anything to help bring her to justice. And another thing; the forensics bods have confirmed that the substance found in Tibbet's bedsit, as expected, is nothing other than lethal hydrogen cyanide. They're comparing the dabs on the two cases and phials with Tibbet's fingerprints as I speak. I expect they'll match. Here's your coffee."

"So, when are we going to have our heart-to-stone chat with Bethany Tibbet?"

"Stone? Oh, I see," Vance chuckled. "You think she's heartless, don't you?"

"It's the way she did it, Jacob—scientific and cold. If Dr Tremethyk wasn't so good at his job, she might even have gone undetected."

"Except that Bethany had an axe to grind, in the shape of her Tibbet crusade, as she made explicit in her diary. That's something to take up with her when we start our little chat with her downstairs. We'll have to wait, though; Myra is seeing her on her own. We can't begin until she's finished, and meanwhile, Miriam is talking to Malcolm. I think our DCI is doing his best to forewarn her against Bethany's ploys and Myra's tactics. The boss feels like you, Brit, that they'll try to hoodwink the jury into thinking Bethany Tibbet is insane. He's desperate for that not to happen."

"We'll make sure it doesn't. We'll nail Tibbet, Jacob. Shall we do the usual?"

"I think so. We've broken many a tough nut with our pincer approach, Brit." Grinning, he clenched and unclenched his hand several times as if to demonstrate cracking nuts.

Later in the morning, Myra Bailey announced that the interview could begin. Behind the one-way glass, the Commissioner, Ridgeway and Miriam Walker, the profiler, looked down into the room where Tibbet and Bailey sat on one side of a table, with Vance and Shepherd on the other. A constable stood with folded arms in front of the door.

Vance set the scene by speaking into a recorder, detailing the date and time, persons present, and the interview's nature.

"I'll begin by asking you, Ms Tibbet, why you wrote the diary entry stating that Arnold was innocent and demanding that we re-open the case? If you hadn't done that, maybe the medical examiner would have opted for a heart attack as the cause of death, and you'd have got away with the perfect crime."

Bethany simpered. "It *was* the perfect crime. But you don't understand, do you? Poor Arnold was innocent. The police are guilty."

"How do you work that out?" Vance said through clenched teeth.

"Poor Arnold was a sensitive soul. He was an accomplished writer, you know. He could have become as famous as any modern poet, like Seamus Heaney, for example. Except that the police ruined everything. That arrogant bitch of a commissioner with her pompous speech triggered him off. You see, he was already upset, but he'd kept it bottled up for years. He was devoted to his little sister, Melanie—"

"Hang on! You're Melanie. You said so yourself, yesterday."

"Did I? I suppose. Anyway, as I was saying, when a pervert interfered with Melanie, she was only seven—can you imagine that?" She glared at Vance as if it was his fault. "Well, when Arnold found out, he went ballistic. The police didn't catch the perv, and Melanie had to keep going to school, poor angel. Then, one day, he sees the commissioner on TV bragging about what she was going to do and how the criminals were all dimwits. Arnold said if the cops were so bloody clever, why didn't they capture the beast that interfered with poor Mel? That was the day he set his poetry aside and started planning to teach a lesson to that self-important cop with brass knobs on. Poor misunderstood Arnold! Look how you lot let him down. You locked him away with a maniac paedophile who killed him. You're responsible for his death!"

"Well, well, that was a long speech, Ms Tibbet. Perhaps I should remind you that Arnold killed six innocent people, so he wasn't the poor misunderstood wretch that you're trying to portray. And, *you* are here today accused of going one worse, destroying the lives of seven people, not to mention the effect on their families and friends."

"*One better,* you mean, copper." Tibbet looked smug. "I took on Arnold's mantle, the poor mite. You lot had to pay for your crimes." Her solicitor whispered in her ear and gave her a reproving look, but Tibbet ignored her and continued, "You let that poor blameless angel, Melanie, suffer again. If you'd been doing your jobs properly, you'd have arrested the drunken pervert before he importuned her on the tram or fell under it at Mitcham Junction."

Shepherd, who had listened with increasing irritation to Tibbet's ravings, decided to intervene, cleverly masking her annoyance with a flat, matter-of-fact tone.

"So, that was what happened to you when you were seven—"

"Are you deaf or stupid, copper? I told you it happened to *Melanie,* not to me."

Vance leant over the recorder and declared the interview suspended. He turned to Myra Bailey. "You might want to explain a few things to your client whilst we have some urgent business to attend to."

Outside in the corridor, Shepherd caught Vance's arm. "What urgent business, Jacob? I thought we were doing quite well in there."

"We were, but I'm floundering with this Bethany-Melanie situation. I need to clear it up with Miriam Walker."

"Yeah, right. She's as crazy as a sprayed hornet. We might as well get a professional opinion."

Miriam Walker admitted that she'd watched Tibbet's performance with increasing fascination. "We cannot dismiss the notion that Melanie Bradshaw is a separate identity of the same killer. If anything, she's Bethany's alter ego. You might say that Melanie is a Doctor Jekyll to Bethany's Mister Hyde."

Vance nodded, pursed his lips, then said, "Do you think we're dealing with a doppelganger, then, Miriam?"

"Not exactly, Jacob. I stand by my initial dissociative identity disorder diagnosis, but it is clear that Bethany identifies Melanie as her alter ego, and you should understand that to mean an alternative self, distinct from a person's normal or true original personality. Discovering one's alter ego will require finding one's other self, one with a different personality. Let's say that Bethany controls her behaviour at different times, which might well lead to memory gaps and/or hallucinations. DID is usually the result of sexual or physical abuse in childhood and becomes a way to distance oneself from trauma. We heard her speak about interference on a tram, and it may not be casual that Bethany refers to paedophilia, which would explain her obsession with trams. Bear in mind when interviewing her that Bethany believes Melanie is a superior, distinct and separate person from herself."

"Yet she's not so crazy as to deny being Melanie. Under pressure yesterday, she owned up. Today, she's reverted to them being two different people," Shepherd grumbled. "I don't want her wriggling off on an insanity verdict."

Miriam shook her head. "I'm not prepared to diagnose insanity, but I will underline her psychological disorder. Bethany, acting like herself, is lucid. Her alter ego is a valuable contributing member of society. Her compassionate attitude to her brother might even be interpreted as a kind of exculpation of her actions. What a pity about Melanie! Do you know if she was brought up a Catholic?"

"She was," Vance said with certainty. "So, do you think that she's complexed and guilt-ridden, Miriam?"

"I'm sure of it, but you won't easily get a confession out of her because she's erected barriers. I suggest you use her alter ego against her by playing on her pride. I believe that you will elicit as much and more than you need for a watertight conviction with that technique."

"See that you do, you two," Ridgeway growled.

The commissioner, who had remained silent throughout the conversation, added, "Build her up to bring her down."

Vance and Shepherd returned to the interview room with a much clearer idea. The formality of setting up the recorder completed, Vance gazed at Bethany with feigned admiration, playing a part. "We've just been saying, Bethany, that you are much smarter than your brother. Arnold was a master criminal, but you made him look like a beginner. I don't mind telling you that you had us running around chasing our tails. Did you spend much time planning your killings?"

Myra Bailey nudged Tibbet without saying anything, but her warning glance was clear enough, to Vance's dismay. Bethany, who had visibly puffed up her chest and looked proud, changed expression like a balloon deflating. She was silent for a moment then said, "I don't want to talk about me. I'm more concerned about Melanie. She's done nothing wrong, and I want the world to know that. She has her manslaughter case coming up, and I want her to clear her name. Melanie's a brilliant scientist, and she's never hurt anyone deliberately. She had nothing to do with what you're accusing me of. By the way, those seven deaths are on your conscience. All you had to do was declare Arnold innocent. Now, poor Melanie has to face the ordeal of a court case, and that's your fault, too. Bloody coppers!"

"Well, we have a bit of a problem, there, Bethany. You must see that the Met can't send Melanie Bradshaw for trial when she's Bethany Tibbet, who's accused of multiple murders," Shepherd said in a sugary voice and smiled sweetly.

Tibbet's reaction was violent. She lunged across the table towards Vance, but because she was cuffed to a chain attached to a ring, she was brusquely brought up short. She sat back down with an expression of sheer hatred on her pretty face. "Melanie has to clear her name!" she spat.

"I'm sure she will, Bethany," Vance said gently. "A brilliant young woman like Melanie, a law-abiding citizen and a model of virtue, couldn't be mistaken for a criminal. And do you know what? You are very like Melanie. I don't think you meant to hurt anyone. That's why you chose such a humane way to dispatch your victims. I reckon you consulted Melanie about the substance you used, am I right?"

"You always were the bright one of the two." She glared at Shepherd. "I only wanted to get even with the Met. I've explained that. Strange, it's not as if I remember doing anything wrong."

Refusing to be duped by Bethany's innocent expression, Shepherd hissed, "Look at this, then. Maybe it'll jog your memory," and she removed the photo of the body of Sister Agnes, taken *in situ*, from a manila folder. The detective had cleverly calculated her choice of victim. She slid the image across the table and watched Bethany's lip curl. "I suggest you wanted to get even with the nuns at your old school."

This incendiary remark fired Bethany up, and Myra Bailey could only look on in dismay.

"It was the only killing that I enjoyed. The others were just examples. All I could think of was that devil's spawn, Sister Joseph, and how she treated poor Melanie. And just think, Mel was such a well-behaved pupil, but it didn't stop bloody Sister Joseph from rapping her knuckles or pulling her pigtails."

"I'll bet you felt more than justified in killing her." Shepherd pointed at the photo. "You were saving other girls from sarcasm and humiliation, weren't you?"

"You know that's a leading question, Detective," Myra Bailey objected.

"Aw, shut up!" Bethany scowled at the discomfited lawyer. "What's the harm? Yeah, you're right. That's the most sensible thing you've said, Miss Marple. By getting rid of this old bag," she tapped the photo with a beautifully varnished nail, "I was removing another of those bigoted fanatics from the lives of downtrodden, gullible Catholics who think they can mindlessly chant their way, bead by bead, into the Virgin's good graces. Our Melanie knows better. She sees God through a microscope. You should ask *her* about the meaning of life."

"I hope I'll get a chance to do that, Bethany," Vance said mildly. "But let me get this right. Are you confessing to removing Sister Agnes from society?"

"Of course. I just said so, didn't I?"

Myra Bailey shuffled uncomfortably in her seat and looked as if she wanted to intervene. Vance, realising this, said quickly, "Look, Bethany, we can make a deal here, you know."

The lawyer leapt to her feet. "I demand a few minutes alone with my client, Detective. I'm not sure I approve of the way this interview is going."

"Put it this way, Ms Bailey. As I'm sure you are aware, we have damning evidence taken from your client's bedsit with her fingerprints all over it. We have a witness ready to testify to her presence near the scene of Sister Agnes's murder yesterday, and we have a partial confession in her own words. I was about to propose an offer in exchange for a full and clear confession so that I can stand up and testify to the good character of Ms Tibbet." He smiled at Bethany, who looked confused but pleased.

Vance ritually suspended the recording and said, "Ten minutes, Ms Bailey. You know the score. I won't attempt to advise you."

Vance and Shepherd received the congratulations of the Commissioner and the DCI, who encouraged them to drive home their advantage.

"Regarding that, Jacob," Miriam Walker said, "continue to play the card of Bethany's good character. Brittany, don't say anything. She's marked you down as an antagonist, just smile encouragingly. I'm sure you'll get what you need. I think it best."

In the corridor and out of earshot, Shepherd muttered, "Bloody cheek! *Antagonist*, am I? You'd think I was a hindrance!"

"Not at all, Brit, but Miriam knows her stuff. Better oblige, eh?"

Shepherd gave an unladylike snort and opened the door to let a smiling Vance through.

He soon had the recorder running and he gazed encouragingly at Bethany. He addressed her lawyer. "So, what's it to be, Ms Bailey?"

The red-lipsticked mouth broke into a broad smile, revealing even white teeth. "After consultation with my client, she is willing to cooperate fully, providing that her good name and that of Melanie," the lawyer discreetly rolled her eyes, and the corner of Vance's mouth twitched, "are underlined by you in court."

"You have my word on that, Bethany." Vance gazed into the startlingly attractive cobalt blue eyes. "I'll go out of my way to stress that you are just as kind and thoughtful as Melanie,"

Tibbet startled him by shouting, "No! I'm nowhere near as good as Melanie. I'd like to be, but I'm not. No need to exaggerate. Just say that I'm not a bad person."

"Of course you're not a bad person, Bethany," Vance, who hated aspects of his job sometimes, lied calmly. "We have to separate the deeds from the person, don't we? Regarding the deeds, now that you have my promise, I'd like you to take me through how you did them, one by one, in your own words. Take all the time you need, my dear. I'm listening, and I think we'll learn from you." His encouraging smile was matched by Shepherd's.

"I chose Avenue Lane because..." Bethany gave them every detail of the killing of Gundega Krūmina, the Latvian citizen. The more Bethany went ahead, the more sickened Shepherd became, but the more she hid her disgust behind feigned interest.

It took the best part of an hour for the blonde to relate all seven murders in the minutest detail. Vance knew that her confession would put her away for the rest of her life, so what were a few words in her favour on his part before a judge and jury? With great satisfaction, he switched off the recording and, to massage Bethany's ego, he said, "In my career, I don't think I've ever come across anyone quite like you, Ms Tibbet. It's been fascinating to hear you out. If you agree, tomorrow I'd love to hear what plans you had if we hadn't interrupted your sequence. Are you agreeable? You won't be needed tomorrow, Ms Bailey, as it'll be off the record and won't be anything we'll use against your client in court. Thank you so much for your cooperation, both of you." He beamed from one to the other in an avuncular way, then nodded to the uniformed officer and said, "Accompany Ms Tibbet to her cell and make sure she has fresh water. She's done a lot of talking."

"Detective," Myra Bailey stood in front of Vance after the officer had led Tibbet away, "you missed your vocation. You should have been an actor! I'll be honest with you, I'm good at my job, but nobody can fight a losing cause like this one. At one point, I even toyed with the idea of calling in a psychiatrist and having her certified as insane."

"It wouldn't have worked, Myra; we had an expert psychologist," he glanced up at the partition glass, "she was prepared to certify Tibbet's sanity before the court. My *unprofessional* opinion," he hastily stressed the word, "is that anyone who kills seven innocent people in cold blood has to be off her rocker."

DI Shepherd looked up from her keyboard and puffed out her cheeks. She wasn't the world's fastest typist, never having learnt to use more than three fingers on her right hand and two on her left.

"Fancy a break from that, Brittany?" Vance enquired. "I've scheduled a chat with Bethany Tibbet, and I'd prefer you to be there."

"Ah, your interview off the record. Is it essential, Jacob? We've got enough to send her down for a very long time."

"As I'm well aware, but she's a fascinating subject and, strictly from a professional point of view, I hasten to add, she provides an amazing insight into the criminal mind."

"I'll say she does! I don't know how I slept last night. Do you need me down there?"

"It's the protocol, if nothing else—"

"Of course, a token female presence."

"You know you're much more than that for me. Not that I can order you to come with me as you're no longer my sergeant, Detective Inspector. I can only ask you nicely."

"Go on, then."

"Please, Brittany—"

"That's enough! You've convinced me. Let's go!" she giggled.

They took the lift down in companionable silence until Shepherd said with a smirk, "I wonder which one we'll get today, Bradshaw or Tibbet?"

"Tibbet, I hope," he grinned, "I know you. You're only trying to rub it in. You said from the start that they were the same person. But I take satisfaction from her two personas being like chalk and cheese. It justifies my being slower than you on the uptake."

"I'll give you that. Miriam was right when she compared her to Jekyll and Hyde. It's a shocking difference. Have you read the book, by the way? We did it for GCSE at school."

"I didn't study it in a classroom, but the concept of doppelganger has always interested me. To be serious for a moment, I sometimes wonder if I should have done like Miriam and studied psychology. Still, I think that you, with your intuitions, would make an excellent criminologist. Have you ever considered taking it up? The Met would back you up one hundred per cent if you did."

"I've never thought about it, Jacob, probably because I've always wanted to be a detective bringing murderers like the Tibbets to justice. I don't think that I could find anything to suit me better."

"It pleases me enormously to hear that. And soon, I can start my campaign of getting to know Russell. Tell you what, Shep, now the case is over, why don't you and I and your finance all go out for a drink after work this evening?

"*Fiancé*, Jacob, and yes, why not? Great idea!"

Vance held the door of the interview room to let Shepherd enter first, then sat opposite Bethany, holding the cobalt blue eyes for a pleasant moment. *She's a stunner, alright, what a pity she's warped as a distorting mirror.*

He smiled encouragingly, but she wiped the smile away with, "Do you think I'm pretty, copper?"

"Yes, Bethany, very pretty."

"Thanks, but Melanie is much prettier—if she'd been taller, she could have been a top model: she's so beautiful." Bethany looked dewy-eyed and smiled as if sharing an intimacy with a friend.

Shepherd suppressed a groan and stared at the wall.

"I'm sure you're right, Bethany, but it's *you* I want to know better, not Melanie, at least, not this morning. Tell me about what you would have done if we hadn't interrupted your series of killings."

Bethany frowned, looked momentarily angry and, in a surprisingly harsh voice for a petite charmer, said, "It's frustrating. I so wanted to punish that bitch!"

"Are you referring to the commissioner, by any chance?"

"Yes, that supercilious Aalia Phadkar, or whatever her name is."

"You got her name perfectly correct, Bethany; I'd have been surprised if you hadn't. What you might not know is that when she was a detective, like me, almost single-handedly, she broke the stranglehold of the Talarico clan on the narcotics trade in London. She risked her life to dismantle that organisation. It took a lot of courage."

"I don't care. All I know is that she wouldn't apologise to Arnold and that it's her fault that he met such a rotten end."

"So, you, as you say, meant to *punish* her by killing your eighth victim. Tell me about that."

Shepherd leant forward in her first display of interest. Tibbet's blue eyes held hers with a challenging expression, and, as if offending Shepherd was the trigger to start talking, she began: "M Eight? Yeah, just a stepping stone to the Big One. I didn't have much time to plan it, to tell the truth. The only thing I'd decided was that it wouldn't be on the Tramlink. I researched the internet and found a disused tram-crossing in Silvertown. That would have been great. The photo showed that the gate was rickety and overgrown, but when I looked into it, the council removed it in 2007 and ripped up the rails in the road in

2012. So, I had to abandon that idea. But it did get me thinking. Why not copy Arnold? You'll remember that he chose a couple of roads that had changed their names?" Her eyes re-challenged Shepherd, but Shepherd was determined to accept the gauntlet. She had a good memory, and now she'd vaunt it. "You mean Allenbury Lane, formerly Primrose Street and Satchwell Road, as was Orange Street?"

"Oh, very good, a fair cop by the fair cop!" Bethany's sneering tone was calculated to irritate, and Shepherd glared at her.

"I decided to do the same, just to set you a little puzzle. Let's say that if I'd chosen the flats at Stephen Lawrence House in Plaistow, you wouldn't have had a clue, would you?"

Vance shrugged, at a loss, but Shepherd said, "Don't underestimate us, Tibbet. We have ways and means."

"Go on then; let's see how good you are."

"Just give me a few minutes to think about it."

"Meanwhile, you can tell me who your victim would have been, Bethany," Vance said gently.

Unseen by Tibbet, under the table, Shepherd tapped out a text message to DS Wright: *What have the Stephen Lawrence House flats to do with trams?* She muted the notification and waited.

"No idea, an opportunist one, I think. I do have standards, though." She reminded Vance how she had spared the schoolgirl in uniform, whom Sister Agnes had substituted. Under the table, in rapid time, Shepherd's display lit up with an incoming message that read: *Stephen Lawrence House flats on site of demolished West Ham Tram Depot offices.*

Shepherd looked smug and, pretending she'd just remembered, informed Tibbet that she knew.

"I've misjudged you, copper; you do have a brain, after all. You could have fooled me with your dumb expression and silly hairstyle."

"We can't all be as wonderful as Melanie Bradshaw," Shepherd said provocatively, in a similar sneering tone to the one used by Tibbet.

Vance interceded before the women fought. "That was clever of you, Bethany. I didn't know of the existence of any such offices. So that would have been your eighth. Will you tell me about the Big One?"

"Yeah, if Smarty-pants there doesn't butt in."

"Oh, I won't say a word, I promise." Shepherd sat back, grinning smugly and slipping her phone into her pocket.

Bethany had looked forward to this moment and given much thought about how best to irritate the cops. It was a question of delivery, because the fact itself was annoying in its own right. She had practised the speech in her head many times in her cell, but unfortunately, she wasn't allowed a mirror in there. Did they think *she* would self-harm when Melanie had so much to live for?

She milked the moment by pretending to sink into a trance. When she judged that Shepherd was becoming impatient, she sneered and said, "If you're sitting comfortably, then I'll begin," aping an old-fashioned children's *Storytime* presenter. "Unlike M Eight, the Big One had a specific target. My brother discovered that Aalia Phadkar has a sister who had three kids. The eldest is Farid. Farid Iqbal is a student at Imperial College, and that's where Melanie could help me. It's an advantage Arnold didn't have. You see, Melanie's flatmate, Jan Moore, is at Imperial, too. Jan's not a beauty, but she has appeal for a certain type of man— there are some who like big booties, you know what I mean, don't you, Detective?" She leered at Vance.

Shepherd snorted but said not a word. "Anyway, Jan's endowed in that sense, and Mel encouraged her to bump into Farid. Now, he's a good Muslim boy and hasn't taken her to bed. In fact, he's been honest with Jan that his family would never accept her, so he won't take advantage of her. Even so, he's not averse to a bit of snogging and going to the cinema or to a fast-food joint with her. So, I planned to have Melanie go out with the pair of them at first. Did you know that Farid studies chemistry at Imperial? So, the idea was that Mel would dazzle him with science. She's much prettier than Jan, and he'd likely fall for Melanie's looks and brilliance. She'd prepared a whole spiel about how the origin of life on Earth is linked to astrophysical ice chemistry."

Bethany smirked again infuriatingly and addressed Vance, "Does the argument interest you? I can tell you how it would have hooked Farid if you want."

"Go on." Vance was curious. If Bethany could sustain this discourse, it meant that she was, indeed, at the MSc level.

Bethany cleared her throat and, adopting a surprising lecture tone that would have done credit to a university don, she expounded: "Understanding how simple compounds gave rise to the complex organic molecules and metabolic processes we see in today's biology is one of the greatest conundrums of modern scientific endeavour. Two key metabolic precursors, vitamin B_3 and quinolinic acid, could have been synthesised in space."

She looked at Vance intently to see whether he was following her. He was. Satisfied, she curled her lip at Shepherd's ill-concealed surprise and continued, "Icy grains, eventually incorporated into comets or asteroids, could be an original site of their synthesis. Meteoric delivery of the organic compounds to earth may have provided the necessary metabolic precursors for the earliest forms of life. It's a plausible theory, copper," she directed this at Shepherd, who as promised remained mute. "You see," she explained, "under vacuum, with very low temperatures and strong UV irradiation that you get in space, complex organics formed in ice mixtures with a defined ratio of pyridine, carbon dioxide and water would do the trick. That's rather different from the Adam and Eve stories those bloody nuns ram down our throats."

She paused, twirled her hair around a finger and then, with a practised sneer, said, "Here's the beauty of my plan. Melanie would have then proposed collaboration to Farid. She would have offered him the chance to measure the compounds' stability under the expected conditions of such icy grains in future research. How could a third-year undergraduate resist the opportunity to do that alongside the beautiful, super-intelligent Melanie? When he'd fallen for it, as he surely would have, I'd have substituted Mel. You'll have noticed how we look alike," she giggled, a laugh too close to hysterical for comfort. "Then, I'd have caught him unawares with my cotton pad soaked in HCN. Neat, don't you think? And nobody would suspect the little Goody Two-Shoes, Melanie Bradshaw," she chortled, and this time there was no escaping the insane gleam in her eyes and the disturbing throatiness of the laugh, out of keeping with the slight and attractive frame.

The light in her eyes contrasted with her calm voice. "And do you know what? I'd have gone to the cemetery in the guise of Melanie, to take the weeping Phadkar's hand and offer my condolences." She laughed wildly but stopped, a mad look on her contorted face. She brought a fist down so hard on the table that Vance started back in surprise, and Shepherd leapt to her feet, ready to restrain the maniac. "But *you* ruined my plan—bloody interfering coppers!"

Vance kept calm. "Thank you for sharing that, Bethany, it was a fascinating insight. Don't worry, in court, I'll keep my promise to you—escort Ms Tibbet to her cell, Constable." A sturdy female officer took Bethany's arm and steered her out of the room.

"Surely, you don't mean to speak in her favour in court, Jacob?"

"Of course, Shep. I don't recall *you* making any such promises, though. You can say what you feel about Bethany Tibbet. After all, one Detective Inspector's word should counterbalance another's."

"You sly old fox!"

"Now, compliments aside, isn't it time you phoned your

finance? Remember, we have a well-earned evening off awaiting us."

"*Fiancé*, Jacob!"

"Oh yeah, sorry, Sarge."

"*Inspector*, Jacob!"

"Oh yeah, old habits die hard! Do accept my humble apologies."

They strolled out of New Scotland Yard to one of their old haunts, The Feathers, each with a jaunty spring in their step.

EPILOGUE
NEWINGTON, AND VAUXHALL CROSS, LONDON

A MAN IN A GREY SUIT BEHIND A DESK IN VAUXHALL CROSS PEERED at the screen of a top-of-the-range portable computer. He was following the trial of Bethany Tibbet with professional interest. While Detective Inspector Vance gave evidence under oath, producing an impassioned appeal to the jury, the man in grey jotted down notes with a Mont Blanc fountain pen.

In the Inner London Crown Court at Newington, Vance outlined the exceptional qualities of Melanie Bradshaw, stressing her intelligence and unblemished conduct, appealing for special consideration during her inevitable reclusion. He contrasted this appeal with the failure of civilised society to prevent the murderous sprees of the Tibbet siblings. He accepted that the woman was a danger to society but, referring to her alter ego, made her seem more human than the cold, calculating monster DI Shepherd portrayed, after taking his place in the stand. Brittany Shepherd was uncomfortable as she testified, finding herself in divergence from her mentor for the first time in her career. She could not know that her testimony was vital to the man in grey to establish an all-round vision of the complex subject that was Bethany Tibbet.

Satisfied, the man laid down his pen, switched on the latest version of a Dictaphone and spoke his thoughts into the machine, including a strong recommendation to his peers. When he had finished his long, convincing monologue, he called his personal assistant, Marilyn Woodward, slid the Dictaphone across his desk to her and requested, post-haste, a transcript produced by her admirable and flawless seventy-five-words-a-minute typing skill and speed.

After a mere thirty minutes' seclusion at the end of a twenty-eight-day trial, the jury trooped back into the courtroom. The jury foreman reported their deliberations by returning a unanimous guilty verdict. Judge Sir Ian Jefford left no doubt that he roundly condemned the *heinous crimes committed by the cold-blooded assassin Bethany Tibbet*, in his words, and had no hesitation in condemning her to seven consecutive life sentences without the possibility of parole. In Vauxhall, the man in grey smiled with satisfaction. This ruling played straight into his hands.

Thanks to the strings pulled by his powerful influence, Bethany Tibbet had served less than a fortnight, spent in isolation. He wanted Bethany to be uncontaminated by the negativity permeating her new surroundings.

Bethany did not expect a visit from anyone, not even Mel's erstwhile flatmate, Ramona, that arch-antiestablishment figure, so it came as a surprise when Ram's antithesis, the embodiment of the Establishment, the man in grey, introduced himself. What he had to say fascinated her—so much so that his interview *went swimmingly*, as he later reported.

The man made it quite clear to Bethany that she would undertake the most suitable training "to complete your already abundant skills-set. My dear, I'll be frank with you. It's Bethany Tibbet we are interested in. You will have to participate in some mental as well as physical conditioning. You have to realise that Bethany Tibbet is far superior to Melanie Bradshaw as far as we're concerned. To serve Queen and Country successfully, dear girl, you will have to be Bethany Tibbet. You can walk tall and you will be allowed to live freely in your Fulham apartment under the name of Melanie Bradshaw. How does that grab you?" He gave her an avuncular smile.

"But be clear on one thing, in your head, there will be no room for what that detective called your *alter ego*. You will not need it, dear girl, as Bethany's ego will totally eclipse it. Now, how does that appeal to you?" He stared into the delightful blue eyes where he read what he desired.

"It sounds to me, mister, that you are offering me the job I was born for. It's much better than spending the rest of my life in this hell-hole. When can I sign on the dotted line?"

"No need for signatures, Bethany, I see that you are convinced. So, from this moment, you are a free woman. Free, that is, to commit your loyalty to Her Majesty's Government—Special Agent Melanie Bradshaw." He held out a hand, eagerly clasped by a delighted Bethany Tibbet—soon to be licensed to kill in the name of the United Kingdom of Great Britain and Northern Ireland.

Within the week, Commissioner Phadkar entered Vance's office.

"Sit down, Jacob. May I?" She took a seat opposite him without waiting for consent. "I've just had MI6 on the phone. This visit is more than a courtesy call on my part. I have to inform you and the whole squad that Bethany Tibbet, a.k.a. Melanie Bradshaw, was released from HM Prison Bronzefield last week, but I'll leave that task to you, Detective."

"What!" Vance half-rose in his chair, but an expression of understanding came over his features. "I get it, Ma'am, MI6 have seen Bethany's potential. She has it all, doesn't she? The ruthlessness, the intelligence, the looks—a perfect little Nikita!"

"I think, Jacob, the interest of MI6 is in no small part due to your superb speech in the Crown Court. We can rest assured that if Bethany doesn't meet Six's rigorous standards, she will simply disappear from the face of the earth. In either case, she can no longer be considered a menace to civilised society. I'll freely admit that I can now breathe a long sigh of relief. My darling Farid isn't in danger from her anymore."

The divinely sculpted countenance of Aalia Phadkar relaxed into the most beguiling smile Jacob had ever seen, and, as rarely happened these days, he felt every inch the Jake the Rake of his youth. He returned her a mischievous, downright roguish, grin.

"Ah, by the way, Jacob, MI6 cautioned me that in due course, Bethany Tibbet will return to her Riverside apartment in the name of Melanie Bradshaw. On no account is a Met officer to take any interest in what will be her strictly law-abiding activities. Please make that known to all of our personnel."

"Well," smiled Vance, "I can't pretend not to be pleased. I always felt that Melanie Bradshaw could offer her enormous potential for the benefit of society. I'd imagined it would be in the scientific, not the espionage field, though."

"Who's to say, Jacob? MI6 moves in mysterious ways." The Commissioner regaled him with another blood-stirring smile. He squirmed in his seat. *Good job you can't read my mind, Ma'am!* The deep pools of her dark eyes, holding his, displayed a little amusement, leading him to think uneasily, *never underrate female intuition, Jacob Vance.*

She continued: "Once again, the tried and tested Shepherd and Vance team have come up trumps. I have a small reward for your excellent work, Detective Inspector. Your new Detective Sergeant, Russell Simons, will report to you to take up service as of tomorrow. Given his relationship with Brittany, I don't need to stress how important it is that you instil the most rigorous standards in your new partner. We can afford no distractions on the job."

"Quite right, Ma'am. I'll see that he toes the line."

"Good, I had no doubts. Now, I'll leave you to deal with what I hope will be the epilogue on the Tibbet case that has been our Cross to bear for the last two years.

Two and a half years later.

Melanie Bradshaw's cobalt blue eyes held those of Dariush Ahmadi's. They were sitting in a private house in Tehran. The nuclear physicist was understandably nervous, and not even the blonde beauty he knew as Denise Barclay, her stunning hair now loose and free of the concealing hijab, could put him completely at his ease. The information he had revealed to her was classified top secret, and if his masters ever discovered his treachery, his life was as good as relinquished.

Melanie restored the hijab so that not one strand of her blonde locks could be seen. "Don't worry," she patted Dariush's hand, "nobody knows we are here, and you will never see me again, I promise. Your efforts and sacrifice will be of immense importance to the Free World. Now, I must leave you."

She smiled, but not for his benefit, as she thought of how pleasant it would be to relax and watch the Thames River traffic from her Fulham flat later that evening. On this occasion, the time lag for the return journey to London would be in her favour. And then, she might be ready to renew acquaintance with Mark, the barman at the Shanakee pub. Mind you, she'd have to keep her occupation secret from him. Her latest mission had been particularly successful; her only regret was that she'd had no opportunity to kill—strictly in the line of duty, of course.

THE END

ABOUT THE AUTHOR

John Broughton was born in Cleethorpes Lincolnshire UK in 1948: just one of many post-war babies. After attending grammar school and studying to the sound of Bob Dylan, he went to Nottingham University and studied Medieval and Modern History (Archaeology subsidiary). The subsidiary course led to one of his greatest academic achievements: tipping the soil content of a wheelbarrow from the summit of a spoil heap on an old lady hobbling past the dig.

He did many different jobs while living in Radcliffe-on-Trent, Leamington, Glossop, the Scilly Isles, Puglia and Calabria. They include teaching English and History, managing a Day Care Centre, being a Director of a Trade Institute and teaching university students English. He even tried being a fisherman and a flower picker when he was on St. Agnes island, Scilly. He has lived in Calabria since 1992 where he settled into a long-term job at the University of Calabria, teaching English. No doubt his lovely Calabrian wife Maria stopped him being restless.

His two kids are grown up now, but he wrote books for them when they were little. Hamish Hamilton and then Thomas Nelson published six of these in England in the 1980s. They are now out of print. He's a granddad and, happily, the parents gratifyingly named his grandson Dylan. He decided to take up writing again late in his career. When teaching and working as a translator, you don't really have time for writing. As soon as he stopped the translation work, he resumed writing in 2014.

The fruit of that decision was his first historical novel, *The Purple Thread*, followed by *Wyrd of the Wolf*. Both are set in his favourite Anglo-Saxon period. His third and fourth novels, a two-book set, are *Saints and Sinners* and its sequel *Mixed Blessings*, set on the cusp of the eighth century in Mercia and Lindsey. A fifth, *Sward and Sword*, is about the great Earl Godwine. Creativia Publishing has released *Perfecta Saxonia* and *Ulf's Tale* about King Aethelstan and King Cnut's empire respectively. In May 2019, they published *In the Name of the Mother*, a sequel to *Wyrd of the Wolf*. Creativia/Next Chapter also published *Angenga*, a time-travel novel linking the ninth century to the twenty-first. This novel inspired John Broughton's next venture, a series of seven novels about psychic investigator Jake Conley, whose retrocognition takes him back to Anglo-Saxon times. In another departure, he published a fantasy novel, *Whirligig*.

Other historical novels followed including the St Cuthbert Trilogy and the Sceapig Chronicles Trilogy. Seeking to expand his horizons, he wrote his first mystery novel, *The Quasimodo Killings*, Book 1 of the Vance and Shepherd series. *The London Tram Murders* is Book 2. In another departure, he wrote *The Remnant*, a sci-fi novel about the Apocalypse.

In all, he has twenty-five novels published.

––––––––

To learn more about John Broughton and discover more Next Chapter authors, visit our website at www.nextchapter.pub.

The London Tram Murders
ISBN: 978-4-82412-821-8

Published by
Next Chapter
1-60-20 Minami-Otsuka
170-0005 Toshima-Ku, Tokyo
+818035793528

7th March 2022